CW00858754

ABOUT THE AUTHORS

Jack Bold is the pseudonym for the writing partnership of Brian Bold and Jackie Green. They met as members of Watford Writers and felt their complementary writing styles would work well for this novel. Both have won, local and national short story competitions and have been published as individual writers.

QUOTA

JACK BOLD

First published in Great Britain in 2017
ISBN 13: 978-1975951443
Copyright © Jackie Green and Brian Bold 2017

Book design by The Art of Communication www.book-design.co.uk
Original images © Shutterstock

To Sandy, Les, Peter and Iris
who always believed in us,
but who sadly never saw the finished book.
We made it in the end!

QUOTA

WHEN LIFE IS JUST
A NUMBER...

...WHO COUNTS?

To Kay,

Enjoy

Bri + Jackie
xxx

DAILY NEWS

ASSISTED DYING BILL GOES LIVE IN 2018!

...r has succeeded despite passionate support from some MPs.
...legislation with a conscience

A bid to legali...
Parliamentari...
vote late on V...
Despite prote...
but insisted ...
states rally a...
'This is the ...
"It is a very ...
confronted ...

DAILY NEWS

DEMENTIA TAX FORCES 95 YEAR OLD WIDOW OUT OF HOME

DEMENTIA is currently the leading cause of death...
2040, it is estimated 219,400...
dementi...

DAILY NEWS

OVER 75% OF NHS SERVICES PRIVATISED. NO BEDS AVAILABLE IN CARE HOMES

DAILY NEWS

1 July 2025

VOLUNTARY EUTHANASIA BILL PASSED IN COMMONS

CAP ON NHS CARE FOR OVER 70S & GOVERNMENT DEMAND LICENCES FOR ALL NEW PREGNANCIES.

DAILY NEWS

25 March 2031

PARLIAMENT APPROVES QUOTA ACT

COMPULSORY EUTHANASIA

Amendment passed on 2nd attempt

CHAPTER 1

James was dead. Kate had to choose who would be next.

She followed her children out of the crematorium into the winter sunshine. Jack kicked the odd clump of grass but glanced at his sister every few feet. Lisa's head was down, nose buried in a handful of tissues. They walked to the limousine in silence, Kate's red heels the only splash of colour in a tableau of black. The world looked the same but was hollow without James. She felt numb. All her emotions were trapped in that coffin with him. She wanted to reach out and touch him, feel his arms around her, breathe in the perfume that was him.

Lisa and Jack were already in the car when Kate heard a motorbike approach at speed. She stopped as it swerved and screeched to a halt, spewing gravel across her shoes. The rider reached into his pannier and removed an envelope bearing the Quota logo. Kate froze; she knew what it meant.

Feeling faint, she grabbed the door handle for support and shrank away from the bike. She jumped as the rider opened the throttle and revved the engine. He thrust the envelope towards her and his voice hissed through the grill of his helmet, "Quota Realignment papers. Refusal to accept will activate immediate arrest."

Her traitorous fingers reached forward and took it.

The rider adjusted the receiver on his headset and his toneless voice made her shiver. "Papers delivered. Appleby Case Two Zero Four Five registered." He swivelled his bike on the path and roared away through the avenue of ancient graves.

Kate pulled the car door open and fell into the leather seat. She placed the envelope on her lap but felt contaminated so stuffed it into her bag. "Home, please," she whispered to the driver. She clasped Mary's hand, watching grief contort her mother-in-law's face. Words of comfort lodged in Kate's throat as the car eased its way out through the cemetery gates.

"Who was that?" asked Lisa.

"I know," Jack said.

Kate turned towards her children and her son's flat eyes stared back.

"He's just delivered our future," he said, "or what's left of it."

CHAPTER 2

When Kate's face appeared on the intelligence wall of Quota Control, Clive moved up a gear and propelled the operator's chair towards the image. At first he thought he had imagined it but there she was. His work in the Ministry of Life gave him access to millions of personal files but it was this particular woman that excited him. Kate was vulnerable now, the opportunity he had hoped for. He must download her full history.

Reattaching fresh finger pads, Clive eliminated the tracker on his workstation and disabled the latest spy software. The timer was set for a six-minute safe window so he needed to work quickly.

He initiated the illegal download the second his co-worker left for his break. He knew Norman would be away for the full ten-minutes. The slob liked his food but that could never satisfy the hunger that gnawed at Clive. He fed on human misery.

The door opened and Norman shuffled back into the room. He squeezed into his electronic chair, still eating a glutinous mess. Clive glanced at his colleague and switched the main screen to the day's official workload.

"Hey, Clive, you up for a double shift tomorrow?" Norman's booming voice filled the room. "The wife's saved enough credits to visit the beach. Any chance you could cover me, mate?" Norman manoeuvred his chair forwards.

Clive realised any closer and his co-worker would see Kate's data and ask uncomfortable questions. "Sure, log me down for it."

With a soft whirr, Norman swung his chair away again and gave a cheery thumbs-up, turning to study his own work screens.

Clive moved towards the wall, blanking his personal monitor as he went. He was surrounded by streams of live data. The digital flow cast a green glow on the ceiling as the images raced around the room. Pulsating figures ran across his arms when he dipped in and out of the interactive material. He was far brighter than Norman but made just enough mistakes to rank mediocre on every test they gave him. No one in the Ministry of Life would suspect what he was up to. Not until it was too late.

At the end of his shift, Clive joined the queue at the security desk, a complete waste of time in his opinion. He would have no trouble bypassing the machine. He smiled at the mass of workers streaming out of the Ministry building: pure lemmings, he thought.

Pulling his collar up against the icy rain, he broke away from the line of commuters, jumped the concrete bollards and leapt on to the crowded Traveline vehicle. He moulded himself into the curved doorway, avoiding all contact with his fellow passengers and stood in silence until they reached the Employees' Hostel.

Inside his flat, Clive swept the dirty plates off the worktable and loaded the data he had stolen earlier. Kate's face illuminated the room, providing colour and warmth to the clinical furnishings. He touched her cheek. The display shivered as his hands explored her features. It was the first time he had allowed a female inside his home.

As he studied her electronic smile, his eyes darkened. "Fucking woman," he hissed at the face he remembered so well.

When they had been students together, he had worked hard to impress her: taking time to explain his theories, writing out endless calculations. Her research was competent at most. She must have been aware that he was streets ahead of both her and the professor they worked for. He was confident Kate would support his outrage when the professor stole his work and published it as his own. But she didn't and was upset by his protests.

"They were your ideas, Clive, we both know that. Be patient. Your time will come." She had been right about that.

Clive knew women were weak. He frowned, remembering the pain of leaving his mother. She had kept him for five years, then given him up when officials discovered he was an unlicensed birth. He had been spared the children's home but realised quickly this was no kindness. The Ministry had recognised his potential, housed him on campus and crammed his brain full of data. They tried to develop him into a little workhorse, groomed him well. He worked it to his advantage and as his thirst for knowledge grew, he made sure he understood every bit of software and how every department worked. If this was his world, he would rule it. He was already planning his revenge.

"Clive," the monitor blacked out Kate's image. Norman's bloated face intruded. "Hi, dude, just confirming you can do my shift tomorrow. Julie and the kids are getting excited about the beach. I don't want to let them down."

Clive's stomach churned as he watched the sloppy faces of Norman and his wife on the wall. They were infecting his space. He was grateful his own outgoing communications were non-visual. He forced himself to sound friendly. "Sure, Norman, no probs."

"I owe you one, man." Norman's huge thumb was still raised as the image faded and Kate reappeared.

It was bad enough that Clive had to suffer Norman's outdated slang at work but he wouldn't have it here. This was his space. He would reset his message encryptions tomorrow to ensure he had total control at home. The maintenance programme had obviously found his illegal changes.

A clap of thunder drew his gaze towards the patio windows in his lounge. The rain lashed against the glass, forming a river of translucent tears that obscured the Ministry building in the distance. He turned back to the keyboard, keen to get started. Kate deserved special attention. Clive's tongue ran across his lips as his fingers flew through cyberspace, entering the secret avenues of the Ministry of Life.

He was ready to play.

CHAPTER 3

Kate stood on the porch and stared towards the breeding sheds. The dark clouds threw a mottled blanket of light across the fields. The farm seemed to hold its breath. Even the animals were subdued. She glanced at her children who were deep in thought at either end of the decking. She pulled James's old dressing gown tightly around her body and made her way over to the rocking chair.

She had managed to ignore the Quota letter for three days. Now she felt strong enough to read it. Flipping the envelope to hide the logo, she slid her finger under the flap, tearing it open.

They had slashed her Family Life Quota. She searched for her children's allocation. Both had been cut to 40 years. That was inhuman, less than half their expected lifespan. The terse words from the Ministry of Life blurred into white space. As the figures swam out of focus, her grip slackened and the letter floated down to the decking. She felt sick. This threatened her entire family.

As a teenager, she had been abandoned by her parents. She had blocked out the panic. Could she do it again? Losing James so unexpectedly had unlocked the anxiety she had submerged for years. Mary was her only support but she was marked for immediate release.

The breeze caught the letter, throwing it against the wooden rails. She sprung from the chair. Her family mustn't see it yet. Snatching it up, she forced herself to read it again. They would come for Mary soon. The thought of losing her was unbearable but she had to protect her children. The Quota breakdown posed an impossible choice.

Kate's attention switched to her children sitting on the porch. They were both struggling with the loss of their father. Lisa's dark hair hung loose and drifted across her face as she rocked aimlessly on the lounger. She had become withdrawn and moody, choosing to spend more time at the neighbour's farm than here. Jack had thrown himself into continuing his dad's work in the farm lab. He looked so much like James, his stocky shoulders filled his t-shirt. He was taking a rare break from the farm's laboratory, sipping a beer, legs stretched out on the steps. They were both cocooned in grief and still needed her.

The Government's warning glared out from the page. "You have one month to provide a preferred breakdown."

Preferred? She would prefer her family be left alone. She would prefer her parents had not disappeared. She would prefer James hadn't died. Mary had become her surrogate mother but giving her more years would leave less for Lisa and Jack. How could she?

She stuffed the letter deep into her pocket and walked down the steps towards the enclosures. Acres of wild pasture stretched before her. The colours of the country had been a shock after her childhood in the claustrophobic city. Now the space and the gentle noise of the animals were the new heartbeat of her life.

James would have worked out a solution. That was his speciality, solving problems. With renewed anger, she questioned his lack of care. The accident had been so unlike him. Had it been pure exhaustion after working long hours on the government food programme? She would never know.

"Mum."

Kate jumped at the sound of her daughter's voice.

"I'm going to Hunter's farm. Their sow's about to drop; they said I could help." Lisa sounded impatient.

Kate turned to speak to her but she was already walking into the house. She decided it would be good for Lisa to get away for a while. They could talk later. She went over to Jack who was finishing his beer. She nodded towards the house, "Why don't you go help your sister?"

Jack looked up. "It's our livestock you should be worrying about, not the neighbour's." He glared at her.

Kate snapped. "Spending hours on research is pointless if it doesn't improve the stock. You might learn something."

She regretted her tone as she watched him stomp off to the lab. He'd be gone for hours now. She should have held her tongue. He was hurting but sometimes his arrogance was out of hand. James always thought it was confidence but she wasn't so sure. She spotted Mary listening at the back door and followed her into the house. Her pocket bulged with the poisonous letter she could not face.

Mary offered her a steaming mug of tea. "He'll come round; it's early days."

Kate took the tea and sat down at the kitchen table. She sighed. "I can't even talk to my own children."

"Nonsense," Mary said, "Jack's feeling the pressure. He thinks he's the head of the family and Lisa's hurting. They both need time."

Time was something Mary had run out of. How could Kate tell her? The government was stealing it from all of them. She felt useless. Even her son was avoiding her. "I hardly ever see Jack. He spends all day in the lab."

"James was the same but having you and the children helped balance his life. Jack's young."

Kate saw her mother-in-law's face cloud over. She was still coming to terms with losing her own son.

The bang of the front door broke the moment and Mary nodded towards the window. "Lisa looks a bit dressed up for birthing work. She's not wearing her protective clothing?"

"I think she must have her eye on one of those new technicians at Hunter's Farm. That outfit only arrived last week. They'll suit her up when she gets there," Kate said.

"I remember when you first met James. You wore heels to feed the dairy herd." Mary smiled. "Those designer shoes looked like cow pats by the time you'd finished. I gave you six months and expected you to drag James back to the city. But I underestimated your courage. You'll need it now."

Mary smiled with satisfaction as she tested a spoonful of the stew. "The old recipes are the best," she said.

As are the people, Kate thought, watching the flames from the stove illuminate Mary's face. The Quota letter scorched Kate's conscience. She was faced with an impossible decision. She would have to betray her children to save Mary.

CHAPTER 4

Grant Spencer eased his new BMW out of the car park onto Putney Bridge Road. He felt sorry for the workers sheltering from the storm outside the Ministry of Life. The advantages of high office meant he didn't have to suffer the crowded Traveline vehicles. His well-equipped car was a perk he had wangled after his latest promotion. He had not been as fortunate getting his Medi Credits increased. They would run out soon and Toby would have little chance. He had to find a way to save him.

Toby was a handsome boy, inheriting his looks and Carolyn's blue-black hair. His childish curiosity always made Grant smile, but the struggle his son faced daily broke his heart. Toby needed constant dialysis to stay alive.

Despite the torrential rain, Grant arrived home close to his usual time. He parked and paused at the entrance of his penthouse apartment, preparing himself for the usual uncomfortable exchange with his wife. The front door opened automatically as he approached and he could hear her shrill voice.

"Toby, sit down, your father will talk to you when he's ready. Don't make me have to call the nurse again." Carolyn's tone was tense and Grant felt a surge of anger as he entered the living room.

"Sitting still won't help his lungs." Grant held his arms out to encourage the boy to walk towards him. "Come on, mate, give your dad a hug. I missed you."

Toby's smile illuminated his pale features as he struggled towards his father. He was small for three but the determination shone in his eyes as he pushed his weak body forward. Arms outstretched, he staggered across the wooden floor.

"Fantastic," Grant said, enveloping him in an enormous hug and lifting him through the air in one swoop. The excitement caused a coughing fit. Carolyn slammed her work down on the glass table and snatched Toby from Grant's arms.

"Won't either of you learn?" Her expression hardened and her grip on the boy's arm made him shriek with alarm.

Grant was horrified that she ignored his sobs, more intent on reaching the call button to summon the nurse. Toby was removed and taken down to his medi-room facility.

Grant strode across the room and grabbed Carolyn by the shoulders. "He's deteriorating. If we don't get a transplant soon, he's as good as finished."

She pushed him away, returned to her workstation, and started keying in stats without a word.

"For God's sake leave the damn work and talk to me." Grant went to the alcohol dispenser and took a measure in one gulp. He waited for her to look up.

She swept her long black hair on top of her head and secured it with a clip. This used to fire Grant up but right now it just infuriated him. Her face was unsympathetic.

"Nothing's going to change. You know permissions for transplants are unheard of." Her tone was harsh. "Face it, Toby doesn't have a chance. I've accepted that, so should you."

"Never," he replied. "I won't give up on him. I've got an opportunity with my latest project to look for a kidney donor."

"You know that's illegal."

"Yes, but I can bury the request in my research."

She looked shocked. "Why risk your ministerial appointment? You're so close."

"If I find a suitable donor, I might be able to negotiate with the family direct. No one else would know. I could offer to improve their Quota, in return. It's Toby's only hope."

Carolyn's eyes widened with rage. "Are you mad? Where would they do the operation? We've worked so hard to get this far. I've spent years charming all those aristocratic boneheads. Are you determined to throw it away?"

"Listen to yourself. This is our son's future at stake. He will die if I don't make this work."

"I know, I know," Carolyn's voice softened and she stroked Grant's cheek, "but we could always have another child, a perfect one this time."

Grant pushed her away and stormed off towards the lift. "I'm going to see my son, he needs me."

CHAPTER 5

"Jack, dinner's ready. If you want to eat you'll have to come now." Kate sighed and stared at the blank screen on the kitchen wall: Jack insisted on blocking the visual image. "I'd really like to see you today."

His reply was terse. "I'm running tests."

Before Kate could respond, he'd cut communication.

"He'll come down if he's hungry. Let's eat ours anyway." Mary started collecting the plates and cutlery from the antique dresser.

As Kate pulled the finished casserole from the wood burner, the entry phone buzzed. At least Lisa was going to join them. The piglets must have come quickly for her to be back so soon. Kate jabbed at the front door release with her elbow as she passed and placed the steaming casserole onto the kitchen table.

She heard footsteps in the hall and shouted as she ladled the stew on the plates. "I'm dishing up, Lisa, come and eat as soon as you've changed." She removed a plate. "Jack's not joining us as usual."

The door creaked and she glanced over her shoulder.

She froze.

Her father stood in the doorway. He was thinner than she remembered, his hair completely grey but still worn in a long plait. He said nothing but held his arms out to her.

"Dad?" she whispered before the rage of her teenage years rose up in her throat. She shoved the ladle back into the pot and stared at her father.

Mary picked up the brandy bottle and poured out two measures. "It's good for shock. Now, both of you drink."

Kate found her voice first. "You're alive."

"Yes, love. Sorry to surprise you." Her father tried a weak smile.

She was caught between the desire to smack his face and run into his arms.

"Drink the brandy," said Mary, "There'll be plenty of time to talk."

He moved towards a chair and leant on it.

"You're limping," said Kate.

"Something I picked up during the last skirmish your mother and I got involved in."

"Mum?"

"She's waiting outside. She wanted me to test the water. She's terrified of how you'd feel about us just turning up like this." He wrinkled his mouth into a nervous grin and looked towards Mary for support.

"Well, I'll go and get her. We can't leave her outside." Mary moved towards the door but hesitated for a second before leaving. "I'll lay some extra plates."

Kate just continued to stare at the man in front of her.

"I know it must be a shock seeing us after all this time. We were so sorry to hear about James."

Kate did not answer.

Her father ran a hand over his thinning hair. "Can't tell you how wonderful it is to see you again, Kathryn."

"Kate. It's just Kate." She picked up the spoon and continued to ladle the stew onto the plates so that she wouldn't have to look at him.

Lisa stormed into the kitchen. "Gran says your dad's here. Has she completely lost it?"

"Get changed, dinner will be cold otherwise."

"But, Mum, I..."

"Don't argue with me, Lisa. Just get those birthing overalls in the sterilizer."

Lisa looked at her grandfather before changing direction and disappearing off towards her room. Kate slopped the last of the stew onto a plate and moved to the sink. She dumped the empty casserole dish in and turned the taps on full blast.

"Kathryn."

She turned and her mother walked towards her, arms open. Despite her anger, Kate collapsed against her mother's small round body. A head taller, she buried her face in her mother's hair. It smelt of childhood.

"Good," said Mary, smiling at the new arrivals. "Now, let's eat. There's plenty to go round."

Kate wrenched herself out of her mother's arms and dragged extra chairs to the table. She could not look at her parents as they offered polite introductions to Mary.

By the time Jack appeared the plates were empty but tension filled the room. Kate felt the wave of unasked questions hover over the table. Jack swept his lank hair from his face to peer at the strangers sitting beside his sister.

"Meet Adam and Sarah. Your grandparents," Kate snapped as she circled the table, snatching up the dishes and adding them to the sink.

"You look great for dead people," Jack joked before tucking into his dinner. "What's your secret? Might come in handy for the research I'm doing."

Kate stared at her uncomfortable family. "Why not catch up? You might actually like each other."

She pulled off her apron and threw the crumpled garment on the table. "I'm off for a bath." A soak would dilute her fury and silence the questions that she couldn't ask. It was her sanctuary. She ignored their shocked faces as she left the room.

Locked inside the bathroom, Kate sat on the stool, her mind in turmoil. A knock on the door broke her thoughts.

"Mum, let me in. I need to talk."

At the sound of her daughter's voice, Kate rose and switched on the water flow to the bath. The pump was noisy but having an independent water supply was a luxury.

"Mum," Lisa shouted.

Kate knew she would have to talk this through with her family but not now. She needed time to think. Lisa's knocking became more insistent. Kate sighed. I have a son who won't talk to me and a daughter I can't confide in. James would have sorted this with a few well-chosen words. She opened the door a fraction and saw Lisa's flushed face.

"Mum."

"I'm so sorry, darling. It's been a shock for all of us. Give me a little time."

"It's not that, there's something I need to tell you." Despite her nineteen years, Liza looked like a lost child.

"Not now love, eh?"

"Just thought we'd have a proper conversation for a change but I should've known."

Kate opened the door wider but Lisa was already strutting down the hallway. "Lisa!"

Her daughter's wavy dark hair bounced off her shoulders in angry bursts, as her pace quickened. Kate watched her stretch the new wrap tighter around her body. She had put on weight. That probably explained her bad mood.

Great, thought Kate. Another intimate mother/daughter moment ruined. She turned to see the water tumbling over the bath's edge and rushed to turn it off. As she soaked in the warm suds, she tried to get her head around her parents' return. Where had they been and why come back after all these years?

Without James, it would be hard enough for the farm to

17

support her and the kids, let alone another two adults. She sat bolt upright and the water cascaded from her body. What would two more mean to their Quota? The letter had not listed them. She would be forced to report her parents' return which could bring down her children's allocated years yet again. That was something she wouldn't do. Her parents had to go. She owed them nothing. They had abandoned her easily enough. Unlike them she would put her children first.

As she climbed from the bath and wrapped herself in a towel, her chest tightened. For years she had ached for her mother's arms, dreamt of this reunion. Could she tell them to go? Suddenly she was angry at James's death. She rubbed the towel up and down her body. Oh, James, why did you leave me in this bloody mess?

CHAPTER 6

Grant eased himself into the desk chair, twirling for a quick view of his office in the Ministry of Life and the River Thames below. It had been a while since he had worked over the weekend but he didn't want anyone interrupting him. His latest secondment, a review of Quota, gave him access to private medical records. He could search for possible kidney donors for Toby. Although illegal, he'd take any risk to save his son.

His boss, Sir Charles Winchester, wanted the Quota Analysis by the end of the week and Grant had nothing to show yet.

He pressed the recognition sector on the electronic tabletop. Access was approved, the main screen window flashing an update. Grant groaned. It wasn't good news. This was his third attempt at analysing the Hertfordshire data and the results were different each time.

Something must be happening to the data between runs. He needed technical help fast but from someone he could trust. Scrolling through the on-call support he spotted Peter, his friend in IT services. They had a history of keeping secrets back to college days. Soon his grinning face flashed up on the table screen.

"What's up, Grant? You don't call me at weekends."

"You aren't usually in on a Sunday."

"That hurts, mate. Anyway, how can I help? You look worried."

"I'm getting inconsistent results on a Herts query. Have there been any recent changes?"

"No updates to Hertfordshire. Maybe some of the data is ageing."

"I suppose that's possible, but I'd expect the results to be moving in the same direction, but they went up and then down."

"I'll give your data a scan with the Sleuth software," Peter said. "It'll only take half an hour and you'll have a log of any changes."

"Ok, thanks. That's another drink I owe you," Grant quipped.

Peter laughed before his moving image froze back to the directory picture.

Grant reviewed the coding for his latest query. He had been trying to test an idea that had been bugging him. What if the Quota life expectancy algorithms were out of date? What if the continued growth of the aged population was still being calculated on assumptions based on 2010 lifestyles? The prediction errors could be huge.

His queries included a genetic question. Officially, he was researching the impact of inheritance and gene therapy but the results should reveal any kidney matches for Toby. He was sure this wasn't confusing the results and was determined to keep it in.

He stood up and walked round his desk before leaning on the windowsill to watch a fast-paced rowing eight coming down river. They were so fit. His son would never have that sort of energy or live long enough to reach their age. He crumpled his last page of notes and ripped them to pieces. He wasn't thinking clearly, time for a break. While the Sleuth software was running, he'd get a coffee.

Carolyn called just after Grant returned to his office. "Remember we've dinner with Douglas Franks, Chairman of the Arts Council tonight. Don't be late, we want to impress him."

"I'll do my best, but Sir Charles needs this report. I'll try and get away by 6pm latest."

"Ok but don't embarrass me again. I won't make your excuses this time."

More pressure, thought Grant. He really didn't need the constant networking that Carolyn insisted on. He checked the status of the data scan. Just five minutes to go. Looking through his emails he noticed the report on population control in China. That could be relevant. He was about to read it when the Sleuth results flashed onto his desktop.

The data had changed. The records of two families had been altered on each of his three computer runs. Someone was manipulating the data and then trying to cover their tracks. The Quota predictions for both families had been reduced and then put back to their original values, but why?

Grant drilled down into the detailed data for both families. The Applebys and the Richards each had three living generations and no obvious illnesses. But both had recently lost their main provider leaving widows in their mid-forties triggering reduced Quota allocations. He clicked the gene profiles for a final inspection.

He could find nothing significant, so why had the numbers fluctuated? Before he could log out, an alert flashed on the screen.

'Possible match for donor query search code: Spencer.'

Grant's finger traced the message. He hardly dared to believe it. Jack Appleby, a 17-year-old, was a 98% match for Toby. He couldn't have hoped for anything better. His pulse quickened as he switched to the profile page and bought up a picture of the Appleby boy, a good-looking youngster, though a bit sullen.

He downloaded the family information onto his mobile and closed the tracker software. The room seemed brighter now as he went to the window and looked at the Thames below. Several families were sitting on the new towpaths, their children screaming as commuter boats whizzed past, causing the river to wash high up the walls almost touching them. He smiled. Toby might have the chance to do the same after all.

The Richards and Appleby families deserved the best for their children but someone was altering their Quota allocations. He must find out who and more importantly why? Were they being threatened with false reduced life years? He'd heard this sort of extortion was happening. He would contact the Applebys to check and he hoped they might be able to help each other.

His mobile buzzed. Carolyn again.

"You needn't bother to rush home. The dinner's off. Your little darling has seen to that."

"What's happened?"

"His counts have dropped and the doctor wants him in hospital now but Amersham is the only one that will take him. They want me to go as you're not here."

"I'll come to the hospital as soon as I can." Grant sighed, his hopes for Toby dashed again.

CHAPTER 7

Jack went to the farm laboratory and locked himself in before switching on his workstation. The optical sensor scanned his iris and access was approved. He checked through the farm security film of the last twenty-four hours.

"Gotcha," he whispered, honing in on the freeze-frame of his newly returned grandparents as they entered the house. Opening the illegally obtained search software, he copied the photo over.

"Search back forty years," he commanded.

Image after image stacked up as his excitement rose. He paused after 300 matches, the earliest nearly 40 years ago. The hair and beard were black, but the man in the "Live and Let Live" T-shirt was easy to recognise as his grandfather, the distinctive scar on his face, fresh and raw in this old photo. Wanted for affray in London, wanted for criminal damage in Paris, wanted for illegal entry in New York, this man was a living history of population control protests for nearly half a century.

Jack was impressed. His grandmother was a beauty too. "Bloody hell," he thought, "Grandad certainly knew how to pick them back then." He allowed himself grudging respect for their brave stand against government policy in those early days. But returning now, when they were old and useless, would just threaten his family's Quota.

He decided to check his protest group chat forum to see if he could find more recent news about them. He was startled by a loud knock on the laboratory door but ignored it and continued entering the password for the forum. The knock came again, this time even louder.

"It's me," Lisa shouted, "let me in. I need to talk."

"Give me a minute," Jack groaned. He waved his hand to blank the computer screen and waited a while before releasing the door lock. He wasn't going to let his family discover his interests, well not yet anyway.

"What were you up to?" Lisa smirked.

Jack ignored the comment and moved back to his seat.

"What's so urgent? I'm working."

She didn't answer, her eyes scanning her father's office, in reality a cubicle, partitioned from the main laboratory. He knew it must be difficult for her. She hadn't been in here since Dad died. Jack had forced himself to come. He needed privacy and he wanted to continue with his father's research, but it had taken huge control to overcome his grief. Now it made him feel closer to his father.

Lisa sat facing him on the leather armchair. He closed down the group site and pretended to be busy but stole a quick glance at her. He saw concern as well as sadness. Lisa had never been the bossy sister and always showed care for him. Maybe it was time he returned some of it.

"You all right?" Jack asked. "Do you want a drink? Only beer though."

Lisa shook her head. "Mum won't talk to me; all freaked out by her parents. Anyone else would be thrilled to see them after all this time."

"They're trouble, that's why," Jack snorted, "and they're going to fuck things up for all of us."

"What do you mean?"

"Our Quota allocation will be screwed. After Dad died, Mum's been sent a reduced estimate. That's how it works but it's us who will lose out."

Lisa looked confused. "How do you know? I don't understand all this Quota stuff."

Jack remembered the hours with his dad going over the Quota regulations. Despite his protests, Jack was fascinated. "Dad explained the system to me," he said, proud of his superior knowledge. "Every family gets a Quota of years to spread over their immediate relatives. The more old gits there are, the less we get."

"What do you mean?" Lisa said.

"Putting it bluntly, our life expectancy is reduced and they keep all the decent jobs too. Even stop us having kids."

"We can't have kids, ever?"

"Who cares?"

"But supposing I want a child?" Lisa said.

"You'd have to find a family with a positive Quota."

"It might be a little late for that."

His sister could not hold his gaze.

"You can't be? You never go anywhere. Well, apart from Hunters. No, you haven't?"

"I need to tell someone. Mum won't listen. I've missed a couple of periods and I can't go to an official clinic for a test."

"Whose is it?"

"You won't like it. It's Tom's."

"Not the old farmer? He's married."

"You have no idea what he's really like. I knew you wouldn't understand." Lisa slumped in the chair, tears welling up in her eyes. Jack moved over and put an awkward arm around her shoulder.

"Sorry, Sis, you're supposed to be the reliable one. I'm the one that's normally in trouble."

Lisa smiled.

"You should talk to Mum though. She knows everyone at the hospital. She must be able to get you a test on the sly. We just need to get rid of her parents first. We don't want the government guys breathing down our necks."

"I'm sorry. I didn't mean it to happen. Tom always seemed to have time for me. Really listens, you know?"

"I'd doubt this is something he'd want to hear. He already has three children." Jack felt his sister crumple against him and held her as she cried. He lifted her head and his tone softened. "Lisa, you do realise you can't have this baby, don't you? It would be an unlicensed birth." He let his words sink in before continuing. "You need to ask Mum. She could even try to get you some serum on the quiet."

Lisa turned and looked at him with astonishment.

"If not, I might be able to. I know you can get the abortion packs on the black market."

"How would you have access to something like that?"

Jack swallowed. It was probably time he told her. "I've joined an online protest group. I might be able to get help through them."

"I knew you were up to something but I don't think I want an abortion. This could be my only chance for a baby."

"Does the farmer know?"

"No. I have to be sure first. You mustn't tell anyone. Not yet. Do you think I should talk to Mum tomorrow. What'll she say?"

"Nothing once she sees this." Jack walked over to his screen and recovered the pictures of their grandparents. "They're bloody criminals," he said.

Lisa stared in astonishment at the long list of news reports scrolling across the screen.

Kate padded downstairs in her dressing gown and paused outside the lounge to tighten the towel around her wet hair.

She could hear her parents' conversation through the open doorway.

"We agreed to tell her everything. That's part of the reason we came home." Her father's voice sounded full of emotion.

"But not yet. Let's just enjoy seeing her a little, get to know our grandchildren," her mother replied. Kate could hear the strain in her voice.

"Sarah, it's time she knew the truth."

Kate walked in and closed the door, turning to face her parents. "I'll second that."

They looked up and she was shocked again at how much they'd aged. Kate had always imagined this scene as a happy reunion. But it was not the joyous homecoming she had dreamt of.

"Sit down, love. We need to talk."

Her mother clearly expected Kate to join her on the sofa but she chose the worn rocker by the fire and sat waiting for them to speak. Her mother's grey hair was pulled up in a colourful scarf and although lined, her face still shone with the kindness and radiance that Kate remembered as a child.

"We had to leave you, Kate. They were coming for us. We'd crossed the line and were branded anarchists."

"You're criminals?" Kate gasped.

"Not exactly, love," her father said, "we just uncovered more than a few government lies. If we'd stayed, they'd have found a reason to arrest us and you could have been at risk too. So we went abroad."

"But why didn't you take me with you. And no contact all this time. I thought you were dead."

Her mother's face crumpled and her father offered her his grubby hanky. "You're a mum now, Kathryn. I've seen the way you look at your own children. Like me you'd do anything to protect them. We had a terrible decision to make. The government guys followed us and left you alone. It was the hardest thing we ever did, believe me."

"We loved you," her father continued, "more than you know. We left money so you could finish your education but could never risk contact. We kept moving and friends all over the world protected us and we worked together to try and make a difference, a better world. We knew it would be hard for you to cope on your own but our friends told us you were safe and happy."

"But why risk your lives in the first place?"

Her father crossed the room towards her. "It was wrong what the government were saying. They were lying to everyone. They still are. We tried to stop them, gather intelligence against them, any way we could. People all over the world had similar problems."

Kate rose and stood facing her dad. "But now you're putting my family at risk, putting my kids in danger. I've just lost my husband, I won't risk hurting Lisa and Jack. You can stay a few days but no more. Just make sure you keep out of sight. That's all I can offer you. I'm sorry."

She pulled her dressing gown tighter and strode from the room. She couldn't look at their faces. She couldn't forgive them.

CHAPTER 8

Grant collected a travel authorisation token from the Ministry office and took the lift to the underground garage. Three grey cars were parked in the charging bay. He climbed into the nearest one and inserted the card into the dashboard. He wished he was allowed to use his own car rather than these nondescript boxes, but he still wasn't a high-enough grade.

The route to his destination had been pre-calculated. Maybe he could override the mileage allocated and visit Toby in hospital on his way back. He hadn't seen his son since the day of his admission. It wouldn't be much of a diversion, the Chiltern Infirmary was just off the main Wendover Road. He smiled to himself as he transferred an image of Toby from his mobile to the navigation screen.

His report had taken all night. Still, the automatic nature of driving gave him time to think and he'd done plenty of that lately. His son's future and the problems of the families he was investigating wound a tight band round his head. As he adjusted the mirrors, he saw his eyes were mere slits. He rubbed his face vigorously to prepare for the drive. The electric engine purred into life as soon as he pressed the pedal and the journey stats flashed across the dashboard: distance 40 miles, arrival time of 2.30pm. He was confident he would be at Sir Charles's estate within minutes of the prediction.

He had been there once before, five or so years ago for a summer party, celebrating Sir Charles's twenty-five years in the Ministry. Carolyn had positively glowed, rubbing shoulders with the rich and famous. Her eagerness to network had embarrassed Grant, particularly her flirtation with Sir Charles himself. His jaw tightened at the memory of his wife's behaviour and Sir Charles's regular enquiries about his 'lovely' wife. Carolyn's ambition was obsessive, pressing Grant to seek career advancement at every opportunity.

He checked the passenger seat for his briefcase. He had brought along a set of summary charts to explain the detail of his Quota analysis. However, he knew he wouldn't need to show them. Sir Charles would just want the bottom line. Was the system secure? Were the Quota targets being met?

The last update had been in the office, six months ago. Sir Charles had stayed for less than two minutes but Grant would get his full attention this time. His heart raced when he thought about the significant revelations in his report.

The route wound through the idyllic Chiltern hills, climbing gently from Amersham, passing Great Missenden and onto high ground around Tring. Grant was surprised this part of the Green Belt round London had been protected for so long. Sir Charles often talked of how his father led the campaign to stop the area being ravaged by the high-speed rail, HS2.

The dashboard display dimmed and Toby's face melted to a flat black as Grant drove the car onto the estate, an indication that satellite monitoring was jammed here. The drive up to the house was almost a mile, through open pastures, past grazing cattle and under the high canopy of ancient oaks that had towered over this land for hundreds of years. The world never stops changing, thought Grant, but the opulence of the British government aristocracy continues undisturbed.

Sir Charles was waiting on the steps of his Palladian-style mansion, dressed in jeans and a tailored blue-striped shirt.

Grant emerged crumpled from the car, already sweating and ill at ease in his office suit. "Afternoon, Sir. Lovely weather. It was overcast when I left London just over an hour ago."

"Micro-climate," Sir Charles said, offering a brief handshake. "Let's take a walk to the Garden House."

They made their way through the flower gardens to a stone building overlooking an ornamental lake. The table was laid with a crisp white cloth and refreshments.

"Help yourself to coffee," Sir Charles said, fiddling with his spoon. He let Grant take one sip before waving the utensil like a baton inviting input. "So what progress have you made?"

Grant was determined to get attention but wasn't sure in which order to drop his bombshells for maximum impact. In the event he decided to drop them together.

"The Quota system is unfair and is being sabotaged," he said, watching Sir Charles intently. The peer raised his eyebrows and gave a dismissive nod of the head.

Grant realised he'd used the wrong word. Everyone had being saying the Quota system was unfair since it had been introduced. "What I mean is the Quota algorithm is wrong and it's creating unfair life allocations." He reached for his briefcase to find his charts.

"Who is sabotaging it?"

"I don't know but I have tracked several unauthorised temporary Quota changes this month."

"Temporary?"

"They were changed just long enough to issue false Quota reports to families. I am sure this is for extortion."

Sir Charles looked up from his coffee, more interested, but waited for Grant to continue.

"However, the bigger issue is that the main Quota algorithm is wrong. It's based on outdated population estimates."

"Have you told anyone else about that?"

"No. I only uncovered proof of the problem yesterday."

Sir Charles stood and paced round the table, frowning. "I want you to keep this an absolute secret. Is that clear? I also want you to do what you can to identify the blackmailers and let me know as soon as you have more information."

Grant nodded. "Do you want to see these charts?"

"Give the whole report to me and I'll look at it later," Sir Charles said, already stepping out of the Garden House, indicating the meeting was over. Grant followed him as he strode back to the main house.

"Thanks for coming, Spencer. Remember what I told you," Sir Charles said, over his shoulder, before he disappeared inside.

Grant stood on the drive watching the huge oak doors slam shut. He felt uneasy as he walked to his car. It wasn't the reaction he had expected and was furious not to have been given a chance to discuss his findings. A tight smile flickered across his mouth. Shame, he thought, it would have been interesting to hear Sir Charles's reaction when he discovered his own family's Quota flagged up in the report.

Checking the read-out on the dash his mood lightened. The brief meeting meant he now had plenty of time to visit Toby.

CHAPTER 9

Clive wound the window down and flashed his electronic identity badge at the teenager. "Clive Boland, Resources Inspector. Is Mrs Appleby in?"

"Might be," the boy replied.

He decided to ignore the attitude. "Where's your power inductor?" Clive asked looking across the Appleby property.

The black-haired youth stopped kicking stones and stared at him. "You are joking," he snapped. "Take a good look, mate, it's a farm. Proper animals even." With a desultory grin he added, "You won't see any fancy electric cars here, just cloning sheds and a lot of shit."

"Great," said Clive. The Quota photo didn't do the lad justice. Jack Appleby had more guts than he'd imagined. "So park it where it will pick up the sun," he shouted, throwing his keys at Jack. "If I'd known it was so primitive, I'd have used an outreach vehicle."

Jack caught the keys with ease, clearly keen to drive a car that could go more than 20 mph. He jumped inside and Clive watched him manoeuvre round the house and park the vehicle alongside a row of solar panels.

Clive walked to meet him and took the keys from Jack's

outstretched hand. "I knew your mum at University. Don't expect she's changed that much." He forced himself to smile, trying to soften the boy's protective stare.

"Funny, don't remember Mum ever mentioning you. Can't have made much of an impression," he smirked.

Clive bit back the urge to hit him and followed Jack's cocky swagger towards the entrance of the farmhouse. The smell of freshly baked cakes greeted them.

"Mum," the boy yelled, "there's some pen-pusher here. Reckons he knows you?"

Kate emerged from the kitchen drying her hands and took a step back as Clive moved towards her.

"Kate."

She frowned. He could see she was confused by his familiarity. He watched recognition dawn and thought he noticed a fleeting expression of concern. "It's Clive isn't it? Goodness, what are you doing here?"

Not the welcome he had been hoping for. Bitch. Softly, softly, then. "I'm sorry to just turn up unannounced like this."

"I haven't seen you since university, must be twenty years at least." She seemed a little more relaxed but didn't move any closer.

"I wish it was a social visit but I'm afraid it's official. I'm a Quota inspector." He lowered his voice to a caring whisper. "First, I must say how sorry I was to hear about your husband." Clive wrenched his eyes away from Kate's obvious pain to stare at the boy.

"Got work to do," Jack said, turning and leaving the room.

"That's my son, Jack," she sighed. "He's finding it tough. Sorry, let me get you a cup of tea and cake." She headed towards the kitchen.

She was still a sexy woman. Her long hair had been cut and her teenage fringe replaced by a sleek side parting. Maturity had given her a slimmer, refined elegance but her breasts looked as full as he remembered. He would enjoy this.

He dropped into the comfort of the huge sofa and waited for her to return. Looking around the room, he spotted a photograph of Kate with her late husband. They looked happy and carefree. Not anymore. Kate had no one to protect her now. He would have total control.

She appeared in the doorway with a tray and set it down on the coffee table in front of him. He hated cakes.

"So, you've enough power for a few luxuries then?" he picked up a slice and took a bite. "Fruit cake, my favourite."

She added another slice to his plate before answering. "The wind turbine is a godsend. The government fund the research buildings but give us nothing for personal use."

"You're lucky to have natural resources." He wiped a few disgusting crumbs from his lap and returned the rest of the cake to the plate.

"Oh, I'm terrified of the regulations. James handled it all." She hesitated before adding, "I've just had a Quota demand. It's terrifying. How do people cope?"

Good, it had been delivered: time to show his super-hero side. "That's my job. I help families work within the government guidelines."

Kate looked up at him, alarmed. "I'm not as worried about resources. The farm's well-run and we manage for food and power. It's this last demand... I..." Her hand shook as she put down her cup.

"Don't worry. I've come to help." He tried to reassure her with a smile. "We go back a long way. I must admit, it can be a bit of minefield."

Her anxiety was clear as she leant forward. "I'm worried about the children. My Quota choice looks frightening."

She did not look terrified enough, thought Clive and decided to add some pressure. He placed his cup down and tried to look concerned.

"We have equations that calculate the balance of a family's output and demand. Without James, I'm afraid you will be in deficit." He let that sink in before continuing. "I know your mother-in-law lives here and she is at serious risk. Your own parents are still registered as unlisted." He paused, "Of course, if they were to return, your Quota would be decimated. But I'm sure you know, as our UK borders are closed, that's unlikely."

She looked startled at the mention of her parents and made a huge deal of stacking the cups back on the tray. "I'm sorry, Clive, you must think I'm stupid but I don't know what to do." She stopped, tray in hand. "My mother-in-law has been called for immediate release. Couldn't I give her some of my allowance?"

"If only it was that easy." He knew Mary's age. "It all depends. The regulations were amended to stop transfers to people over 70. Too many families kept transferring years as soon as a new child was born." He sat back in the sofa. "All very predictable really. The inspectors couldn't manage the thousands of transactions. So sick elderly people slipped through the net, using up resources we didn't have." He shrugged. "They had to close the loophole."

Kate's despair was increasing so he decided to press the point. "I'm afraid things do look a bit grim." He lent forward and grasped her hand to comfort her. She flinched. Disappointed, he let go. He calmed himself. This needed patience. After all, he held all the cards. "But I'm here for you, Kate."

"That's good of you." He could see the crockery tremble as she picked up the tray and glanced towards the door. "My mother-in-law will be struggling to feed the animals. I really need to help her."

"Of course. I'll leave you a download about your Quota options. You can read it later."

She smiled and Clive could see relief soften her features. Was it to be this easy?

"Just call me, if you still need help," he added, "after

all, what are friends for?" He decided he had done enough for now.

Bait set. Game on.

When he reached his car, Jack was looking it over. "Would you like a proper drive?" said Clive, sensing an opportunity to groom the boy.

"Might do."

"It's fully automatic so you've only got to steer and brake."

Jack nodded and grinned. Once inside, Clive went over the controls and handed him the keys. Jack drove at full throttle down the hill into the village and screamed to a stop outside the pub.

Clive turned in his seat. This boy enjoyed danger. "You obviously like fast cars?"

"Yep, but that's about as close as I'm ever going to get," said Jack, "I can't even get a place at university, let alone a bloody half-decent job."

He could hear the anger rumble through Jack's words. He could use that. "Yes, it's tough. Until the government improve the allocation of resources, it's not going to change."

"I've learnt loads from my dad in the lab but I can't see myself ever getting off the farm." Jack looked frustrated and glared out from under his floppy fringe.

Clive decided to stoke the fire a little. "There are a lot of people that feel like you, Jack, and the government will have to listen at some point. The elderly have had their time; they need to make way."

Jack twisted in his seat, pushing his face nearer Clive's. "That's never going to happen. The old gits just don't give up. Even my grandparents have turned up like a bad smell."

Clive was about to push the little prick's face away but was too interested in hearing more. "You must be pleased."

"You reckon? If I knew what they're really up to, I'd feel better."

Clive had been tracking Jack's entries in the protest chat forum and knew he was ripe for the picking. "You sound like a bright lad. If you want to do something about it, you should join a protest group.

"Too right. I'm not about to watch the old buggers bleed our resources."

"Well, there's an active group in Rickmansworth that might interest you. I'm going to their meeting next week. Why not come along?"

"I know them." Jack grinned. "I've been posting to their website for ages."

Taking a card from his wallet, Clive scribbled an address and date and gave it to Jack. "I hope to see you there. Now, as I value my wheels, I'd like to drive." He opened the door and Jack reluctantly changed places. He smiled at Jack's sulky expression on the way back to the farm. Clive waved goodbye and watched the boy shrug and walk inside.

As he passed rows of breeding facilities, he looked at the diminishing farmhouse in his rear view mirror and knew for sure Kate's parents had returned. She must have been hiding them. She would be terrified, just how he liked it. Desperate women were always much easier to control.

CHAPTER 10

Sir Charles was bored. One of the downsides of achieving high rank, he supposed. He retrieved his umbrella from the luggage rack and followed the attractive blonde along the aisle to the carriage door. He had been watching her for most of the train journey from Tring and they had exchanged smiles. He was tempted to make an approach but she might live too close to home. His sex life had lacked a certain excitement since he had bored of his last mistress and he couldn't resist the opportunity to help the woman with her case.

"Thank you," she said, "I was impressed to see you finish the Times crossword so quickly."

"It was yesterday's paper," Sir Charles lied. "I often use that trick to impress a beautiful woman."

"That was honest," the blonde replied. "Is that the only reason you travel by train?"

"No. I like to drive but it's not so easy with all the restrictions."

As they reached the end of the platform, she hesitated. "Well, if I ever need the answer to yesterday's crossword, I know who to ask."

She sashayed towards the underground entrance, her

pencil skirt focusing Sir Charles's gaze. He knew he had turned down an opportunity but he soon found himself thinking about Carolyn Spencer.

He really must take up her insistence of dinner in town. Although far from his usual type, she had been his part-time mistress for ages. Spending time with her now might give him another view on Spencer's Quota suspicions. He smiled, imagining pillow talk with Carolyn.

He was meeting Stuart Sutton from the Home Office for lunch in a well-known restaurant. It would be reported as a social meeting between cabinet civil servants, fond of their wine. The Rendezvous was popular with high-ranking officials. The secure dining alcoves blocked all electronic surveillance.

Stuart was sipping some white Burgundy when Sir Charles arrived.

"Hello, Bummer," he said, "I think you'll enjoy this, especially as I paid for it."

Sir Charles scowled. He hated the nickname acquired at Eton playing rugby alongside Stuart. He had earned a reputation for being slow to the bar just because he took longer to change. "Don't be so bloody childish."

"Sorry. I couldn't resist it and you were late. This is the best I've tasted for years." Stuart poured a generous glass of the white Burgundy and passed it across the table.

Sir Charles took a sip. "I suggest we do our business first then we can enjoy the wine without any pressure."

"So, has your man Spencer come up with anything?"

"Yes. He's proved it isn't too difficult to find the Quota algorithms are out of date."

"So it's possible our tame protest groups might find out too?"

"They may need a little help from us. Is your insider ready to leak Quota information?"

"Absolutely. He works in that area so he's believable and

he has contacts."

"We need to decide how best to do that. I think we could convince the PM that a controlled Quota protest is the government's best opportunity for winning the next election. I'll give you the analysis report and leave you to work out the details."

"Ok. I'll get back to you next week with a firm plan."

"There's another thing. Spencer's discovered the extortionists are at it again."

"I thought we'd sorted them."

"These must be new ones. I told Spencer to get onto them as soon as possible. They're probably insiders with privileged Quota access and there aren't too many of those."

"Ok. Keep me posted. We don't want any of that getting out," Stuart said. "Now what do you think of the Burgundy?"

Halfway through the second bottle, Sir Charles had divorced himself from government business and was regretting he hadn't got the name and contact number of the blonde on the train.

He would call Carolyn tonight.

Kate walked into the farm kitchen and rushed towards Lisa who was bent over the sink. Her head hung low; she was retching.

"Whatever's wrong?" Kate tore off some paper towels and handed them to Lisa. "You look awful."

"Nothing, it's just the smell of those pancakes."

Kate boiled the kettle. "You had nothing for breakfast so at least have some tea. It might help."

Lisa sipped some water, dropped into a chair and shook her head, "No thanks, Mum."

"You usually love pancakes. Mind you, they're a nightmare for the hips and those overalls are looking a bit snug."

"Great. Thanks, Mum, you know how to make a girl feel

good." She turned away but not before Kate could see she was upset.

"Oh, love, I was only joking. Actually, a few more curves look good. You've always been a bit skinny. Boys like a little something to hug. You never know, you might get more interest."

She watched her daughter's face crumple. A keen runner, Lisa had always been proud of her flat stomach. But Kate could see a definite curve now. Her imagination might be working overtime but she had to ask. "Oh, no, Lisa, you're not, not..."

Lisa's face hardened and she stared at her mother, her silence speaking volumes.

Kate rammed the paper towel back in its holder, "Haven't I got enough to worry about?"

"You?"

"Yes, me. Another problem I didn't ask for. Thanks for that." Kate could not look at Lisa. She turned to pick up the plates and scraped the remains into the refuse bin.

"Oh, right, 'cos I planned the whole bloody thing, didn't I?" Lisa yelled.

Kate spun round. "Our Quota's bad enough as it is. Have you any idea what I'm dealing with?"

"Right, so it's all about you as usual. At least he listened, which was more than you ever did."

"So, it's my fault you threw yourself at the first bloke that smiled at you." Kate tried to drag the words back but it was too late. Lisa's distress was evident and she hid her face in trembling hands.

Kate knelt down, wiping Lisa's tears away with her finger. "I'm so sorry. Look at me, love. It'll be ok. I promise."

Between sobs and a whole box of tissues, Kate heard the entire story. The middle-aged farmer next door was responsible. Lisa had been working over there for months but Kate had never suspected a thing.

"I'll wring his neck. He's old enough to be your father.

What were you thinking?"

"I'm so sorry, Mum." She hesitated. "Jack thought you'd be able to get me a test. Just to make sure. I don't want you to say anything until we're certain. Even then, I know he'll just go mad."

"Go mad? You wait until I see him." Kate stopped, as Lisa started crying again. "You're right. Don't worry. We'll sort this out. I think I can get a test kit home if I'm careful. I know the girl in the lab at work, so it shouldn't be too difficult." She glanced at the clock. "You go up and wash your face. My parents will be over from the feeding rooms in a minute and I don't want them finding out."

"What were they like, Mum? When you were young?"

Kate thought back to her own childhood, in the city. She had grown up amongst medical students and her parents held open house for all the political activists in the district. She sat on their laps as they discussed a better world, talking late into the night.

The government called them undesirables but they all looked out for her. One by one they stopped visiting and every now and then she would come home from school to find everything packed in the car and they would move on yet again. Once she started at university and lived in the hostel, she hardly heard from her parents. It was as if they had lost all interest. She threw herself into her studies and then met James who offered her the first secure home she had ever had.

After the wedding, they returned to his childhood farm and a rainbow of green fields and crops. But she never forgot the heated arguments that surrounded her disruptive childhood and panicked every time she saw her own children fighting. She tried to keep the peace at all costs but losing James had broken the security she valued above all else. Now her daughter needed help too. Could she cope?

"They were different, that's all, just different. Go and get dressed then help Mary with the young calves. I need to go to the hospital early if I'm to get that test for you."

"Thanks, Mum."

"It's ok. Everything's going to be alright."

Kate watched Lisa drag her feet down the hall towards her room and glanced at James's photo on the shelf. Good God, she thought, why did you leave me? She reached up to touch his face. "So where do I find a new hero, when I need one?" Her eyes settled on the card Clive had left.

Maybe, that's what friends are for. She picked it up, turned it over and stared at his contact details on the back.

CHAPTER 11

Clive was pleased to get the call to encourage more Quota protests. He would attend the next Young Britons meeting in Rickmansworth. If Jack Appleby came, it would be a great opportunity to start grooming him.

He arrived early and sat in the car park, watching those arriving. From ministry downloads he could identify any known dissidents. Glancing up from the scrolling faces on his mobile, he made a note of any new alliances. Overt and covert liaisons were an important part of group dynamics.

He soon spotted Jack parking his electronic scooter. He smiled. The boy had taken up his suggestion to attend the meeting. He looked tense. Clive saw his eyes assessing the others striding towards the entrance and heard him shout obscenities at a young boy who was approaching his scooter. The anger scored years on Jack's face: something Clive would use later to blow Kate's family apart.

Many protest meetings took place undercover but the Young Britons were a recognised organisation openly promoting the development of youth culture, and the Rickmansworth group met regularly at the Mill End Community Centre.

At this meeting, local councillor John Fox had been

invited to discuss new opportunities for the young. Very clever, thought Clive, to get him along. It gave the group legality, and he was impressed when the chairman told him he had even managed to get a grant from the council to fund their equipment. Members subscribing to the group's secret website had been messaged to stay on after the main session. Clive knew Jack was one of these, although he hadn't attended a meeting before. A password would gain them access to another room later in the evening. Clive counted just over thirty attendees, a mixture of teenagers and twenty some-things, mainly male.

Councillor Fox took the podium after a brief introduction by the chairman. "In Rickmansworth, we are dedicated to giving young people a better deal," he opened, echoing the hypocrisy of so many older people.

The first heckler made the mood of the meeting clear. "Prove it, you slimy bastard!"

"We are investing in a new apprentice scheme which will offer training in civil maintenance."

"Road sweeping and shit shovelling," shouted a lad at the back. There was a chorus of laughter. Whilst Clive wanted the first part of the evening to fuel discontent, he needed the group to be angry rather than entertained by their mockery. He stood and moved to the side of the hall so he could eyeball the last heckler and calm things down, for now. "Give the man a fair hearing. He didn't have to come. He isn't going to solve your problems tonight, but any help is a positive step."

The chairman nodded. Clive's confident authority seemed to be accepted and the speaker was able to finish his talk. His proposals offered some new opportunities but they weren't discussed. Just the usual complaints of the young erupted in the shouting that followed.

"Why are the old blokes hanging on to all the good jobs and we get the dross?"

"Why are the old allowed to work as long as they want?"

"Why do university fees rise at double the inflation rate?"

The councillor attempted to respond but was drowned out by constant interruptions.

A ginger youth, whom Clive had recognised in his dissidents file, broke the impasse. He ran to the front, so agitated that it looked like he might become violent.

"We shouldn't bother to talk to these government arse holes," he shouted to cheers. "Let's show them we aren't going to put up with this anymore."

Clive jerked his head at the chairman. Get control of the meeting or you'll lose it, the gesture said. The chairman reacted as his lieutenants moved alongside the angry boy.

"Your committee agrees," he bellowed. "We are going to force the government to take notice of us. And we have a friend here tonight," he added, pointing at Clive, "who can help us do just that."

Clive smiled but said nothing. It was time to close the meeting.

A disgruntled and disaffected group drifted away to find temporary oblivion in the Rickmansworth bars whilst the hard-line activists, including Jack, reconvened in a smaller room. Clive took immediate control, his presence commanding attention.

"We all know that the big issue influencing government policy is increased life expectancy. The sick and old squander more and more resources. Quota was meant to deal with this but it doesn't address your needs. You are still deprived of meaningful work by the active old."

Everyone was listening now.

"I am sure you are all fond of your grandparents but should it be at the cost of your careers? How much is their later life costing your generation? Many of you will be forced into full-time education well past your 30s. Over-educated and under-used. The old have had their day. It's your turn now."

There was a stifled cheer from one youth and Clive paused, giving the group a moment to think about their own aged relations. He knew it was easier to get them to focus on specific targets than a vague enemy.

"The government needs to change the Quota system. Too many families are hiding their old dependents and finding ways of using scarce resources illegally. They're robbing your futures to pay for theirs."

"So what can we do about it?" said the ginger haired activist. "Our parents do what they want."

"We need to persuade the government they are wrong. They must see that employing the young makes sense."

"So what are you suggesting?" the chairman said.

"Get the truth out. Create on-line campaigns. Encourage the Quota owners in your family to withhold their taxes. Then take to the streets at the right time. You won't get change by just whining. Use me as your contact on the inside." Clive added, "I have access to those in power and I will use it for you anyway I can. Without you, this aging society will collapse and they know it."

"Thank you," the chairman said and the rest of the group cheered.

After the meeting, Jack approached Clive.

"Good to see you here," Clive said.

"Thanks. I have been thinking about what you said. Should I report my grandparents? They've just turned up at our farm. They'll screw our Quota and I don't owe them anything. I do a lot of work for this crap government and I deserve some reward."

"You should," Clive said. "If they get sick, the authorities will find out anyway and penalise you. Send me their details and I'll try to minimise the damage on your Quota. I want to help your mum. She is special to me too, but I'm sure you know that, Jack."

Jack nodded agreement. He shook Clive's hand and said

he'd keep in touch.

"The meeting went well in the end, thanks to you," the chairman said.

"Yes," Clive agreed. "I think they're ready. The movement is building and nothing changes without a fight."

He strode back to his car. The pieces were coming together. He was establishing a power base with these young dissidents. He flicked Kate's image back on his dash and grinned. She would be begging for his help any day now but would the payment be worth it? He leant forward and placed his outstretched fingers across her face.

He would make sure it was.

CHAPTER 12

Grant reached out and touched his son's limp fingers lying over the side of the medicot. It had been a close call. The latest dialysis had barely lasted three days, the second one since Toby had been admitted at the weekend. He was deteriorating fast and his medical credits were almost exhausted. Grant was grateful for his ministerial privileges that allowed access to this specialist renal unit. The Amersham hospital was one of the few still active.

Although his condition had stabilised, Toby's only real hope was a transplant. When the credits ran out, he would be put on an early release list. Grant saw the reports weekly. Compulsory euthanasia was widespread, but please god, not his son. He would find a way to get Toby a transplant. An illegal operation in the UK it might be, but he was sure it could be done somewhere. He wasn't going to listen to Carolyn moaning about risking his promotion.

He kissed Toby's cheek and tucked the worn snuggle bear inside the bed. "Sleep well, little man," he whispered.

It had been a long night. He had come here alone, while Carolyn was off on another of her networking weekends. Yawning, he stretched and picked up his coat. He knew what he must do. A young nurse stared at him as he passed her on his way out of the hospital. He guessed he looked a mess and rubbed a hand over his stubble. It was the least of his worries now. With his coat collar turned up, he walked into the dawn mist, heading for a wooden bench in the grounds.

He took out his phone and tapped the contact number. It was early, so Kate Appleby should be home. She would have received her reduced Quota allocation by now and would be feeling vulnerable.

There was a long pause before the phone was answered.

"Jack Appleby."

Grant swallowed with surprise. He struggled to remember his planned words. This was the boy, the possible donor. He must keep calm. "My name's Spencer, Ministry of Life. I'm processing your Quota assessment. Please put Mrs Appleby on the phone."

"What at this time of the morning?"

"This is an official request."

"She's at work."

"I need to speak to her urgently. I know she's a medical assistant. Which hospital is she attached to at the moment?"

"You work it out. You seem to have all the answers."

The phone went dead.

Well, the boy had guts, Grant thought. Most people were only too eager to keep on the right side of government officials. But he was correct about one thing, with his security clearance it would only take a few seconds to pull up Kate's employment record. As soon as the information appeared on his phone, Grant turned to check the entrance sign. Central Hospital 12. Amazingly, she worked at this one. After a long troubled night, his spirits lifted.

He hurried back into the hospital and identified himself to the receptionist. She was quick to direct him to Kate Appleby's unit, located in a secure section.

"Can I help you, sir? This area is for staff only." The

security guard blocked his progress. Grant was not used to being intimidated. He jabbed his ministry card at the man like a weapon, "Stop wasting my time. Where I can find Mrs Appleby?"

"Sorry, sir. I... I didn't realise. Just down the hall there, she's on a break in the rest room. Shall I show you the... "

"No. I can see for myself." Grant strode past. He knew he had been unreasonable but what he was about to do was illegal. He wiped his forehead, loosened his tie a little and sped up.

Reaching the staff room, he pushed the door ajar and looked inside. He recognised Kate Appleby from her data photo, an attractive woman, taller than Carolyn and shapelier than he had expected. She was putting some equipment into her handbag and looked up, startled, as he entered the room.

"Stealing hospital equipment is a serious offence, Mrs Appleby," he said and watched the blood drain from her face.

She dropped her bag on the floor and some of its contents rolled towards him. He picked up a cylinder and read the label, a pregnancy test. So she had another problem he could exploit.

"It seems we have something to discuss," he said, pocketing the kit. "I assume you'd like to talk this through." He felt a little guilty at the fear he saw in her eyes.

"Who are you?" she said.

He flashed his pass.

"I've never done anything like this before, really, but I'm desperate."

"It's a desperate world, Mrs Appleby. Now we can talk or perhaps," he patted his pocket, "you'd like me to take this to the hospital management."

"No. No. We can talk here. We won't be disturbed."

The room was furnished with a leather sofa, a low table, and several chairs. He waited for her to sit and took the chair opposite.

"You can have the pregnancy test kit back and I'll say no

more about it, but you need to hear me out first."

"But... "

"I am a senior official from the Ministry of Life," Grant said, waving his ID again. "I know your Quota has been reduced and after stealing the test kit, it's obvious your position is worse than I realised."

"Please, please don't report me. I'll put it back." Her face mirrored the sort of pain he had been enduring recently. He softened his tone. She seemed an honest person. She had not attempted to deny her actions.

"I am in a position to help your family, Kate, if you help mine."

"What do you mean?"

He leant towards her. "My son is dying. He's just five years old and he's dying." His voice broke and he had to look away for a few seconds.

She waited.

"He has kidney failure and his only chance is a transplant. I'd given up hope of finding a suitable donor, but yesterday, I found a match."

"Well, that's great. You must be so plea..."

"It's your son, Jack. He's a 98% match, the best I could hope for."

She stood. "Just a minute. What's going on here? You burst into my room, looking like a tramp, but claiming to be some sort of official and you start demanding that my son gives you a kidney! I ought to call security."

"You're right, this must look weird, but my son, Toby, is in a ward upstairs and I've been with him all night. I know I don't look good but I am a minister and here's the proof that Jack is a suitable kidney donor." Grant pulled a paper from his pocket and offered it to her.

"I am sorry about your son," she said, her expression mellowing. "But you can't seriously think I would agree to something like this. I know how dangerous that operation is.

You wouldn't get permission for it, and I would never put Jack through something like that. Why would I?"

"Because we both love our children and would do anything to protect them. You help me give Toby extra years and I'll give you the same for your family. Think about it, Kate. I could make your worries go away."

"Sorry I can't and I won't," she said and made for the door.

"Aren't you forgetting something?" Grant stood and removed the test kit from his pocket. "You can hardly risk another pregnancy, another life for the government to assess. Whose it is?"

She shook her head violently.

"My son's upstairs in the critical renal unit. His name's Toby Spencer. Go and see him. See what I have to lose before you make up your mind."

He grabbed her arm. "And Kate, promise me you'll think about it. We both have a lot to gain."

She looked at him, her face flushed.

He released his grip, turned towards the door to go and hesitated. "Here, as a gesture of goodwill. Take it." He gave her the pregnancy kit and stood looking into her eyes. "If we're careful here we could both do well out of it. I'll be in touch, but don't take too long deciding. My son doesn't have much time to spare."

He left, closing the door behind him. As he walked towards the lifts, Grant decided to update Carolyn. Where was she? He had tried her mobile repeatedly and then her hotel. The conference organiser said his wife hadn't booked in. Typical, the one weekend he had Toby to himself there was a crisis. She would blame him as usual. Now he had made contact with the donor family, he wished Carolyn would see sense about a transplant. But if not, he would not hesitate to risk both his career and his marriage.

Toby's fate now depended on Kate Appleby. He would

prefer to get her help willingly but if necessary he would find a way of forcing her cooperation. He hoped it would never come to that. He already liked her.

CHAPTER 13

On the second floor of the hospital, Kate hesitated outside Toby's room. She moved closer to the viewing panel and could see his small body plugged into the monitoring machines that surrounded his bed. He looked pale.

"He had an awful night. Poor kid's deteriorating rapidly." The ward nurse interrupted Kate's thoughts. "It's a crime we aren't allowed to do more." The nurse touched Kate's arm before moving down the corridor towards the next critical care room.

Kate held her palm up and waited for the security scanner to release Toby's door. She stepped inside and drew closer to the sleeping child. He was beautiful. She swept a curl of unruly black hair back from his damp forehead. The darker skin around his eyes gave him a haunted look.

Toby whispered. She leant forward to listen. "Mum," he croaked. "Want Mum."

Kate took one of the sponge sticks from the glass of water by the bed. She ran it gently along his cracked lips and saw a smile start to form and then fade as his eyes searched hers and slid away. He must be feeling abandoned. She remembered how that felt. Her mother had never been around when she was sick.

"Yes, love," she replied, "I know, I know." She tucked his arms back under the covers and waited until he fell asleep again. She slipped out of the room towards the exit and car park.

On the drive home she remembered having a stream of neighbours looking after her when she was small. She had never found anyone she could rely on. Not until she met James.

She glanced at the silver chain hanging from the dashboard and smiled. Her husband's photo stared out from the open locket. Even he had left her. Knowing his death was an accident did not ease the pain.

He was the foundation she had built her adult life on. He had been there in the early days when she learnt to help with the farm and later when the children came along. He had always been her biggest fan. He welcomed her contributions in the laboratory, as he turned the farm into a food research centre. Her qualifications were useful but she found the clinical studies did not give her the satisfaction that nursing offered. People needed her. She was trained to help them. She liked that.

James had a natural understanding with Lisa and Jack, even when they were babies. He had a confidence they responded to. When they were older, she watched James throw himself into the harmless bundle of arms and legs. She felt awkward, over protective and unable to join in the boisterous games. The sullen stares they threw back made her feel like an outsider. She realised now they were pleas for affection. She always seemed to get it wrong. The stream of temporary carers she had as a child, made it difficult for her to believe anyone loved her, even her own children. She needed to get it right now.

She turned off the motorway towards Sarratt. The lanes grew narrow and branches whipped backwards and forwards in the driving rain. Jack would need all the help he could get to bring the animals in. He was wiry but had his dad's strength, unlike Toby.

She thought of Toby's dad. His offer to help with her family's Quota came at a high cost. His child needed a transplant but the risk involved for Jack could be substantial. It was not a decision she could make at the moment, she could still see Toby's face too clearly.

Grant was obviously doing everything possible to save his son but what if Kate didn't go along with his suggestion? He was a powerful man. Maybe she should appear to consider his offer just to buy some time, not that Toby had much to spare.

As she drove slowly through the flooded lanes she considered her other option. Clive also had insider knowledge and influence. At university she had never felt at ease in his company but he wasn't asking for anything and appeared to want to help her. Could she trust telling him about her parents' return? She would have to. He was shrewd and would certainly find out eventually.

She remembered him as a bit of a loner in his younger days but he had always seemed to like her. His temper, when his work was not credited, was frightening and she had even feared for the professor that had stolen his research. When the professor was given an unexpected scholarship abroad, Clive seemed to forget about him, so she had relaxed.

Clive was a clever man and if he said he could get around the system she had no doubt he would. She would give Clive a call. What did she have to lose?

She pulled into the farm's security enclosure and waved her hand across the scanner to gain access. The government had insisted on a high level of screening after James had started his final project but the children were always powering the system down so they could invite their friends round. It had sent James mad but she turned a blind eye.

At least they had friends, although she needed to talk to Jack about the hours he spent on chat forums. James used to run a report to check on his activities. She felt it was as bad as reading someone's diary but he might have been right. Lisa might not have got pregnant if she had been watching her more closely.

She parked the car and ran through the downpour to the front door. The weather was worsening year on year but the government still insisted it was on top of climate control. Most of the population had already stopped believing them. Her parents were adamant the government had been lying for years.

She shook the water from her coat and hung it in the sterilising room before going into the kitchen for a hot drink, her mind still in turmoil. Her parents were laughing around the kitchen table with Mary and her children. She had not seen her mother-in-law giggle like this for months. She watched her trying to hold her drink steady as laughter erupted. Even Jack had a wry smile on his face.

For a brief second, she felt immense comfort at having the whole family around her again before reality sank in. She was tempted to tell her parents not to get too comfortable but said nothing and poured herself a mug of tea.

"We were just telling Mary about an artist who lived with us. He painted 3D images of politicians on our toilet walls in various stages of discomfort. Constipation Cabinet he called it." Her father's remark set off more laughter.

Kate snapped. "I wasn't aware we had so much to celebrate." She dropped her bag on the table and removed a small plastic box which she passed to her daughter. "Some new embryo tests for the spring lambs." She stared at Lisa's puzzled frown until her meaning was clear. Lisa took the sterile container and rushed from the room.

"Mum's always been a party pooper," said Jack before he picked up his lab coat and left too.

"Had a hard day, love?" offered Mary, blotting her tears on her cardigan and trying to submerge another giggle that threatened to erupt.

"It was a tough one."

"I'll go and check on Lisa for you. She's looked a bit down lately. Not really herself." Mary patted Kate's arm before following her granddaughter upstairs.

"Dinner will be ready in an hour," her mother said, picking up the empty mug in front of Kate, "Do you want a refill?"

Kate looked at her mother and swallowed the tart response forming on her lips.

"I've been showing Mary some of the European recipes we picked up on our travels." Her mother continued. "We've made a Ukrainian stew tonight."

Kate paused and studied her mother's thin face: she was gaunt, her eyes blood-shot. Probably her age, she thought.

"You look worried, Kathryn. Have there been problems at the hospital?"

She recognised real concern in the words. but twenty years too late.

Her mother turned away from Kate's intense gaze and started fussing with the oven. "Haven't seen one of these old stoves for years, so much better than the hi-tech bloody contraptions they use nowadays."

Her father walked across and put a gentle hand on his wife's back before taking the cloth from her and cleaning the hob himself. They still showed love for each other.

"Are you ok, Mum?" Kate asked. The words were out of her mouth before she could stop them.

"Course," said her mother, turning around with a quick smile.

"Now, Sarah, we can't keep up this charade. Remember what we agreed, love?"

She watched as her father guided her mother to a seat and beckoned for Kate to sit with them. "Your mother's ill. It's why we came back."

Kate dropped into the chair. "What's wrong?"

"Cancer, treatable nowadays of course but with our record we won't get the treatment she needs at NHS hospitals."

"I'd help," Kate said, realising she meant it. "But without medical credits I'd never get you into my hospital."

"We know, Kate. We wanted to see you and the family before taking the next step."

"What next step?"

"There's a private research hospital we have contacts at. It's unlicensed, not government run," he smiled at Sarah.

"Isn't that dangerous?"

"No, the government turn a blind eye, probably because most of the ministers use it themselves."

"People will usually find a way round a system if their families are threatened," said Kate realising it was exactly what she hoped to do. "It's like the poor boy I saw tonight at the hospital. He'll die if he doesn't get the transplant he needs but his family have just run out of credits. It's criminal."

"Bit like us," said her dad.

She smiled and they all found the common ground they were searching for.

"I want to help him but I just don't know how. His father is a Government official and he has offered to increase our family Quota if I let him use Jack as a kidney donor. He seems certain he is a good enough match."

"Surely that's Jack's decision, not yours, but if he doesn't get involved, this hospital could do the operation. Sick children have higher priority there, unlike the bloody government hospitals."

Her mother looked at her with regret and sadness. Maybe it was time to let go of the past, thought Kate. After all she had hardly been a model parent herself. She softened but could not bring herself to speak. It was still too early.

"Well, let's get that dinner sorted," her mother said, moving towards the oven. "Didn't you say you were going up to talk to Lisa?"

Kate's thoughts came crashing back to the present. "I'll go up now. Yes, I must talk to her. Something that needs sorting. I'm sorry about the cancer, Mum, really I am."

She waited for her mother's nod and then rose from the table and left to find Lisa. She climbed the stairs with mounting concern. She hoped the pregnancy test would turn up a negative result but in her heart she already knew.

Kate paused to listen before entering Lisa's room to check Mary had gone. With a surprising sense of relief, she realised her parents' return might offer the support she needed. She knocked gently and opened the door to find Lisa with the serum kit in her hands.

"Mum, what are we going to do?"

Kate felt her daughter's fear and tried to reassure her. "We'll work it out."

"I can't go to the clinic for the embryo test. I don't have a partner or even enough credits to get the pregnancy licence. They'll abort it." Lisa's face crumpled.

"Would that be such a bad thing?" The words were out of her mouth before she could think. Kate's eyes slid away from Lisa's searching stare. What a stupid thing to say. She met her daughter's gaze, she had seen that look before, and it was defiance.

"Mum, that's not going to happen. I know I've been really stupid but that's hardly the baby's fault." She placed her hands on her softly curved abdomen and raised her voice. "It might be wrong but it feels good. I'm scared but deep down I feel happier than I have felt for ages. Is that mad?"

"No, love, no it's not. I just had to ask, see if you were sure. It's not going to be easy but we'll get through it together. I think I'll be able to smuggle the Correction Serum out as my friend Maggie works in the lab. I know she did it for her sister."

"I'm not sure I want it. I know it's been used for years but it just doesn't feel right. Is it safe?"

Kate smiled, she was thinking like a mother already. "I felt the same but it's no different from the old vaccinations really and it will ensure your baby has no disabilities and a cancer-free life." She walked across and hugged Lisa tight. "It's the best start you could give your child."

She stroked her daughter's hair and the protection she had felt when Lisa was born surfaced all over again. This raw emotion was the core strength she drew on now. "We'll work it out. You get some sleep and we'll talk again tomorrow when I get back from work. Your grandparents were telling me about contacts they have with an unlicensed hospital."

"Unlicensed?"

"Yes, it sounds a bit scary but they have looked into it already. It's probably the only place we could go for your scan and delivery. We'll check it all out before we decide though."

"They seem to know a lot of things, Mum. Grandad's so funny too. I'm glad they're here, aren't you?"

Kate turned to face the bedroom window and watched the moon's glow highlighting the lambs in the feeding fields. She waved her hand to activate the blackout filter. "Yes," she said. "I think I am." Kate closed Lisa's door and decided to run a bath.

She needed thinking time.

Wallowing in the foamy water, she listened to a few of her husband's favourite tracks. The gentle rhythm of the orchestral chords washed over her and the frantic clatter of her thoughts slowed to a murmur at last. The music faded and her mother-in-law's voice burst through the speaker.

"Sorry, Kate, I know how you feel about being disturbed in the bath, but he says it's urgent, some Ministry official about Quota. I'll patch it through."

Although Kate knew there would be no visual connection, she automatically lowered herself in the water as Clive's voice filled the room. "Apologies for the late call, Kate, but I've had some disturbing news. A reliable source says your grandparents have returned."

Kate sighed. She should have told him. This would not look good. The water lapped around her as she closed her eyes and tipped her head back against the cold porcelain and groaned. "Sorry," she muttered as she sank lower in the water.

"Where are you, Kate? Are you in the bath?"

Her eyes flew open. She had an uncanny feeling that he could see her, was there in the room with her. A rush of water cascaded down her body as she stood, grabbed the towel and stepped from the bath.

"You are, aren't you? Pity I don't have visual."

She could hear his breathing. Kate's eyes scanned the room and checked the red eye monitor in the corner. The light was out, so why did she feel so nervous? There was an uncomfortable silence before Clive continued. "Just joking, Kate, but I do need to talk to you. I am in the north-west sector tomorrow seeing a client so I will pop by your hospital. It's important. This is serious: your parents return will damage your Quota allocation."

"Of course."

"If I am going to help, I need you to be completely truthful. No more secrets."

Kate's chest tightened as she pictured Lisa's swelling stomach but she couldn't risk it. Not until she knew she could trust him. "No, I understand, of course I do. I'll talk to you tomorrow and no secrets, I promise."

His tone lightened. "Great. I look forward to seeing you fully clothed this time." She heard a breathy laugh before he cut the call.

She shivered, pulled the towel tighter and hurried into the bedroom.

CHAPTER 14

Kate awoke with a start. Clive's call had unsettled her last night so she hadn't fallen asleep until around 2am. She looked at the clock and groaned, realising she was a good half hour late already. She rolled the duvet back and dragged herself out of bed. She raced into the shower and let the warm water stream down her face, trying to empty her mind. She told herself she had overreacted.

Clive was a high-ranking Quota official with the skills to help. His tone had an uncomfortable intimate tone but if he was the only man who could help, she would learn to deal with him. After the shower, she checked the time. She hated rushing but there was no option.

The traffic was light so she caught up a little time but was still late. She parked her car near the hospital charge unit, slammed the door and ran towards the entrance. Nudging her way through the queue of patients, she hurried towards the reception desk, registered Clive's details onto the visitor screen and headed for the stairs.

She rushed into the staff room to change into her shift uniform. After ripping open the sealed pack, she wedged her feet into the sterilised shoes. Six forty-five. Damn.

"Late night?" the agency nurse joked as she passed. "Hope he was worth it!"

Kate frowned and continued walking. These young nurses had only one thing on their minds. Was she ever like that? She adjusted her cap, took a deep breath and entered the ward, hoping she looked calmer than she felt.

It was a busy morning with ten new admissions and a download from central records to co-ordinate. With her research experience, Kate was always asked to manage the data reports and monitoring system but it was not something she enjoyed. She would rather talk to old Mrs Matthews than manage the data stream that documented her last breath.

It was midday when she walked into the clinical office. She removed her sterile ward clothes and pushed them down inside the shredder, slipped into the blue admin outfit and clipped the monitoring belt around her waist. After entering her personal code into the belt, she pulled out a pair of interactive glasses and adjusted the lenses.

She sat at the table-top and sighed. She was too tired for any problems this morning. The last update had taken hours of extra work. The icons came alive as she murmured, "Let's get this done."

She concentrated on tracking the information with her fingertips, watching test results whizz across the softly illuminated display to disappear into the patients' files. She didn't hear the office door open. The hand on her shoulder was totally unexpected and she recoiled in shock.

"I'm sorry, Kate. I didn't mean to frighten you." She saw Grant's eyes soften and he moved back a little.

"How did you get in?"

"I was on the third floor. Toby's condition has worsened." She could see the panic in his eyes as his voice grew louder, "I need your decision."

"For God's sake, Grant, you'd better close the door. Someone might hear us."

66

He appeared slightly dazed as he leant against the steel frame and drew his hands through his short grey hair. He was a big man but seemed to crumple inside his suit jacket. "Please," he said quietly.

She took a few seconds to reply. "I haven't had a chance to talk to Jack yet. If I'm honest it's not something I can see him doing and I'm not sure I'd let him anyway." She moved back. "I'm sorry."

He looked broken. "But you're my only hope. I don't have enough credits to keep Toby here any longer. You have to help me."

Kate could see the pain in his face and spoke softly, "I know he's fragile. I saw him yesterday." She touched Grant's shoulder and decided to trust him a little. "I might be able to help you in another way. My family have contacts with a research hospital that handles transplants. It may be possible to transfer Toby there. It's risky but I could find out for you. Don't give up yet."

The dark shadows and overgrown stubble underlined the strain he was under. This was not the powerful man she had witnessed earlier. She helped him to a seat, filled a paper cup with water and held his fingers around the container.

"I haven't slept properly for days," he said. "I don't know what to do. For the first time in my life I feel so helpless, so utterly alone."

"What about your wife? How is she coping?"

His hand tightened around the cup. "She's more worried about the effect on my career. I'm afraid Toby doesn't fit the designer lifestyle she had in mind."

Kate was surprised at this intimate disclosure but ignored it. "Try not to worry."

Grant seemed to find his composure, drained the water and tossed the cup in the bin. Kate's attention switched to an alert scrolling across her Comms glasses. After tweaking the image she realised Clive was on his way up to see her. She felt uneasy; she did not want these men to meet. She had too many decisions to make first.

"I'm sorry, Grant, I have a lot of data to process, I really need to get on."

He straightened. "I'll leave now but please don't let me down, Kate. I'm relying on you and so is Toby."

"I'll be in touch, I promise. Now you really have to go." She took off her glasses and smiled.

He looked directly into her eyes, "Make sure it's soon. Please," he said, shaking her hand. Kate followed him across the room and watched him disappear around the corner.

She closed the door and before she had reached her chair, heard an urgent knock. Oh no, she thought, surely Grant wasn't going to pressurise her again? It was Clive.

"You ok, Kate?" he hesitated, "Were you expecting someone else?"

"No, no. Come in." she felt flustered. "Would you like a drink?"

"I was planning to take you to lunch."

Kate flinched under his intense gaze. "We could go to the staff restaurant but I don't have long," she stammered, fumbling with her monitoring belt and struggling to switch it to standby. She stabbed at the table-top display power button and cursed when it was slow to respond.

"You look stressed. I'll take you out for a bit. Looks like you could do with a break." Clive strolled over to open the door. "There's a café in the park over the road." His mouth stretched into a wide grin. "My treat."

The protest dried on her lips as she folded her glasses into her uniform pocket. Kate felt his hand on the small of her back and was propelled out of the room.

"Leave everything to me," he insisted.

She forced herself to relax. She must be getting neurotic. He just wants to help. She smiled at Clive and walked out.

The weather was fine so they chose a seat outside the

café, opposite the lake. After a quick look at the menu, Clive disappeared into the wooden chalet. There were many families enjoying the sunshine and she thought how Grant's son Toby would have loved it here.

Kate watched Clive as he walked towards her, tray in hand. He was not a handsome man. His thin floppy hair framed an almost gaunt face which had an intensity she realised she found unsettling. At university she had sensed he had wanted a personal relationship, but his interest in her cooled around the time she met James.

A small child ran in front of Clive, nearly causing him to drop the tray. He thrust his foot out and for one horrified moment she imagined he was going to kick the boy. He looked across at her and laughed loudly. No doubt about it, her paranoia was getting out of hand. She had too much on her mind.

"Pesky kids, thought I was going to drop the lot," he said with a nod. He placed the tray on the plastic yellow table and sat next to her. "Eat up and I'll let you know how much trouble you're in."

Kate sat back in her chair and listened with a growing sense of disbelief. The situation was worse than she imaged. He explained that the return of her grandparents completely altered her status as they were seen as non-contributing dependents. This and their past involvement in outlawed protest groups would affect her family Quota irretrievably.

Clive told her the government no longer saw her aged parents as a threat; it was the young militants they were worried about, but they would still have a negative effect on her Quota. He showed her his calculations. Kate was shocked. Her mother-in-law was facing a Compulsory Exit order, with her parents following within weeks. Her children's life expectancy had been lowered to mid-forties.

Her distress was obvious and Clive reached for her hand.

"But, Kate, it doesn't have to be like that. You're lucky.

I can manipulate the data. I've done it before. It's foolproof. The suits upstairs won't have a clue." Clive leant back in his chair and a cocky smile spread across his pale face. "Problem solved."

"But what if they find out? I've heard of whole families disappearing when they've tried to avoid their Quota."

Clive gripped her shaking hands. "Trust me, that won't happen. I know the system inside out. They have no idea what I'm capable of."

His hands gripped hers so tight. She could feel his nails pinch her wrists and his eyes seemed to worm their way into her thoughts. She wrenched her hands away and a cool breeze combed the tiny hairs on her arms. "It's getting cold." She glanced down at her watch. "And it's time I got back."

Clive stood and waited for her to get closer. "Before you go, perhaps you'd like to tell me what Grant Spencer wanted today? He looked upset as he was leaving." He blocked her way.

Kate knew she would have to come up with something quickly. "His son's ill. I was just trying to help. Why, do you know him?"

"The Ministry's a small world and if you're thinking of getting involved with him, there are a few things you should know."

On their way back to the hospital, Clive talked of Grant's high profile in the Ministry of Life and his reputation for advancement and getting his own way. "Not many people would take him on and if his scheming wife's to be believed, there's a whisper he might be up for a top ministerial job. He has asked for help, hasn't he?"

She wondered how much she should tell him. She needed Clive and if Grant's promotion was at risk, he could inform on her entire family once his son had the treatment. She didn't intend to go ahead with the transplant idea anyway so why get involved?

"Grant wants me to help his son get treatment, a transplant, maybe."

"Why would you risk that?"

"Like you, he said he could manipulate my Quota."

Clive turned away and seemed to be considering his answer. "He's lying Kate. No-one could pull that off and get away with it, except me. Ignore him; he's just a desperate man trying to save his son." He flashed a smile and held out his hand. "As a small bonus, I'll check him out." Before she had time to complain, he kissed her cheek.

Kate watched him melt into the crowds and felt a soft chill caress the nape of her neck. She wiped her cheek. The kiss had unnerved her. Had she made the right decision? She hoped she hadn't caused Grant trouble. He clearly cared for his son and she wanted to help if she could. But Clive had been adamant. Grant was someone who knew what he wanted and used anyone to get it. She could see that herself. He was a powerful man wielding his influence, so why did the butterfly in her chest beat its wings so wildly?

The alarm on her uniform lapel flashed out a ward emergency. She pushed the respond button and hurried towards the hospital. Her worry about Clive was pure paranoia. She had to ignore both men and concentrate on her patients.

CHAPTER 15

After leaving Kate, Clive drove back to London at high speed. Sorting out the Appleby's Quota had paled into insignificance. Someone was getting in his way. He was annoyed with himself that he hadn't taken measures against Grant Spencer when the arrogant bureaucrat had first crossed his path.

He'd heard that Spencer had spotted his illegal manipulations, but Clive was confident that he couldn't be identified directly. It would take a long time before suspicion would fall on him. After all, wasn't he one of the government's special agents? But he had been too complacent. He should neutralise Spencer now. The guy was meddling, competing for Kate and with the same bait.

Clive switched on his spy software from the car transmitter. He requested a scan of Spencer's personnel files and a list of surveillance sources in the neighbourhood of his flat. He should have the results by the time he reached his own apartment. He was determined to take action tonight.

He set up another search on Spencer's wife, Carolyn. Her continuing absence from her son's bedside looked suspicious. Most mothers would have been there day and night. So why hadn't she visited once? He displayed her image on the car's master screen and recognised her immediately. She had been at one of Sir Charles's jamborees several years back. He remembered wondering why she had been flirting so blatantly with her host. It was going to be worth having a closer look at her activities too.

As Clive's sense of control returned, his anger mutated to a powerful lust and thoughts of Kate flooded his mind. He wanted her more than ever before. For years he had battled to forget his early infatuation but seeing her again had revived and strengthened those feelings. The compulsion to have her felt irresistible. He couldn't play the long game anymore. She was available and his for the taking. He would have her now. Trembling with expectation he touched the car screen and retrieved a recent picture of her, then speaking slowly into the on-board communicator, he arranged a meeting.

After a quick stop at his flat for a shower and change of clothes, Clive was back in his car. He activated the tracking blocker so he could drive to his next location undetected, the secret place he used for his liaisons.

On arrival at the entrance to a regency terraced house in West London, he punched in his personal access code and was alerted that his guest had arrived ten minutes earlier. She was ready, waiting for him in the first floor front bedroom. He fought to control the frenzied anticipation that threatened his performance but rushed up the stairs and pushed open the bedroom door. The red light picked out Kate sitting half-naked on the edge of the bed. She turned towards him with an inviting smile and reached down to run a fingertip up her inner thighs. Clive was on her in an instant. She screamed as he threw her onto the bed, turned her over, and ripped off her pants. With animal fury, he released twenty years of repressed lust in a violent rape.

"You bastard," the girl whispered as Clive lay gasping on

top of her. "You'll pay top whack for that."

He groaned and rolled on to his side. The holographic projector was turned off and the Kate lookalike reverted to her normal appearance, a hard-faced, twenty-something, he hadn't seen at the Virtual Brothel before. She disentangled herself, collected her scattered clothes and slammed the door as she left.

At that moment his phone rang. It was the real thing this time. He let the message service pick up. Kate was calling for help but she could wait. After all, hadn't he waited years?

CHAPTER 16

Grant sat sipping a beer in the raised area at the back of the Coach and Horses, a pub he had noticed passing through Rickmansworth. He would have driven straight home after visiting Toby, but a chilling message from Sir Charles had pushed him into a dark mood and he needed a drink.

He couldn't face Carolyn and her usual histrionics yet. In truth, he didn't enjoy being with her much these days. They had stopped having sex over a year ago and her demand for separate rooms had killed any intimacy. Toby's health should have given them lots to talk about but Carolyn seemed to have abandoned the boy to the carers. He never saw her playing with him. And now, with his condition critical, she had dismissed the boy as an irritant to her social mobility and decided that fate could take its course without her involvement.

From his vantage point in the bar, Grant could observe the progress of dates, the friendly posturing of football fans and was just in earshot of several older men debating the future of the world.

Their shouting and raucous belly laughs shattered his concentration. A curious group, he thought, wondering if it was only fondness for drink that had brought them together. The bald-headed man, with a potbelly, was clearly a labourer, the man in the suit probably an office worker while the third man, bearded and with a cultured voice, sounded like an academic.

Gradually their conversation became more serious and interesting to Grant. He shifted his chair so he could hear them better. It wasn't often that he listened to what ordinary people were thinking. He grimaced to himself, calling these guys ordinary.

"My grandson's nearly thirty and still can't find a proper job. What sort of life is that, sponging off his parents," the labourer said.

"I've nieces and nephews just like that. There just aren't enough opportunities for the young," the office worker agreed. "This government has got it all wrong."

"That's every family's story these days," added the academic. "I do my best to give youngsters skills and then the government raises the pension age so no one retires."

"I would go tomorrow if they gave me a decent pension," the bald man said." I shouldn't be digging up roads at seventy."

"Of course, you shouldn't," the academic said, "but the moment you stop, the government population policy will consign you to the knackers' yard."

Grant squirmed. That's just what he had been charged with organising. Sir Charles wanted him to set up a project to cull any over-seventies who were using medical services more than the norm. With average life expectancy reaching a hundred, how could you deprive a temporarily-ill seventy-year-old years of reasonable life? He guessed it was a cynical attempt to curry favour with the young and he desperately wanted to find a way of sabotaging this latest initiative.

He started berating himself for getting involved in the Quota programme. And then he realised, his position inside the Ministry of Life might give him the power to change things and he was going to try his hardest to do that.

He didn't think any of the protest groups would be strong

enough to overturn government policy but attacks from the inside might. His report to Sir Charles had shown that the Quota Algorithms were flawed and that a relaxation of the policy was fully justified. But for reasons he didn't understand, the government would not be moved by logic.

He wondered how much the cabinet and senior civil servants were protecting themselves from the Quota threat. Maybe a little delving into their individual family situations might throw up some anomalies. Yes, personal interest was the most powerful lever of change, a threat always won over reason. He would start with a detailed look at Sir Charles' relations. If he could be threatened, there was hope for everyone.

His musings were interrupted by a push from the fat man. "What are you looking at mate?"

Grant hadn't realised that he had been staring at the man, seeing him as the focus of his attempts to save the able-bodied seventy-year-olds. "I am sorry. I was lost in my thoughts."

"Well, piss off and get lost yourself"

The drink had made the atmosphere threatening and Grant decided it was time to leave.

"I'm sorry," he said again and edged quickly past the group to the door. Despite their hostility, he felt better for meeting them.

He paused on the way to his car to read a message, continuously bleeping on his phone. Damn Sir Charles for pestering him in his free time. But it wasn't him. His resolution to break Quota evaporated as his hands trembled. Three curt words seemed to signal the end of any happiness in his life.

Medical Credits Exhausted

He must remove Toby from the Amersham hospital tomorrow. Where could he take him now? He leaned on the nearest car. He had thought he would find a way to save Toby but he had failed. He could hardly breathe and a passer-by stopped, seeing his anguish.

"You all right, pal?"

Grant recognised the labourer from the pub, no longer part of an angry group.

"Yes, thanks. Just felt breathless for moment. I'll be ok."

The man nodded and walked on.

Grant forced himself to take deep breaths and to start thinking calmly. He could only come up with one option now, the research hospital Kate had mentioned. Maybe they could help but would they treat the child of a government minister? He couldn't ask Kate again about her son donating a kidney. He knew it wasn't right. Like him, she wanted to protect her children, particularly after just losing her husband.

It was nearly 11pm, too late to make a begging call really, but he had to do it. Kate answered after a few rings, her voice calm and strangely caring.

"Hello, Kate Appleby," she said, as if she was expecting the call.

"I'm sorry to ring so late Kate, it's Grant Spencer."

"I thought it was the hospital. I'm on call tonight. What do you want? Is it Toby?"

"Yes. He's a lot better after dialysis but I've no credits left so I have to remove him from the ward. I wanted to ask about that research hospital. Do you think they would take Toby? I'll pay whatever it takes."

"I don't know. My father's taking my mum so I could ask him about taking Toby too."

"Can I talk to him? I'm desperate to get something organised."

"He's asleep. I don't want to wake him but I promise I'll ask first thing tomorrow."

"That might be too late. They want to release Toby immediately."

Kate paused before replying. "Toby could stay with me till my parents leave in a few days."

"Could you really care for him at the farm? I don't know

where else to take him. My wife's against anything illegal. I don't want to tell her."

"Yes, I think I can manage. Meet me in the hospital reception at eight tomorrow morning before the doctors' rounds."

"Thanks, Kate. How can I repay you?"

"I'm a nurse, Grant. It's what I do. I'll see you tomorrow."

Grant felt tears of relief. Hope wasn't gone. Something was happening. He decided he didn't want to go home tonight and risk talking to Carolyn.

He sent her a message. *Working late, won't disturb you, staying at the Ramada*

He got into his car and drove to his regular hotel in London. They always had spare rooms. As he parked, he received a reply from Carolyn. Ok

He was surprised she was still awake and disappointed she hadn't asked about Toby.

CHAPTER 17

Kate was up early. She found Mary hunched over the kitchen table concentrating on a lengthy document. After reading the final page, her mother-in-law wrenched off her glasses and dropped them on to the wooden surface.

"Are you ok?" Kate asked, pulling out a chair to sit on.

Mary eyes were red rimmed. She tried to laugh but it almost choked her. "Seems I've got rid of those damned early starts." The letter shook in her hand. "Can't complain. Poor Mrs Patterson got hers at fifty-five, just a week after her husband passed." She turned to Kate with a defiant grin.

Kate grabbed the paperwork and checked the date. "How do they get away with this?"

Her throat burned with outrage. Mary was a healthy, caring, woman who just wanted to stay with her family. It was cruel. She moved to the dresser and pulled her husband's whisky out from the back and poured a large measure. She pressed it into Mary's hands.

"I'll try Clive again. He'll know what to do." She tried to sound confident as she watched Mary, glass in hand, unable to lift it to her lips.

Kate sat and scanned the crumpled pages .The government

literature had been blunt. Mary had one month before her Quota deadline and Early Release. Since the borders had closed, most healthy pensioners signed up for the travel option, deciding to have one final adventure. She read on. The government offered to increase grandchildren's Quota if the elderly took a partner with them. As a widow, Mary was not offered that option. After years of medical neglect, old people with ongoing health problems opted for skilled nursing and an injection to end their suffering. It was ironic to think thousands had campaigned for assisted dying more than 30 years ago and had never imagined this might be the result. Mary's choices were grim but Kate knew they had one more card to play.

She grabbed her phone and tried Clive's number and hoped he picked it up this time.

"Kate?"

"Thank God you're there. Mary's had her Exit notification. You have to do something, now."

"It's ok. That's just an automatic mail out. We still have time." His voice dropped. "You do trust me, don't you Kate?"

Did she? Something in his voice made her tremble until she looked at Mary's face. "I do, of course I do," she stuttered.

He continued quickly, "You mustn't talk to anyone. No one must know you've received the notification, no one."

Clive explained he would need a few days to work on the data. It was dangerous work and he would contact her when he was ready. She felt relieved. They had bought Mary some time, time that five-year-old Toby was running out of. She sighed.

"What's wrong? I thought you'd be over the moon."

"I'm still worried about the little boy in my hospital."

"The Spencer kid will have to take his chances like everyone else. His father thinks he's a big noise. That's his problem. The little brat will probably die soon, anyway."

"My God!" Kate could not silence her shock.

After a pause Clive's voice softened. "Listen, Kate. That

might sound harsh but it's your family you have to worry about. You still want me to help, don't you?"

"Well, yes, of course, but he's just a little..."

"Focus, Kate. Believe me, it's the survival of the fittest. That is, unless you have friends in the right places, eh?"

The guilt sat like a huge lump in her throat but she had to swallow it. Mary was crying softly in the chair. She knew what she had to do.

"You're right, of course, Clive, but I'm worried about the deadlines they've given Mary. We don't have much time."

"Time's a valuable commodity. You'll get everything you deserve. I promise."

She put the phone down and put her arms around Mary. "It's going to be alright. He can help us I'm sure." Kate decided to ignore the unease stirring in her stomach.

"Well, I'd better make myself useful or your friend might change his mind." Mary stood and wiped a hand across her cheeks. She avoided glancing at the papers as if they would infect her and crossed to the oven.

As she looked through the open window at the lambs, Kate's thoughts turned to Toby. Her animals received better care than him. His pale young face haunted her. How could she let him suffer when she knew she could help? She needed to talk to her father.

She found her parents clearing the long grass from the backfields that framed the lambing fence.

"You've let this go, Kate. Come spring, the young ones will get tangled on all this electronic gadgetry eating the overgrown grasses." Her father stopped hacking the undergrowth and smiled up at her.

"At the moment I'm more concerned about the little boy I saw at work yesterday. I've come to ask for your help."

"We're driving down to the research hospital on the Isle of Dogs soon. Do you want us to take him?" asked her mother. "Nothing's guaranteed but the doctors help children as a priority. We'd have to know more about him first but it might be possible."

"Kate, you can't go worrying about every problem you come across." Her father's face was full of concern. "You must concentrate on your own family."

She bit her lip.

"Are you ok, Kate? You look like you've so much on your mind." Her mum drew her close for a hug.

"You have no idea." Kate was horrified when her tears erupted as she felt the familiar softness envelope her. Years of emotion poured out. She looked up and saw the mother's love she had yearned for.

Her mum held her tighter. "I love you, darling. We just couldn't risk contacting you."

There were tears in her father's grey eyes. "We loved you enough to leave you."

She buried herself in her parent's arms until she felt strong enough to continue. "When I lost James I knew life would be hard but I had no idea how tough it would get."

"We're here for you this time," her father said.

"Now Mary's received her Exit papers, I'll be even more alone."

Her father's face glowered with indignation. "Bloody government! I remember when our grandparents looked forward to retirement. Now they treat the elderly like cheap labour and make them work until they drop. That and the withdrawal of decent medical care, even for children. What the bloody hell do they think they're doing?"

Her mother led Kate towards the trunk of a felled oak and they sat down together. "We've travelled all over the world supporting protest groups but governments everywhere continue to ignore people and just want to balance the national debts." She put her arm around Kate and continued. "They've been lying for years about resources while the rest of us pay the price. We need to harness the people's anger and fight smart now."

Her father nodded in agreement. "We came back for your mother's treatment but we want a fair deal for everyone. We need to hit at the heart of Quota headquarters and blow their corrupt intelligence sky high."

Kate listened in silence. The thought frightened her but she could see justification burn in their eyes.

"We're well known to the authorities so have nothing to lose but we don't have the contacts to help Mary with her pension call up. Many of our friends have gone into hiding and escaped for a few years but eventually they're discovered. The only way to make the people we care about safe is to hit the system from within."

She was about to tell her parents about Clive's offer but was afraid they would stop her getting involved. She decided to focus on Toby's problems. "Toby's only hope is a transplant. If you could take him, he stands a chance. His father's an important Ministry man. I'm sure he would help to keep the authorities off your backs."

"I don't like the idea of his father."

"Don't judge, Adam," her mother turned to Kate. "We would have to know more about the child's condition and his father's motives but the poor mite should be given a chance."

"Won't it put you in more danger?" Kate asked.

Her father lifted his hands. "Nothing new there."

They all grinned and started discussing the arrangements and contacts they would need. By the time they walked across the fields back to the farmhouse, Mary had breakfast on the table and was looking far less stressed.

Kate checked her watch, grabbed her car keys and gave Mary a quick kiss before leaving for the hospital. As she drove down the country lanes in the early morning sunshine she decided Clive wasn't the only one who could help people after all.

CHAPTER 18

"Where we going, Daddy?" Toby said, as Grant adjusted the seat belt and buckled up his son. He looked a little better.

"To a farm, Toby, and there will be animals to play with."

"Oh, I love aminals."

Grant was always amused by this malapropism.

Toby's eyes grew wider. "Will there be lions and tigers?"

"I don't think so," he said, "but you'll definitely see some real sheep. They're as soft as your own snuggle bear."

Grant had met Kate at the hospital as planned. She had done more than he expected, arriving early and checking that Toby had completed his treatment and would be safe for another week. She had also procured emergency medical supplies for their journey. Grant was moved by her charitable response to a stranger who had forced his problem on her. He felt he could trust her with Toby's care. She waved him to follow as she drove past in her ancient car before turning out of the hospital car park.

Kate's farm at Sarratt was only ten miles away and in less than twenty minutes they were parking on the gravel yard outside the house. Grant had ignored several messages from the office, having set his receiver to automatic response mode.

He listened to them quickly before leaving the car. There was nothing that couldn't wait.

"Come on, Toby," he chuckled, "let's explore." He lifted his son out of the car and onto his shoulders. Kate smiled as she came over to them.

"Where are the aminals?" Toby asked.

"Let's see if we can find some, shall we?" Kate led them round the barn to the field where sheep were grazing. Grant lowered Toby to the ground and held him close to the fence so he could stroke one of the young lambs. He grinned as he saw the excitement on his son's face.

"I'll show you some more later," Kate said and squeezed Toby's hand. "But let's go in now. We don't want you getting a chill."

Grant walked alongside her towards the farmhouse, while Toby waved noisy goodbyes to the sheep. Kate stopped walking and turned to Grant, her face serious. "Promise me you won't tell anyone my parents are here. It would destroy our Quota."

Shocked by her lack of trust, he was almost brusque with his reply. "After the risks you've taken to help Toby, why would you ask?" He touched her arm. "I've no faith in the Quota regulations either and I'm determined to change them."

"Thank you," she said. Her warm smile made Grant want to kiss her. He turned away and caught up with Toby, scooped him up on to his shoulders and carried him towards the house.

As they entered the kitchen, a grey-haired lady was peeling potatoes. Grant felt at ease in the homely surrounding, so different from the cold elegance of his apartment.

"This is Mary, my mother-in-law," Kate said. Grant smiled at the woman who nodded back. He felt Toby pulling on his trouser legs, trying to hide his face.

"I spy a hungry boy," Mary said, standing with her arms open. "Would he like some ice cream?" She looked across at Grant. "We make it on the farm."

Toby answered the question by walking towards Mary. She took his hand and led him towards the door. "Come with me and let's see what we can find."

Distracted by Toby's reception, Grant hadn't noticed a man enter the room. He was stunned to be confronted by someone whose picture he had seen many times over the years. A name came to him immediately.

"Adam Stone. I didn't realise..."

"You know my father?" Kate looked shocked.

"I've seen photos of him. Your father was a leader of the Quota protest in its early days. Our intelligence services were always tracking him."

He watched Adam's face darken as he snapped. "What are you doing here?"

"His son is the boy we agreed to help. He's here because I invited him, Dad." Kate hurried across the room to close the door, before adding. "Grant needs us and has promised to protect us."

"Name's Spencer," Grant said, dropping his hand when Adam refused to shake it. "I'm a government official, but I think we have more in common than you realise. I probably have more to lose than you at the moment."

"How's that?" Adam said. "What's to stop you informing on us once we've helped your boy? Your lot have hounded us for years. Why give up now?"

Grant could see he needed convincing. "I'd be suspicious too. I'm on your side, irrespective of Toby's situation. I've given a report to the Quota Minister that proves the system is flawed and discovered things my colleagues would be keen I keep quiet, believe me."

"Are you talking about Sir Charles bloody Winchester? The bastard will ignore your report like he's ignored every similar one over the last decade."

Grant swallowed. "I think the government's attitude is changing. They've decided to leak some of my results to protest groups."

"They're just trying to stir up problems for their own political motives."

"Dad, let's leave the politics for the moment, eh? You can swap stories with Grant later," Kate said. "We should be talking about Toby. Do you think we could get him into that hospital?"

Grant was pleased the conversation was back on Toby.

Adam grunted. "Maybe, but it's not certain."

"What do we have to do?" said Grant.

"He'll need to be assessed by the admission doctor before being allowed access. There are hundreds of people looking for treatment. They can't take everyone."

"I've brought his medical records from my hospital," Kate said. "Can we use them?"

Grant stayed silent. He knew it wouldn't go down well if he said he would pay whatever was asked.

Adam stood considering his reply.

A slim woman rose from the old chair by the fire and walked towards them. "It's not the boy's fault his father's a ministry man. He's doing his best for his child, same as we did, Adam." She turned to Grant. "I'm Kate's mother, Sarah."

Grant recognised the same almond eyes as her daughter. He took Sarah's offered hand and nodded gratitude for her support.

Adam's expression mellowed. "You're right of course. If we can do anything to help Toby's chances, we will. I know people in the hospital. I'm sure they'll be able to offer your son a lifeline."

"Grant can help you get to the hospital safely," Kate said. "He has ministerial privileges so his car won't get stopped at police checkpoints."

There was a moment of hesitation before Grant moved forward and offered his hand. Adam looked at the concerned faces around him before gripping it firmly. "You're on approval and I'll be watching every bloody move, Spencer."

"Thank you," Grant sighed. A collective grin of relief broke the tension.

"Now, let's get that boy fed and sort out his bed." Kate said.

CHAPTER 19

Clive had spent hours analysing a week of grainy CCTV digitals from outside the Spencers' apartment. They revealed a special visitor on nights that Grant was out. He decided it was time for him to pay his respects to Mrs Spencer.

It was a cloudy night as he made his way down the elegant avenue packed with modern executive homes and watched the Jaguar cruise by him and turn left towards Parliament Square. He recognised the car, although it had false plates. What stupidity by Ministry staff to assume that such a classic car could be concealed so easily? Or was it an example of Sir Charles's arrogance? He might regret that.

Clive crossed the road and pushed the access button marked Spencer. He stood out of sight of the surveillance camera and the door was opened immediately.

"Greedy boy," purred the sultry voice from the control panel. "Back for more?"

He took the express lift to the penthouse apartment, pausing briefly in the hallway to view the sparkling beauty of London below. Lucky sods, he thought. His sparse apartment overlooked a concrete sea of identical boxes. He pushed at the open door and Carolyn Spencer staggered towards him, her silk gown gaping open, offering more than a glimpse of temptation. Her scream silenced the voice of lust that was already threatening his control. He lunged across the room towards her, worried about the open doorway.

"What the hell?" She backed away but he grabbed her outstretched hand before she could reach the security alarm. He found himself pressed hard against her and felt her make a feeble attempt to escape before she followed his eye line towards her exposed bosom.

"Touch me, little man, and you're as good as dead."

Clive's excitement mounted. He covered her mouth with his hand and hissed, "Tarts should always know when to shut the fuck up. When I talk, you listen."

He kept her body against him and withdrew his hand, running a finger across her plump lips. He gasped as she bit him hard. "You bitch."

She pulled away, tightened her gown and twisted to face him. "Get out or you'll be sorry."

He laughed. "Think your white knight's coming back to defend you? Not a chance. You cause him bother and he'll just move right on to the next tart. I know that. You know that."

"You know nothing. Who are you?"

"Really, Carolyn, I expected better of you. Is this any way to treat a visitor?" He crossed the room and lowered himself into the soft leather chair. Playing with an empty glass on the coffee table he glared, "Pour me a drink and you'll find out what I do know."

"Get it yourself."

"Now you're testing my patience and that's not good." Clive leant forward and gripped the edge of the chair. "Don't make me wait. You'll regret it."

She hesitated then moved a little unsteadily in front of him. His hand whipped out and snatched her arm.

"No ice mind," he stared into her eyes and didn't release his grip until she looked away. "That's better. We'll get along just fine."

She returned with a full glass of whisky, slapped it on the table in front of him, before sitting opposite and refilling her own glass with wine. "Ok, five minutes then I call security."

Clive ignored her and wandered across to the huge balcony doors to take in the view. "It would be a pity if you lost all this," he said, waving his glass at the skyline.

"That's never going to happen," she said, "with friends in high office." She threw him a confident smile.

"What would your husband say if he knew you were shagging his boss?"

She stopped smiling. "Grateful, if he had any sense. He certainly owes his ministerial career to it." She took an obvious glance at a pendulum clock on the wall behind him. "You now have three minutes," she added, toying with her mobile.

He was impressed at how quickly she had regained her composure. He admired her attitude. "Your husband won't have a career if I expose him. The illegal operation he is organising for your son would ruin him, though I find it interesting that you have so little involvement." Now he had her attention.

She gripped her wine glass tightly. "I don't know why he's bothering. The boy's sick. I've told him time and time again he'll just hold us back. I've never understood his obsession with the boy."

"You think a father shouldn't fight for his child?"

Carolyn's head shot up. "His father?"

Clive grinned. "He's not the father?"

"Don't be ridiculous. Your time's up." She started tapping her mobile.

"Carry on, call who you like. The security guys will love your story I'm sure.

She put her phone back on the table. "Who are you?"

"Let's just say I'm not a fan of your husband but I'll keep quiet if you help me."

She looked flustered now. "What?"

"Your husband's researching the Quota system and I don't like his conclusions. You keep me informed of his activities and I'll be satisfied."

"I have no idea what he does." She threw her hands up in exasperation. "He works long hours, all very boring I'm sure, and when he eventually gets home, runs straight to his little cherub. He hardly talks to me nowadays."

She crossed the room to light a cigarette and blew the smoke between perfectly painted lips. Clive's pulse quickened but he needed to keep his mind on business tonight.

"Get him to talk. Find out who he's meeting, and his opinions. If you get me the information, you keep this lifestyle and your lover." He raised his glass.

Carolyn groaned with tired resignation and slumped down on the end of the sofa. She leant forward, ground the cigarette into the ashtray and stared up into his eyes. He grinned. He had her.

"I think we understand each other now. We're alike you and me." He leant across and stroked her arm. "More alike than you realise." She didn't move away.

He had his accomplice but he wanted more. It took a few moments before his control returned.

"I'm going now but I'll be in touch."

He strode out of the flat, closing the door with reluctance. When he reached the street, he looked up. Carolyn was on the balcony, watching him. He waved. There was no response. She would be an enjoyable challenge, one he could almost taste, but first he had another delicacy to line up. This one had even more reason to be grateful to him and he would make sure she was.

CHAPTER 20

Kate felt a soft touch on her cheek and woke to find Toby kneeling by her bed, his face close to hers. She took a second before she remembered why he was here.

"Dad said I could see the aminals again," he smiled and pulled the covers back. "Pleeeeze."

She looked at his pale face tinged with an aura of excitement. She hoped the research doctors could help him. His dark hair flopped over his forehead and his chubby feet were pummelling the carpet in excitement. "Ok, Toby. Just go get your coat and I'll be down in a minute. You can help feed the pigs before you leave."

He was out of the door yelling for his dad before she had rolled back the duvet. Her heart was as heavy as his was light. Soon the dialysis would not be enough and an illegal transplant would be his only hope.

She remembered her parents' discussions late last night. She had been amazed to hear how many top-flight consultants had been passionate enough to start up the research hospital on the Isle of Dogs. Over the years they had continued to revolutionise medical practice, while the country suffered the government's closure of facilities and outlawing of new treatments.

Of course she had heard rumours of these independent hospitals but had assumed they were badly resourced and staffed by unqualified, disgruntled medical staff. She had no idea they represented some of the most talented and experienced doctors who had been horrified at the government's refusal to take on the successful new treatments they were developing.

She was angry that young children like Toby weren't getting the treatment they deserved. She had believed the government's propaganda that, due to diminishing resources, their policy of Quota restrictions was the fairest way forward. No more. She had the means to help one child and support her mother though some difficult treatment and she was determined no one would stop her.

By the time Kate reached the front door, Toby was fully dressed, eating the remainder of his breakfast and asking his father whether pigs liked toast.

"Sorry, Kate, the only pigs Toby's ever seen were in books. But if it's going to hold things up, we'll leave straight away." Grant said.

"My parents are still saying their goodbyes to Mary, and Lisa's not even awake yet, so we've a few minutes and it'll save me feeding them later." She watched as Grant fastened the buttons on Toby's coat and pulled his boots up. He was gentle and obviously loved his child deeply. Why was his wife not here? It wasn't something she felt she could ask.

He looked up and saluted, "Feeding patrol, ready and able."

Kate laughed and hurried them out the door towards the pig enclosure. She picked up the bucket and gave Toby a handful of the specially prepared feed and showed him how to ensure all the squealing animals got a fair share. There was a lot of pushing and shoving but the more noise the pigs made, the louder Toby giggled.

As they all walked back to the house, Grant stopped.

"Kate, I don't know how to thank you and your family. I do understand the risks you're taking. If you ever need help in return, you would ask, wouldn't you?"

Kate thought immediately of Lisa and her mother-in-law and regretted not going to Grant for help in the first place. He seemed a kinder man than Clive, whose agenda she still wasn't sure of. She might be glad of a back-up plan. "Thanks, I may take you up on that."

"I'm not sure how much time I'll have after I've blown the whistle on the Quota system. I'll be facing some powerful enemies. So if I can help, I'd need to do it soon."

She looked over his shoulder and could see her father helping her mother into the car. "Not now, you've got to go. But I will talk to you, Grant. Really I will."

She watched him walk to the car. Her parents were packing the last of their meagre belongings into the boot. Just a few bags, not much to show for a lifetime together.

She giggled at Grant's exasperated face as Toby zigzagged across the drive towards her. "I didn't kiss pigs bye."

He grabbed her hand and pointed towards the pig shed but she bent down and looked directly into his eyes.

"They're very full after all that food you gave them and would be very cross if we interrupt their nap. I'll go and tell them you'll be back soon."

"They'll forget."

"No, they won't. No one could forget your grin, Toby. I'll be sure to come and let you know exactly how they're doing." She could see Grant coming towards her with an apologetic smile.

"Come on, Tobes. Everyone else is in the car and if you don't get in, the greedy grown-ups will eat all Mary's biscuits!" Toby gave Kate's skirt a quick hug before walking reluctantly back to the car.

Grant leant forward to say something but his eyes told her much more.

"Go, Grant, go quickly. You have a difficult journey and my father said the earlier you get to the hospital the better chance you have of being seen today.

"I just hope he gets in."

"We've double-checked everything. It's down to his test results and the doctors. But my parents have a lot of influence."

"I can't thank you enough... Kate..."

"Just go, please. I'll be down at the weekend as I want to see my mum before she starts her treatment too."

"If there is anything, anything I can do for you."

"I know and you may regret that offer. You go look after your son, he needs you."

Kate felt herself lean into Grant's strong body as he embraced her but pulled away just before his face touched hers. He stood back and looked equally shaken.

"Thanks again, for everything," he said.

Lisa joined her at the door in her dressing gown and waved as the car wound down the farm track.

"Sorry, Mum, I didn't wake up in time to wish Toby goodbye. I don't know what's wrong with me, I feel so tired all the time."

"It's normal in the early months, Lisa." After all the upheaval with Toby and Mary, she had put Lisa's problems to the back of her mind. She felt terrible looking at her daughter's worried face now. "We need to get those tests and injections sorted. It has to be done before 12 weeks."

"Don't, Mum, I know but I just can't face it. I tried to go and see Tom at the farm yesterday but I couldn't. Do I have to tell him?"

"He's the father and yes, I think you should. I don't think he's going to be over the moon but at least I don't want to actually strangle the bloody man anymore."

"It wasn't his fault; I knew what I was doing."

"That's debatable."

"Mum, I'm not a child. Since Dad died you've been so

wrapped up in work and stuff, you've hardly noticed I've a life to live too."

Kate looked at her daughter and recognised the folded arms and stance that was so like her father's. Maybe she had taken her eye off the ball. She had certainly failed to notice the extra time Lisa had been spending at the neighbouring farm. "Of course you have. That's why we must get these tests and decide what you're going to do."

"No. Mum. It's me that decides. It's my baby, my life. I can sort this."

Lisa stomped back inside and slammed the door. Kate could put some of it down to hormones but there was an uncomfortable truth in what she had said. Oh God, James, if only you'd been here.

She looked out at the cloud of dust in the distance, as Grant's car reached the perimeter fence. The black vehicle rolled over the horizon. She felt like running after it and shivered, remembering Grant's touch and Toby's innocent face. No, she had the animals to feed and must talk to her daughter again before work. Her parents had recommended delaying any contact until the weekend. She would have to manage until then.

The wind was picking up and the branches whipped back and forth. She feared for Mary, Jack was always locked away in his room and she had upset Lisa. What a bloody mess! But watching the storm clouds gather, she bit her lip, determined to do better. She was a fighter. Maybe she had inherited some of her parents' spirit after all.

CHAPTER 21

Jack checked the Young Britons' forum daily, but while bubbles of discontent floated up across the country there were no posts from the Rickmansworth branch. He was pissed off, all that shouting at the meeting and fuck all since. Clive had tricked him into believing this group would make things happen. Obviously not. He would have to look elsewhere for action. He so wanted to be out there. He hated being stuck on the farm. All he could do was to continue his father's research.

His grandparents might have been more help. They must still know groups worth joining. But they hadn't paid much attention to him. The old lady was sick and he guessed they were probably past it now.

Mum wasn't bothered about him, talking non-stop about the kid who needed a spare part. She was always too interested in everyone else's problems. She hadn't spoken to him properly since Dad died, just moaned he never came to meals on time. Lisa wasn't getting much support either and she was pregnant, for fuck sake. He felt sorry for her. She was more worried than she let on. What did they have to do to get their mum's attention?

He searched for any upcoming protests but nothing was

listed on the web. Bored, he was about to switch back to his favourite interactive porn site when there was a message alert in his secure mailbox. "We need to talk, now."

Jack took off his helmet and set the alarm on his scooter at the Rickmansworth Community Centre. Someone tried to pinch it every time he rode it off the farm but there was no other way of getting here easily. He didn't know why he'd bothered to come anyway. What was so urgent that the YBs wanted to see him immediately when they'd not called for weeks? Was he being singled out? He would have preferred to have someone with him but only Lisa knew he was involved and he couldn't bring her. He approached the building, determined not to be a pushover.

The Centre was much quieter than on his last visit, the corridors empty. In the main office, a young woman was bent over a desk. He mentally scored her bum ten out of ten and had to swallow before speaking and then wasn't sure what to ask. The girl turned and looked at him intently. He felt his face burn. The girl was stunning, with long black hair, and full lips. He gave her another ten.

"Hello," she said.

"Hi," he stammered.

"Philip's waiting for you in the Conference Room. Turn right out of here and it's the fourth door on the left."

Jack grinned before walking off down the corridor, trying to look confident. His heart beat quickened, pumped by desire and apprehension. He fought the urge to turn round and check if she was watching him.

The conference room door was open but he knocked anyway.

"Come in."

He recognised the chairman from the last meeting, sitting at the top of a long table, a dark haired man with penetrating eyes.

"Thanks for coming, Jack. I'm Philip."

He tried to sit close to the door but the man waved for him to come closer.

"I like to have a chat with new members and see how committed they are."

Jack swallowed; he could feel the perspiration building on the back of his neck.

"I've not joined to muck around."

"I am sure you haven't, but you have to understand what you're getting into." Philip stared at him, long enough to make him feel very uncomfortable. "Whatever we discuss in this room stays in the room, do you understand?"

Jack nodded. This was starting to feel more like a bloody interrogation than a chat.

"Our public image is a youth club but underneath we're a militant group, committed to get change by direct action, with violence if necessary. Are you up for that?"

"Of course," Jack said, trying to sound confident, "if I agree."

"I see you have attitude. I just hope that won't be a problem," Philip said, picking up a piece of paper from his desk and scanning it quickly, "because you have the potential to be a key player here, Jack.

"Why's that? I've no experience."

"You've some connections that could be very useful to us. We saw you knew Clive Boland but you've had some other interesting people at your farm too, haven't you?"

"How do you know? Have you been spying on me?" Jack's face reddened. "You've no right."

"Hang on, Jack. If we didn't vet everyone who wants to join us, we wouldn't last long. We watched your farm for a while and checked out your family background."

Jack fidgeted on his chair.

Philip continued. "Listen, if you're a genuine supporter, your contacts could be priceless. We're always looking for people like you. You could help us open many doors and change things."

"I hardly see anyone."

"First, you have heritage, Jack. Your grandparents have been leading protesters for years and your father was involved in secret food technology research. And now, you've just had one of the top Quota officials at your farm."

Jack frowned. Who were they talking about? The only recent visitor had been the little boy's dad and Jack hadn't been introduced. "Who do you mean?"

"Are you telling me you don't know Grant Spencer?"

"Who? The only bloke that's been to the farm is some guy whose kid is sick."

"That was Spencer. He's a high achiever in the Ministry of Life. You might be able to get us some valuable information."

Jack felt flattered but anxious too. He wasn't sure he could be as useful as they seemed to think. He had hardly spoken to his grandparents before they left the farm; he'd only seen Clive a couple of times and he'd never met this Spencer bloke.

"I can't tell you anything."

"I think you can, Jack. You just don't know what's important. Perhaps we should start with your father's work. What was that about?"

Jack shuddered. He missed his dad so much. For the past year he'd worked alongside him on the food enhancement programme. He knew what his dad had achieved and that he shouldn't talk about it. How could he give out details to someone he had only just met? He would bide his time. "Don't know much, really," he lied.

"Do you have access to his files? You could have a look for us."

"I will but there aren't many left. The government inspectors were quick to clear the lab after Dad died."

"That's interesting," Philip said, "and that makes it even more important you have a closer look. Let me know what you find as soon as you can."

"All right."

"Ok, let's leave it there for now. Thanks for coming. I hope you've realised that you can make a difference. We'll be having another group meeting to discuss some real action. I'd like to see you there."

Philip stood. Jack wasn't sure whether to shake hands so nodded briefly before shuffling out of the room. Could he really trust these people? His dad had told him many times that he shouldn't tell anyone about the work. He mustn't betray him. His mum wouldn't understand; she didn't know the half of the research going on at the farm. He was sure his dad hadn't told her.

"Do you want a coffee or a coke?"

Jack snapped out of his distractions and noticed the girl standing by the reception doors. She was smiling. Shit, she was gorgeous.

"A coke would be good, thanks."

"Not here. I thought we could go to the drinks bar round the corner."

"I'd like that."

Jack decided things were looking up after all.

CHAPTER 22

The new lambs were bleating inside the pens. They mirrored her impatience. Kate marked up the feeding charts, annoyed Jack still hadn't returned. She could have done with his help around the farm. She was finding it difficult not knowing how her parents and Toby were getting on at the hospital. She pulled the barn door closed and was concentrating on tapping the long security code in when she felt a hand on her shoulder. She jumped.

"Sorry, Kate, I didn't mean to scare you." His arms had caught her momentarily but as she gathered her balance, his grip tightened.

It was the first time she had been this close to him and she was amazed that such a slight man was so strong. She could feel his breathing quicken as he drew her closer.

"Christ, Clive, you almost gave me a heart attack." She tried to move away but he held her still. She glanced at her overalls. "Mary will go nuts. These were clean on this morning." She forced a smile and he released his grip but did not move away.

"I don't know," he said, looking up and down her body. "They fit you very well."

Kate felt his eyes burn through her clothes.

"But, hardly glamorous, I agree. If you want to change, I'll walk back with you." He looked towards the house. "I've a few details to go through before I can sort Mary's problems. Thought I'd come over rather than phone." He stared pointedly at her bosom. "More personal."

Kate kept her distance as they walked in silence towards the house. She showed him into the lounge and shot upstairs to change. She had to stop herself checking the door, worried he would come up uninvited. Brushing her hair vigorously, she told herself not to be so paranoid.

She hoped Lisa had finished in the bathroom. After tapping on the door she walked in. No daughter in sight but towels everywhere. She showered and took a few minutes clearing up then came down the stairs, hugging a pile of wet bath towels.

She heard Lisa laughing from the lounge and realised Clive must have already introduced himself. Damn. This was a meeting she would have rather avoided. Lisa was hardly likely to tell him of her condition but she could be thoughtless and it would only take a throwaway line and a man like him wouldn't need a diagram.

She dumped the dirty towels in the laundry and hurried toward the lounge. As she opened the door Clive was bent over Lisa with his arms gripping her shoulders and his leg pushed in between her feet.

"What the hell is going on?"

"Oh, Mum, your friend's giving me some self-defence lessons."

Clive grinned and let Lisa complete the move. He flipped on to his back and lay perfectly still while she raised her hands in mock victory. She helped him up and he gripped her hands just a little too long for Kate's liking.

She was fuming. "What an earth do you think you're doing?"

"Pretty girl like her has to know how to protect herself."

Kate butted in before Lisa could say anything, "You need to get out of that dressing gown and go into town. The test syringes have all gone and Jack won't be impressed when he gets back."

Lisa looked annoyed but turned a broad smile towards Clive. "Thanks for the intro."

"Just building your confidence, but you'll need more lessons if you're serious about learning properly."

"Lisa, the car's out the front already charged, so you'd better get dressed." Kate held the door open and stared at her. Lisa tightened her dressing gown and stomped through.

"Really, if I didn't know better, I'd think you were jealous," Clive smirked.

"Don't be ridiculous. If you've a lot to get through, we'd better make a start."

"No rush. I thought we could relax for a bit first." He lifted a package from his holdall on the chair and pulled out some wine, "Red ok with you?"

It was the last thing she felt like but she could not afford to upset the man. "Lovely. I'll get the opener."

She was busy searching through the kitchen drawer when she felt Clive push up behind her. He forced her against the unit, pinned her hands down to the worktop and started nuzzling her neck.

"You're gorgeous, Kate," he whispered. "I'm not surprised your daughter is so beautiful. She reminds me of you. It bought back some pretty hot memories."

"Clive, let me go. Mary will be in any minute now."

"Considering the trouble I'm going to, she'd hardly complain if you show me how grateful you are. How grateful are you, Kate?"

She felt the pressure of his knee behind her forcing her legs apart and his sharp teeth as they travelled up her neck making tiny bites. She trod down on his foot and used the slight release of his grip to jab her elbows back into him. He collapsed onto the floor and she ran out of the door.

She slumped against the porch railing, telling herself to breath and was relieved to see Mary hurrying across the driveway in alarm.

"You look terrible, Kate, what on earth's wrong?"

She did not want to frighten Mary, so she lied. "No, I'm fine, really. It's just a bit hot in there that's all."

"I'll get you some water."

"No. I said I'm fine." By the startled look on Mary's face, she knew she had upset her.

Clive appeared in the doorway. "Unlike your daughter, you have no need of self-defence lessons." He waved the bottle in his hand. "A guy could die of thirst here." He smiled warmly at Mary. "If you can find me an opener, darling, it could be your lucky day. I'm about to save your life." His tone changed as he walked back into the house and shouted over his shoulder, "I'll be waiting, Kate, when you're ready, eh?"

Mary looked concerned but Kate followed him back into the house. So, that was the price for her dear mother-in-law's life. She hoped she could pay it. As she walked into the lounge with the bottle opener, she could feel Clive's eyes follow her every move.

"Take a seat, Kate. I'll shut the door. We don't want to be interrupted, do we?" He moved to the doorway but Mary stood in the entrance, arms folded.

"Is Kate ok?" she said, staring across the room pointedly.

Kate fought the urge to ask her to stay. "I'm fine. Clive has some info to go over so he can help us."

"You do want me to help, don't you?" Clive's voice was soft and calming.

"Yes, but..."

"Then the quicker we get started the better."

She knew Mary would not give up easily

"I just wanted to..."

Clive's voice became terse. She could hear he was losing patience. She watched him draw an electronic tag from his trouser pocket and gestured for Mary to take it. "My car's over by the barn. Check it's still in the sun and stay with it and make sure it doesn't cut out." Kate heard the frustration in his voice. "One day they'll realise just how much I'm worth and give me a decent one." He finished by slamming the door in Mary's face.

Kate almost cried as she heard her mother-in-law's footsteps disappear down the corridor. She perched on the edge of the sofa and tried to face what she knew was coming.

Clive poured the wine and held it up. "Now, let's start with a drink. Loosen you up a bit."

She felt clammy and started to tremble. It was now or never she thought as she lifted the large glass of wine and took a small sip before setting it down on the oak coffee table.

"I can't afford to drink, too much," she said lightly, "I'm working later." She smiled with what she hoped was a confidence she did not feel. Maybe she could stall him, put him off.

"I checked your shift. You're not due back till after the weekend. A little drink with your personal hero's not too much to ask surely?"

Kate was shocked he had gained access to her personal rota. He sat close to her on the sofa and held his full glass towards her lips.

"You wouldn't want me to drink alone, would you?"

"Of course not." She took it and downed it in one. If she had to see this through, she would need all the help she could get.

Clive snatched the empty glass and set it on the table. Kate jumped as his hand gripped her knee and slid up her thigh. He pulled her closer and she could smell his breath on her face. Bile rose in her throat and she fought back tears. It had been months since she had been touched this way, but this was twisted intimacy and not the longed for tenderness she remembered.

She closed her eyes and her husband's smile burnt a guilty image inside her lids. She tried to block out his loving face with Mary's despair. She hoped it would give her the strength to carry it through.

Her head was yanked back and she felt his mouth against hers, so hard his teeth drew pinpricks of blood on her resistant lips. Her muscles tensed as he forced her legs apart. She tried to close her emotions down, freeze her fear as his fingers clawed their way inside. She felt grubby and a scream rose in her throat. He pulled away just far enough to look straight into her eyes. The intensity frightened her.

"I've waited a long time for this." His fingers continued their assault, while his grip tightened around her neck. She felt so helpless.

In the distance, she heard a car door bang and her daughter's voice calling her from outside. She felt Clive's body tense.

Kate realised her daughter was back. "It's Lisa," she said, trying to pull her skirt back down.

He whispered in her ear. "Perhaps she'd like to join us?"

The thought nearly made her vomit. She had to think and outmanoeuvre him. She decided to appeal to his ego. "Do you think I want to share you, Clive?"

He looked uncertain.

"You're too special," she whispered.

He smiled and loosened his grip long enough for her to reach down and readjust her ripped underwear. "Why not pour us another drink and I'll get rid of her. I won't be long, I promise." She smiled, before easing herself out from under him and off the couch. She just hoped her legs would carry her to the door.

"Make sure you're quick. Don't disappoint me now."

She concentrated on getting out, her legs shaking so much

she could hardly walk straight. Closing the door, she leant against the frame until her breathing returned to normal.

Her jittery legs threatened to give out on her as she walked to the kitchen. She reached the front door just as Lisa came rushing through.

"Bloody man, how dare he speak to me like that?" She pushed past, ripped her coat off and flung it at the chair. "I thought I'd pop round to the farm on the way back from the wholesalers to tell him my news. You were right, Mum, he just looked horrified. Like I was some sort of alien. I didn't stop long enough to get the full rejection." She dropped into the chair and looked broken.

Kate stood, rooted to the spot. She could not even comfort her own daughter. She just wanted to run upstairs and scrub herself clean. But she couldn't leave her. Not with Clive in the house.

Lisa raised her head and looked at her mother for the first time. "Christ, what's wrong. It's not Mary is it?"

Kate wiped her lips with the back of her hand. "No. It's..."

At that moment Clive came through to the kitchen waving the empty bottle. "Got lonely in there." He walked up to Lisa and lifted her chin with his finger. "Oh, Lisa, who's upset you? Tell me and I'll kill him."

Lisa giggled but continued to stare at her mother. Kate knew she had to convince her she was fine, make her go upstairs and get Clive out of the house.

"I need to talk to my daughter. She's not feeling great. Some bug that was going around the hospital, actually. I think I might have it too. I need to get the antivirus drugs." Clive took a step back and she realised she was on to a winner. "Yes, it's nasty, highly contagious."

He looked unsure and was staring at Lisa. It was at that precise moment Kate's stomach decided to rebel. Her insides convulsed and she vomited all over Clive's very smart shoes.

"Christ, woman, what the hell do you think you're doing?"

He hopped about like a man who had been burnt and grabbed a towel to wipe the mess off his feet.

"I'm so..." This time she managed to get to the sink.

"Mum. Mum... you ok?"

Clive looked from one to the other and walked back to the lounge. He reappeared with his bag two seconds later and swept through to the front door. "We'll do this another time."

Before she could stop her, Lisa had followed him out of the house. Kate wiped her lips and looked through the window. She could see Lisa flicking her hair away from her face and talking animatedly to Clive. She leant into the car and handed him a note. Then he was gone.

Kate never wanted to see him again. The price, she decided, was one she could not pay. Her eyes widened when she saw Lisa's cocky smile as she almost skipped back into the house. Lisa liked him. Kate clenched her fists and stared at the empty drive. She needed Grant.

CHAPTER 23

Grant thought the clock must be wrong. He was sure it was half an hour since the doctor had taken Toby for examination. He checked his tablet again and reluctantly accepted that only ten minutes had passed. The waiting room was empty. Adam and Sarah were in the Oncology department. Despite their different lives and attitudes, he was getting on well with them. He would have welcomed their company.

The door opened and Mr Morgan beckoned Grant to join him in his room.

"Toby's a great lad," he said. "I know you are well aware of his problem so I'll push on and tell you about the treatment options. There are only two, either a new kidney or dialysis for the rest of his life."

"Can you give him on-going dialysis?" Grant heard the pleading in his voice.

"I have to be frank, no, we don't have the resources. We give short-term care but we can't provide support for an unspecified time. However, we could give Toby a new kidney."

Grant frowned. "I don't understand."

"Using stem cells from Toby and a 3D printer, we can build him a tailor-made kidney."

"But wouldn't a transplant be better? I know a boy who may have a compatible kidney.

"Is he willing to take the risk of donating one?"

"I don't know, I haven't asked him."

"Well, that's a possibility but time is short and my advice is to let us give your son an artificial kidney. We've been creating new organs for years and they have a very good outcome percentage."

"How good?"

"80% of our kidneys are working fine after 10 years. We could make one for Toby in a week." Mr Morgan handed Grant a card. "Here's the password to our website. You can read up on our research and then we should have another chat."

He stood. "Toby will be back in the Children's Ward in an hour if you want to see him. By the way, how's Dr Adam Penn? I notice he recommended your consultation."

"He's fine," said Grant, in surprise. "I only met him recently. I didn't know he was a doctor."

"He's not practising now but he's famous here, one of our founding fathers. He worked at Bart's hospital in the city. He and many of his colleagues fought against the cuts to medical services and raised the money to establish this unit on the Isle of Dogs." Mr Morgan smiled.

"You can see where our Bark's nickname comes from."

Grant returned to the main waiting room, his opinion of Adam greatly enhanced. There was still no sign of him or Sarah, just a young woman trying to calm her screaming baby. He left the room looking for a refuge and followed the signs to the hospital café on the twelfth floor. There he joined a queue of white coats. Contrary to his expectations, the medics were mostly young, recently qualified he surmised, an indication that the anti-Quota movement was attracting new doctors, despite the opportunities in the outside world. He winced at that phrase.

This seemed more real than anything beyond these walls.

He bought himself a coffee and found a table by a window where he could look out over the Thames. The river seemed to connect all the strands of his life. Visibility was good and he was surprised to see his own apartment block in the distance, on a bend in the river. He imagined being able to wave to Toby from his balcony. How strange he'd never known this towering building was a hospital.

"How's Toby?"

He was woken from his daydreaming by Sarah, smiling by the table. He felt the warmth of friendship in her greeting.

"They've offered to make him a new kidney using a 3D printer."

"This hospital can do incredible things. You must be so pleased there's hope. Did they say when they could do the op?"

"They suggested a week but I haven't agreed to it yet. I want to find out more first and talk it over with my wife. But how are you, Sarah?"

"Fine. Adam said it would be ok. They've given me a scan and other tests so they can target my treatment. I'll have to stay a couple more days for injections, but now they use immune therapy, there's none of that horrible chemo that they used before. Look, Adam's in the coffee queue, would you like a refill?"

"Yes, please, but let me pay."

Sarah waved away Grant's offer and went to speak to her husband.

"I hear they can help Toby," Adam said when he joined the table.

"Yes. It seems so," Grant said. "I can't thank you enough for bringing him here. And I heard you had a big part in setting up the hospital."

"With many others," Adam said with a tired grin, "but that was a long time ago. Anyway, now you can see how treatments have advanced without government constraints."

"I can and you seem to be able to attract lots of young doctors. Do they work just here?"

"Yes," Adam said, "they aren't allowed to have jobs outside. The government turns a blind eye to us if we keep things to ourselves. They don't want the general population to know what treatments are possible. They block all reporting of medical breakthroughs."

Grant took a sip of his coffee. He had lots of questions. He risked asking a few but didn't want to appear too probing; he knew he was still on approval by Adam.

"What else can they do here?"

"They specialise in treatment of cancer, heart problems and dementia; the illnesses that affect most people at some stage."

"The hospital must be very expensive to run. Where does all the money come from?"

"There are many rich benefactors who may want treatment for themselves. The government is comfortable with the hospital doing research on people who might die anyway through Quota. Some ministers are also secret patients. We have to compromise with the bastards, hoping that someday our research can be offered more widely."

Grant frowned. Then he realised Adam could be referring to him. "Of course I'm one of them."

"You're beginning to see the light. Instead of getting rid of people, the government should be investing in the development of cheaper treatments. Now you're benefiting personally, does that make you feel guilty about your job?"

"Don't be so harsh on Grant," Sarah said. "Toby isn't cured yet."

"I've only been involved in Quota research for a couple of months. Most of my career has been in the business sector," Grant said. "Not really an excuse, I suppose. But in my defence I've told my boss that we don't need this type of population control anymore."

"You won't be the first to tell the government that. Getting them to listen is another matter. But maybe we can find a way of working together."

Grant was moved by Adam's continuing passion. This doctor had spent his life trying to overcome the unfairness visited on the country. He ought to play his part too.

"I'd like that. We should talk later in the week. I need to see my wife, Carolyn, and show my face at the Ministry. But this visit has confirmed my view of Quota.

"I hope so," Adam said, nodding his head.

"We'll watch over Toby while we're here," Sarah said, tapping Grant gently on the arm.

"That's very kind," he said. "I'll just say goodbye to him."

Grant made his way to the Children's Ward. The sister at the nursing station directed him to the activity area. He was delighted to see his son playing with several other youngsters. Toby saw him and waved before carrying on with his game. Grant had several missed calls, two from Kate, but decided they could all wait. He needed to see Carolyn. He messaged her as soon as he left the hospital. There was an almost instant reply. She was working from home and wanted to see him. He headed for the apartment.

"Where have you been? I haven't heard from you for two days." Carolyn confronted him as soon as he came through the door. "And your office has been chasing you; sounds like you've taken your eye of the ball."

"I'm sorry. It was difficult to call but I think I've found a hospital that can help Toby."

"You aren't still hoping for an illegal operation are you? Just think what would happen if the authorities found out." Carolyn's face twisted with contempt. "How many times have I told you to let nature take its course?"

Grant leaned against the door, taking several deep breaths

to control his temper. His career was all she ever cared about but he wasn't giving up. "I want to show you something," he said and beckoned her to come outside with him.

"I haven't got time for any games."

"This is far from a game."

Carolyn closed down her laptop and walked out onto the balcony.

"See that white tower on the horizon? It's a research hospital." Grant said, pointing down river, "That's where Toby is now. They can build him an artificial kidney and he can have a normal life. It's what we've always dreamed of."

"So you're willing to risk your son on a research project as well as your career?"

"The consultant assured me that Toby will be fine. We're out of medical credits and finding a transplant donor could take ages. I think we should go ahead with the operation. It's Toby's last chance."

"You'll do what you want regardless of my opinion."

"I don't think we have a choice. I just hoped I'd have your support."

"Of course. But make sure it doesn't mess up your promotion. Why are they chasing you from the office anyway?"

"They want more analysis on my Quota project. Someone is altering records and they want me to find out who it is." Grant decided not to mention the Over-70s Cull project.

"You'd better get going then."

"I'll see you this evening. Maybe we can visit Toby together later."

"Fine," said Carolyn and returned to her desk. Grant watched her scowling at the figures. He felt the need of a shower more than ever.

CHAPTER 24

Clive's gaze wandered to the turbulent river outside. The stormy water echoed his rising passion at the thought of Lisa's young body. His favourite restaurant on the South Bank was a bit pretentious but perfect for impressing young women. He had used it many times.

He scrolled through the wine list and narrowed the choice down to two. The sparkling wine from Kent and the Anjou Rose wine that he suspected Lisa might prefer.

His thoughts turned to the first few women he had tracked through Quota and manipulated to his advantage. Initially, he had enjoyed the power and their grateful attempts at pleasing him but it became too easy. No one denied him, all too eager to save their own loved ones from premature death. He preferred to make it more personal, using his research to seek out those who had crossed him in the past.

First on his hit list were staff from the government care unit who had bullied him as a young boy. He was an unlicensed birth and often abused until tests revealed his high IQ. The Ministry realised he had potential and could be of more value within their ranks. They awarded him a place at university, an education that he was using against them now.

His next target was the professor at university who had stolen his research. The pathetic, middle-aged wife, had begged for her husband's life. Denying her pleas, after he had abused her body, was sweet revenge. He had sharpened his skills on them all. He realised now that Kate was the one he'd always wanted. She would satisfy him, fill the vacuum. The others had merely amused him.

His video alert sounded. It was Carolyn. She must be keen. She had impressed him at their first meeting and he knew her pretence at indifference had been all show. Women were so predictable. After years of unsuccessful attempts at attracting them in his twenties, his drastic change of game plan had brought success. The huge risks gave new depth to his pleasure. He had to admit, Carolyn would be an interesting challenge.

He dragged a hand through his hair and straightened his tie before opening the video connection. Her steely eyes stared into his. "I hope this is worth the interruption, Carolyn, I am about to eat, or couldn't you wait to see me?" He was pleased to see annoyance crease her rather beautiful brow.

"Grant's on to you," she snapped.

He sat forward in his chair and waved the approaching wine waiter away. "What?"

Her luscious red lips stretched into a smile and she leant forward until her mouth filled the small screen. "He knows someone is manipulating Quota and he's determined to stop them. He's going to find you, Mr Cocky."

Clive's hand tightened around the phone.

"It's you isn't it?"

"What have you told him, bitch?"

"Nothing. But if I keep you up to date what do I get for my trouble?"

He wanted to cut that smile right off her smart-arsed face but this was something he could deal with later. Greed he understood. She cared nothing for her husband, just her

119

own neck. If he was wise he could use her ambitions and her connections. This was the break he was looking for. He must get rid of Spencer; using his wife made it all the sweeter.

"Ok, Carolyn, I see we have something in common. Self-interest."

The lips widened and the throaty laugh made him tremble with excitement. This woman could be useful to him in so many ways. He could see the blonde girl on the next table glance at him with interest. Sex seemed to filter through the air around him. How delicious.

"I'll be calling you. Just make sure you've got something worthwhile to tell me next time." He cut the connection before she had time to answer. The bitch would have to be taught a lesson, but he had plenty of time for that.

He looked up and saw Lisa hesitating by the entrance. The flimsy material fluttered above her knees in a whirl of indecision. He caught the waiter's attention and asked him to show her over and bring a bottle of champagne. When she reached the table he smiled and kissed her cheek. She smelt of youth.

"Oh, my God, I've never been anywhere like this." She blushed as the waiter took her jacket and seated her opposite. Clive took her hand and was pleased to feel the shiver it produced as he stroked his finger up the inside of her wrist.

"Then it's about time I introduced you to the high life. Welcome to my world, Lisa."

He could hardly take his eyes off her throughout the meal. Even her laugh reminded him of her mother and he wondered if she had inherited Kate's soft skin. The disaster at the farmhouse had not pleased him but he was throbbing with the anticipation of having both mother and daughter. It would give him an opportunity to exploit his power over the entire family.

The warmth of his smile was almost genuine as he leant forward to pop a strawberry into her mouth. This served to silence her teenage rant about her mother's lack of trust: an old story but one he could use to his advantage.

"Lisa, you have to prove to her you are an adult. Make your own decisions. You must live your own life. Make your own mistakes."

She looked distraught at this last remark, her young face fraught with pain. "Clive, I knew you'd understand. I just have to tell you..."

He wasn't into hearing the emotional claptrap that silly girls of her age dwelt on, so was relieved when the waiter interrupted with the coffee. Clive grinned at her and asked if she would like a liqueur. She looked uncertain so he made the decision for her. More alcohol would make her easier to handle later.

He couldn't decide whether it was worth booking a room for the night. He was more concerned about Carolyn's news and planning his next step to neutralise Spencer's attempts to track him down.

Lisa was a ripening plum: she would wait. He stared into her eyes. She looked up through her eyelashes and ran the tip of her finger along her pink lips. He imagined wrenching her clothes off and picked up the napkin, dabbing his mouth to calm down.

"Thanks, Clive, it was an amazing meal." She moved closer and he placed a controlled kiss on her lips. Yes, soft and as ready as could be. He would enjoy the chase and his prize.

"I'll call a cab. We wouldn't want your mum worrying now, would we?" She was about to argue but he put a finger to her moist lips. "We have all the time in the world."

He ushered Lisa out of the restaurant and used his scammed credit card to pay a passing cab driver to take her home to Sarratt. She waved an excited goodbye. He guessed she had not travelled by taxi before.

As he walked to his flat along the riverbank, he could see the revolving lights on the roof of the Ministry of Life blinking in the distance. Laughing aloud he knew he stood out amongst the sombre commuters who shuffled their way into the underbelly of London and home, but for once he did not care. The transport camera zoomed towards him as he glided down the walkway, smirking about his evening.

When his front door closed and the sensors locked behind him, Clive noticed the alerts flashing on his watch. Lisa forgotten, he sat down in his coat and with a flick of his hand, transferred his tracking program to the wall screen and opened the first message.

Jack Appleby had been interviewed by the Rickmansworth group and, according to the hacked info streaming across his wall, was of great interest to the cell leadership. This suburban group had started to irritate the Ministry and Sir Charles had mentioned them last month. Clive thought them harmless but had agreed to monitor their activities, more for his own benefit. He had used these groups as a diversion from his own Quota manipulations in the past but might need to shut them down if they became too much of a nuisance. He made a mental note to keep a close eye on Jack.

The second alert was more worrying. The tracker on Spencer's car had been deactivated and he had been off the radar for almost fifteen hours. Together with Carolyn's message, this sent shivers of excitement through him. What had the high and mighty Spencer been up to? He'd soon find out. The room was bathed in a luminous glow from the stream of information filtering across the walls. He smiled. Playing with other people's lives thrilled him to the core. Love was a weakness he exploited. But his hunger was never quite satisfied. Maybe this time?

He enlarged Spencer's face and merged the data tracks to overlay both Kate and Lisa's images. He walked up to the interactive wall until his eyes were level with theirs. His hand delved into his coat pocket.

A sharp crack sliced the silence as he rammed the six-inch blade into the pupil of Grant Spencer's eye. "Game on," he hissed.

CHAPTER 25

It was one-fifteen in the morning when Kate heard the gravel crunch and scatter outside the house. She pulled the curtains aside to see the cab's wheels stop. The internal light caught the excited grin on her daughter's face as she climbed out of the black taxi. A London cab was a rare sight in Hertfordshire. Where had Lisa been and more importantly, who with?

Kate should have been working tonight but her shift had been cancelled. More proof of the continual cutbacks. She knew Lisa would have expected her late return to have gone unnoticed. It had not.

"Mum?"

Kate watched her daughter's face fall for a second before she recovered and rushed across the kitchen to hug her. She reeked of alcohol and would have enjoyed the unexpected show of affection, had it not been fuelled by drink.

Lisa giggled and shuffled out of her jacket to pour herself a glass of water.

"Pity you didn't drink more of that earlier." She watched the excitement drain from Lisa's flushed face.

"It makes me feel good. Wouldn't hurt you to try a little fun sometimes. You never know you might actually like it."

Lisa pulled out a chair, dumped the glass down on the table, and sank back into the seat. Her expensive dress was rumpled and cascaded around her in a froth of aubergine. The silk straps had slipped down her pale shoulders. Lisa smiled. Kate realised she had no idea what her daughter was thinking. What was going on behind those beautifully manicured brows? She had gone to a lot of trouble to look her best tonight.

"So, was he worth it?"

Lisa sat up and frowned. "What you on about? Just a boring birthday party with Charlotte, it was rubbish though." She avoided Kate's question and studied the glass she was drinking from.

"You haven't seen her for ages."

"I thought some of my old college mates would be there, wasn't going to hang around that long anyway."

"Well, you managed to hang around till after midnight."

"Had trouble getting back, didn't I?"

"So exactly where in Rickmansworth did you find the London cab then?"

Lisa slammed the glass back down and scrambled to her feet. "I'm tired."

Kate caught her arm as she passed and held on firmly. "I'm tired, tired of listening to a load of lies. Who did you meet in London? Why don't you want me to know?"

"Because, this is how you always react." Lisa snatched her arm away and opened the door to leave. "Like you always tell the truth? I spend half my life thinking my grandparents are dead, then they turn up, like a couple of lost hippies."

"That's different."

"Oh, yeah, cos that's your life, not mine. I've found someone who's actually interested in what I have to say and doesn't come covered in shit and carrying a shovel. He's smart and knows just about everything."

"And you know nothing."

"I know I want to get out. This farm's your life, not mine.

I've decided I like expensive restaurants, food that I haven't nursed to maturity and a man whose slightest touch makes me tremble."

"So who is he? The only men that come here are people I know, Grant and Clive."

Lisa avoided her gaze. "Shows you how much you know then, doesn't it?" She grabbed her coat and left the room in a whirlwind of resentment. The door slammed and reverberated through the quiet house. Kate shivered. She opened the door and ran down the hall after Lisa.

"You've already made one mistake. Don't make it worse by making an even bigger one."

Her daughter froze and turned slowly to face her. "It's my choice, who I see and what I do. My decision, my life, not yours. Got it? You haven't a clue about anything, Mum. You don't listen to anyone, ever. Not even to Dad. I just wished he was here, not you. He'd understand."

Their faces locked in silent anger, eyes hard and unflinching. Kate looked away, horrified by the coldness in her daughter's stare. She steadied herself against the wall and watched Lisa run towards her room and heard the door slam.

"For God's sake, some of us are trying to sleep." Jack appeared in the hallway rubbing his head and yawning.

"Sorry. It's your sister. She's been out and won't tell me who with."

"Quite right too. It's a bit late for a talk on the birds and bees for our Lisa." He grinned. "Fancy a drink, now I'm awake."

Kate watched her son as he made the tea. He had the same efficiency of movement as his father: careful, studied. Everything returned to its proper place. Most men were messy in the kitchen but both James and Jack treated it like another lab experiment, planned and methodical.

"You're just like your dad, so careful."

"Apparently not, or he'd still be with us."

"You're right. It was so unlike him to take risks."

"You really have no idea about him, do you? He was always taking them. You should see the stuff he was doing in the lab. Half of it was illegal."

"Don't exaggerate. Your dad wasn't like that."

"Mum, did you know him at all? Some of his research in those last few months before he died looked pretty ground-breaking, then it trailed off completely."

"He said it was boring. Food production is hardly world shattering." Kate laughed. Jack was always winding her up. It was something he was very good at but he wasn't smiling now.

"You just don't listen, Mum. I know what I'm talking about."

"Not you as well? Lisa accused me of never listening. Is there anyone in my family that still likes me?" She grinned and took the cup of tea from Jack.

"She's right, you don't. Dad stopped trying. That's why we were always in the lab as kids. He loved explaining it all to us. Lisa was always more interested in the animals but I was fascinated by the science of it all."

"I thought he was just giving me a bit of peace after my night shifts."

Jack leant against the kitchen cupboards and raised his eyebrows. "Well, it's down to me to keep that lab making money. I don't get paid to stroke the fluffy lambs anymore. Go easy on Lisa. She got involved with that shit down the road, so if she's found a half-decent guy now, that's a plus as far as I can see."

"But I'm frightened she's out of her depth. She has no idea what some men are like."

"And you do, Mum. Yeah, right."

He kissed her cheek and padded out in his grubby socks. He looked so much older all of a sudden. Maybe both her kids had outgrown her. Did they need a mother? They certainly didn't seem to like her at the moment, so it was no surprise they had both forgotten it was her birthday. Perhaps she should have worked tonight after all.

She walked into the kitchen and took out the bottle of wine she had saved to share for the family dinner no one had time for. She poured a large glass and raised it in salute to a photo of happier days. With a hollow 'cheers', she leant closer to study the happy faces of her children when they were young enough to still need her. She could see them writhing with uncontrollable giggles. She could hear their bubbly laughter echo around the empty kitchen.

It was so easy when they were kids. Or was it? Even then it was James they called for and his sense of fun that bought squeals of delight as he threw them back on to their beds, searching for imagined monsters.

She always worried too much. Did James too? Was that why he did not talk to her about his work, why Lisa lied to her now and why Jack seemed to know more about her family than she did? She thought back over the past few months and realised her family was falling apart.

She had asked her parents to help but could she trust them? After all, they had abandoned her in the past. She thought she could trust Clive but shivered at how that had turned out, and while Grant genuinely wanted to help, he had his own problems with Toby.

Sitting in the silent kitchen she knew it was down to her. James had been strong; he always seemed to know what to do, seemed prepared for anything except his accident. How could he have allowed it to happen?

She remembered his tears as he held Lisa the day she was born. She had been crying for a different reason, terrified of the massive responsibility. "Don't worry," he said, "I'll always be there for you. Always protect you and the family, Kate." But he hadn't.

The day before he died, he'd told her to trust him, told her their future depended on it. Didn't he know he was meant to be her future as well as her past? Her memories were precious: she had few from her own childhood and was determined her children would have many. James had teased her about her memory box but always wanted to know when she had added anything. She had squirreled bits and pieces away and continued to add to it as their own children grew. He knew it was one of her most precious possessions.

After her parents disappeared, she would take out the family photographs and the notes her mum had written each time they'd been away at protest meetings and rallies. Later on she had added James's tender letters and her children's booties and baby pictures were tucked inside the box's glowing mahogany sides. Now everything was electronic, she treasured these old hand-written notes and personal threads to the past. She had not been able to open the box since James died; it was too painful. He had never forgotten her birthday. Every card he had sent had been kept.

She walked up to her bedroom, sipping the rest of her wine and remembered those cards. He would not have forgotten her birthday, ever. She had an overwhelming urge to look inside and see them again. Reaching under the bed she pulled the wooden chest towards her and unlocked it. Even the numbered padlock was an old relic of her father's and she pictured him smiling at her childish insistence that her treasures be kept safe.

She rolled the rusted digits until they aligned and unhooked the heavy lock. With a deep breath she opened the lid and unlocked her memories. She took out a bundle of birthday cards. James had hunted high and low for these old-fashioned printed cards. Some had been funny and some had gorgeous handmade adornments, real flowers or sparkly jewels. She read his words, sometimes cheeky but always with love. She kissed them and returned them to their plastic wallet, keen to uncover deeper memories inside the chest.

The first layer was a testament to her family life and she

held photo after photo. Chubby faces grinned out at her and another life filtered back. A young mother, nervous and full of anxiety but so full of love, she was desperate not to lose them. She had been terrified they would not love her back.

She picked up the lower partition and uncovered older memories of her own childhood. Poems her mother had written and photographs of her riding high on her father's shoulders. Her fingers delved deeper and amongst the familiar treasures she found a small package, one she did not recognise. A note in her husband's handwriting was wrapped around an obsolete memory stick.

Her husband's voice whispered through the words on the thin piece of paper, telling her he loved her and the children. Heartfelt apologies followed, he had put his own life in danger but the information on the memory stick was important, so critical he said, used intelligently, it could save them.

Kate stared as the tiny memory stick in her hand as he urged her to take it to someone she trusted, someone who had the power to use it, to make their lives safer. A warning not to tell anyone else, not even Jack. He would not risk his son's life. There were enemies in the government; men who would stop at nothing to keep this information quiet; she must keep it safe.

Was he was trying to help her? Was this really the key she needed to save her family? A searing pain tore through her. Was he killed for this information?

She stared at the letter in horror. In a trance she refolded the note around the old memory stick and buried it in her pocket. Closing the box, her fingers trembled as she reattached the lock and pushed it into the darkness under her bed. She knelt on the floor and hid her face in her hands.

No. It wasn't true, it couldn't be. But had he given her a key from the past that might secure her future? James trusted her judgement. Knew she would do the right thing. A tear slid down her face as she realised he had believed in her all along.

Her fingers delved into her trouser pocket and tightened around his note and the memory stick to check it was still there. If he had left this for her, it was important. He trusted her. It was time she did the same.

CHAPTER 26

What am I doing here? thought Grant, as he touched the entrance pad at The Ministry of Life. It felt like a lifetime since he had been in the office; in fact it was less than a week but one that had changed him forever. Could he continue for the sake of a career he was no longer sure he wanted?

"Nice to see you, Mr Spencer," The security guard grinned as Grant made his way to the lift.

He grunted but kept his eyes focused ahead. The door to his office was open. Had his unexpected absence been a reason for someone to check on his activities? His concern reduced when he saw the bundle of new reports on his desk. He had insisted Sally, his research assistant, get paper copies of external research. They were so much easier to flick though than screen versions, but how many times had he told her to lock the door after her visits?

He couldn't be sure who else might have exploited his open door. Security demanded a bug scan if a Grade 5 office had been compromised. He must organise this as he wanted to ensure no one saw what he was planning. It was illegal.

He picked up the silver frame from his desk with the picture of Toby and carried it to the window where the sun warmed the boy's face. Grant smiled, filled with the hope that now he might watch his son become a man. If only he could persuade Carolyn to be more supportive. She had loved their son as a baby but lost interest when his illness made him a burden. He'd take her to see Toby that evening and maybe they could see Mr Morgan. He couldn't give the go-ahead, without being more aware of the risks.

As Grant turned back into the room, there was a buzz from his message manager which had detected his movement. A flood of messages scrolled across the far wall; several opened as Grant focused on them, but he was soon tired of this unstructured review.

"Set priority filter to urgent," he said, too lazy to return to his desk to key in the command. Three messages passed this filter, one announcing the Christmas party and two terse demands from Sir Charles for an update on the 70s Cull Project. What a cruel and unnecessary exercise. Grant winced at this reminder of his day job. He voiced a curt reply, suggesting he could meet his boss tomorrow morning, before returning to his desk.

He forced himself to sift through the research papers until he found the latest demographic reports for China, India and Brazil. These countries had abandoned population controls ten years earlier, deeming them unnecessary, as their average population age had risen beyond sustainability without more young people. The flu pandemic of the 2020s had hit China hard and exacerbated the male surplus created by their ill-conceived one-child policy of the late 20th century. It showed the mistake of playing god.

Now these countries were prospering again. More evidence, Grant thought, to persuade this government to end or at least modify Quota. He found his copy pen and, after extracting key lines from each report, made a single sheet summary. He would hand this to Sir Charles, make it difficult for him to ignore the facts.

Grant's head drooped as the emotional trauma of the last few days took its toll. He needed a black coffee, or he'd be napping at his desk. The door to his office burst open and a red-faced Sir Charles eyeballed him, breathing heavily. "When I call Spencer, you come. Do you understand? How dare you put me off till tomorrow?"

"Sorry, sir," Grant said, standing with apparent deference, "I've just come in and need time to prepare things."

"Where have you been?" Sir Charles walked behind Grant forcing him to turn into the glare from the window.

"My son has taken a turn for the worse," Grant said.

"I don't care about your son. He has a mother. You have a job and I need someone who delivers. Have you finished the 70s Cull Plan?"

Grant felt his temper rising. Why should he go along with this policy? He wanted to trade his career for principles but realised he was in a better position to fight Quota with his job than without it. "I'm still finalising the numbers," he lied. "But my last report shows we are using the wrong assumptions. We don't need a cull."

"You may be clever, Spencer, but you amaze me with your naivety," said Sir Charles, now speaking with deliberation, "Of course the Quota rules are unnecessary but how else do you think we could have controlled the power of immigrant groups? What do you think would happen if we admitted that? We'd be driven from office and the country bankrupted by compensation claims."

Grant gripped the arms of his chair. Yes, he had been naive. He'd let ambition deny his common sense and accepted the government's propaganda, like most of the country. "Surely, you aren't intending to continue with this?"

"It's not up for discussion. I want the Cull Plan by tomorrow. Understand?" Sir Charles held his gaze until Grant nodded consent. "Good man," he grunted and marched out of Grant's office, his Cuban heels beating his retreat.

Grant was awake now, energised by angry resolution. He picked up the single sheet he had prepared earlier and tore it to shreds. The time for rational persuasion was gone. He'd prepare a Cull Plan for tomorrow and include someone from Sir Charles's family in the target list. Grant's fingers trembled with excitement. Today was the beginning of the end of Quota.

CHAPTER 27

"Tea?"

Kate dragged her eyes open just in time to see her mother-in-law put the welcome drink by her bed.

"Oh, love, you look exhausted."

Kate was not surprised. She had been awake half the night. "I'm really worried about Lisa. I think she's been seeing Clive."

"God, I hope not. Strange bloke. He shook you up last time he was here. You never really explained."

Kate shivered remembering his touch. "He's a nasty, manipulative man. I don't want him anywhere near her."

Mary frowned. "You've had so much to deal with since James died and Lisa's gullible. I can't work out how that blasted farmer fooled her into an affair. You're right to be concerned but if Clive turns up here, he'll have to get past me first." Mary stood, smoothed down her apron and walked towards the door. Opening it she added, "Now drink your tea, love, and I'll run you a nice bath."

Kate had tried to soak away many a dilemma in the bath. She was grateful to have Mary. It was funny but, since she had lost James, her whole world seemed to have imploded. Maybe her parents' return was timely and she needed more people she could trust around her.

The fear she had agonised over during the night knotted into a tight ball of anger in her chest. She would not let anyone hurt her family. Clive had to be stopped, had to be stood up to. He was a bully using his insider knowledge to feed his own lusts. She needed help from someone she could trust. She remembered the connection she had felt with Grant and knew she had to try and get through to him again.

Mary popped her head back around the door. "The bath's ready. You're not working today, are you?"

"No. I'm going to try and speak to Grant at the Ministry building in London. I'm sure he'll help with our Quota problems and your demand from the Ministry."

Her mother-in-law stood in the doorway and looked a little unsure. "That sounds great, although I don't want you to do anything dangerous, Kate. I would never put the family at risk. You know that, don't you?"

"I trust him and I'm sure he won't let us down." Kate threw the duvet aside and walked over to hug her. They had become closer since the funeral. She missed James but could not imagine the pain of losing a son as Mary had. How would she react if it turned out not to be the accident they had believed.

A brave smile spread across Mary's face. "I'd better get a move on myself. Jack's room's a nightmare. I took a drink in first thing but he'd already left."

"Funny, he never said anything about going anywhere today."

"They never want you to know where they are at that age, do they? I didn't have to worry about James. He was always buried in his lab, until he met you."

Kate smiled, remembering how he had often left her in the middle of the night to drive back to continue his research. She had no idea what any of her family had been up to lately but she would find out.

"I'd better have that bath if I'm going to make the early train." Kate smiled as she watched Mary pick up the empty cup. "Thanks, Mary."

She checked the bedside table and saw the memory stick on top of the scrap of paper James had left for her. Mary had enough to worry about at the moment so she decided not to say anything. As Kate walked towards the bathroom, carrying her clean clothes, she hoped Grant Spencer would be willing to help.

Three hours later, Kate stood in front of the huge Ministry of Life's interactive information screen and felt her confidence weaken. She hadn't realised the complex extended so far back from the Thames. It was more like a village. The virtual tour map warned the public about wandering into restricted areas unattended. This was a high-security environment and the travellator, that took her into the main reception building, buzzed with cameras twisting like heat seeking missiles.

She sensed a dozen eyes watching her every move and almost gave up when she caught sight of the armed guard. Before she could ask anything, he glared and waved his gun towards the row of receptionists behind the wall of glass and steel. She waited in the queue.

"Yes?" said the flat-faced girl as Kate approached the desk.

"I would like to see Grant Spencer, please."

"Pass?"

Kate wasn't sure if this was an instruction or a request. "I'm sorry..."

"Your pass?"

The abolition of polite requests, as an efficiency measure, was a big mistake, thought Kate. She hated the way government officials dealt with the public nowadays and was so annoyed she decided to test her newly discovered self-belief.

"He wouldn't be pleased to hear I'd been kept waiting. I'd let him know if I were you." Her tone was confident and she gave the girl her finest smile.

"I'll see if I can contact him. Wait, please."

Kate decided she had won the first round and was thrilled to have squeezed a please out of those glossy lips. When Grant appeared in the lobby she gave the aggrieved girl a wave and walked over to greet him. "Thanks for seeing me at such short notice. How is Toby doing?"

"Comfortable but we've a long way to go yet." Grant looked around and swiftly ushered her outside. "I'm sorry, Kate, but it's better if we talk in the café on the corner. This place has more bugs than the London dungeons."

He showed no annoyance at her unexpected visit and seemed pleased to see her. They chatted about Toby as they walked to a trendy coffee shop on the Thames path. Grant placed a strong hand on her lower back as he guided her through the busy tables towards one of the sofas at the rear of the café. After their coffees were delivered, Grant held a finger to his lips and placed a tiny device on the table. He fiddled with its position a few times before he seemed satisfied and then spoke.

"This must look over-the-top to you but believe me it's necessary. The Ministry is paranoid about security and have recording sensors in most cafés now. This device will scramble what we say." He relaxed back on the sofa and gave a warm smile. "It's lovely to see you again, Kate."

Despite her best efforts, she could feel herself blush and hoped it did not clash with the scarlet dress she was wearing. She was determined not to get flustered. Frowning a little, she switched to a more business-like tone. "I'm sorry to interrupt your morning, Grant, but," she lowered her voice, "I want to take up your offer to change my Quota, if you can. I'll do anything to help you look after Toby."

"You've already done more than I could have hoped. I'll look into it straight away."

Kate fished into her bag and pushed James's letter across the table. "I'd also like you to look at this." She watched his face. At first he seemed slightly embarrassed by the sentiment but then she saw the intrigue grow in his eyes as he re-read it a second time.

"So, where is the file?"

She handed him the memory stick. "I know it's very old but I was hoping you would have something that could read it. I can't think why James didn't just use his normal data stream."

After turning the stick over, in the palm of his hand, Grant looked up. "Because he knew this would be more difficult to decipher. I used these years ago but they've been obsolete for some time. It feels so plastic!"

She laughed and their eyes locked. She felt the chemistry. It was a shock to realise she could even think of a physical relationship with anyone this soon. Suddenly aware that his eyes were drifting down towards her neckline, she gripped the locket that held her husband's picture and felt a wave of guilt flood through her. Determined to keep the conversation on track she asked, "But can you get the information out?"

"I can't but I know a man who can."

Kate was upset, thinking he was being too frivolous. "James seemed positive this information was dangerous. It may even have been linked with his accident. I'll understand if you don't want to get involved." She turned and pulled her jacket towards her.

He moved nearer and covered her hand with his. He lowered his voice. "Kate, I'm sure you're right."

She stopped.

"This could be evidence of a government cover up about their Food Programmes. If they've been putting people's lives at risk, it's inhuman. It may add weight to my Quota research and help force the government to admit they are in the wrong."

His deep concern drew her in and she knew her instincts had been correct. "I do trust you, Grant, but could this be dangerous for all of us? If James died to get this information then we have to be careful."

"James must have been quite a man."

"He was." She drained her coffee and picked up her bag. "Thank you. I know it's risky but we both have a lot at stake here."

"You're right. We are dealing with powerful men and we have to work together to keep our families safe."

She could see he was sincere. "My parents would be pleased to hear you say that. Mum said you were happy with the hospital and the doctor's prognosis for Toby. You must be so relieved."

"Yes. It's not going to be easy but they can offer him a chance. I had no idea artificial transplants were possible." His face darkened a little. "Well, I suppose they're not to most people." He patted the pocket that held the memory stick and smiled. "Maybe this will help change that."

"Let's hope so. But do be careful, please." She rose and he placed her coat around her shoulders.

"If you're visiting your mum at the weekend, I may see you there. I'd like to run a few ideas past your dad." He paused. "It would be nice to have an excuse to spend some time with you again too."

She smiled at him and as they embraced to say goodbye, she felt excited. How ridiculous. She could not stop grinning as he left. She walked to the café pay desk to charge her mobile. She had been so tired this morning she had forgotten.

While she was waiting for security updates, she heard a voice that made her shiver. She gripped the table edge. Looking up, she saw Clive and guessed this was a popular watering hole for ministry staff. He was a leaning towards a young woman in the booth opposite. He was in earnest conversation. Kate could see the girl was nervous. Clive turned his body towards the girl and slid his hand up her skirt.

Thank God his interests had moved on. Maybe he had forgotten about Lisa. This was good news but seeing him was a shock. She lifted her mobile with shaking hands and dropped it. As it clattered to the floor, she saw Clive look over and recognise her. Steadying her emotions, she made herself smile. This was what she wanted after all. She should try to act normal, let him know she did not need him now.

She watched him speak briefly to the girl and then leave the table and come towards her. She froze. "Here, let me help." Clive picked her unit off the floor and handed it back to her, holding her hand a little too long.

"Thanks," she managed to sound calm.

"What brings you here? Couldn't keep away, eh?" He ran a finger down her jaw line and she managed not to move.

"Bit of business, nothing important." She looked across the room and could see his table companion busy gathering her belongings and trying to make a swift exit. Yes, she thought, suddenly worried for this unknown girl, go while you can, love.

"We have unfinished business ourselves if I remember correctly." He followed her gaze just in time to see the back of the young woman's heels as she left the café. A flash of anger flooded his face but it was gone in an instant as he switched his focus to her. "A work colleague, she was already complaining she'd be late back, scatty cow, can't think why I bother with her. Have you eaten? I was just about to order."

Kate forced herself not to back away as Clive led her to his table and struggled to look interested as he ordered lunch and drinks. It was time for her to be strong. She had to deal with him.

He topped up her wine glass. "I don't use this place as a rule, it's crammed with boring ministry staff, but I wanted to catch that little tramp from records. She's always in here. What did you say your meeting was about?"

"I didn't but I do have something to tell you." She noticed she had his full attention. "I've managed to sort Mary's problem so we won't need your help after all."

The dark look in his eyes made her falter but she was determined to do this properly now she had gathered the strength to face him again. "But that's not really what's worrying me. It's Lisa, she's been seeing someone and won't tell me who." He did not flinch.

"I'm not surprised. We all have our secrets, don't we?"

"She's young and very vulnerable. Some men may see that as an opportunity. A very weak man, that is. She looked into his black eyes and could see that hurt.

"From what I remember of her, she could fend for herself. She's very like you, after all." His laugh made her tremble.

"Clive, I'm not here to play games. From now on, she's off-limits."

To her surprise, he looked almost pleased. "Jealous, Kate?"

She could hardly believe his arrogance. She snatched up her coat. "I seemed to have lost my appetite. Don't contact me or my daughter, ever."

He looked like he was about to strike her and she staggered away from the table. She left the café as quickly as she could, although her legs felt near collapse.

She could barely breathe. She made the tube station in under three minutes and boarded the moving staircase. It was only then she felt brave enough to check behind her. He hadn't followed her. Surely he had got the message now. She felt cold as she sat on the train homeward. One stop from Rickmansworth, her mobile buzzed, notice of an incoming message.

Big mistake... Clive

CHAPTER 28

Grant ran his fingers along the plastic end of the memory stick, intrigued to be holding something from Kate. He hadn't seen one of these for years. There must still be billions of them around, forgotten and useless without the proper readers, their valuable data inaccessible. The so-called progress of the digital age had created more secrets in a decade than paper had in a thousand years.

He was sure this stick's contents would be important. Kate's husband, James, had been a leading light in food technology research for years. Why had he hidden this data? Grant understood now Kate's concern that James's death might not have been an accident.

He was sorry he had left so abruptly and would have enjoyed spending more time with her over lunch. The report for Sir Charles was far from complete and he mustn't miss the deadline. Kate said she was visiting the hospital to see her parents at the weekend so he hoped to meet her again then. In a strange way she felt like family. In the café there hadn't been a pause in their conversation. He couldn't remember chatting with Carolyn so easily.

Grant took a last look out of the window. He may have

imagined it but he was sure it was Kate he saw, in her bright red dress, heading towards the tube, on the far side of the river. With increased motivation, he returned to the job in hand.

He checked the latest analysis. It listed more than 50,000 over-70s in Hertfordshire alone and a similar number without medical credits or with a bare minimum. Extrapolate these numbers to a national level and one would be considering potentially culling over 10 million. Age cleansing on a Nazi scale. Ridiculous and inhuman. What sort of people could consider this? Grant knew who they were: the privileged few in power whose own details weren't accessible to him. Or were they? Their data must be there somewhere for security purposes or for accessing medical services.

He checked again to see if Sir Charles's family had any members in his report. There were none and Grant himself wasn't listed. He assumed ministers above a certain grade were excluded. If he got their records he was sure he could have a more persuasive meeting with his boss. Peter, his friend in secure data services, would know what other information was available and he might be able to help with the memory stick too.

Grant activated his security protection before using his mobile. "Hi Peter, how are doing mate?"

"Hello, pal. Are you ringing to fix a time to buy me that beer you promised? From the tone of your voice, it sounds like you are about to add to your drinks debt."

"I know you love the excitement of solving technical problems. We've had a few over the years haven't we? You should thank me for exercising your incredible intellect."

"What is it, you smooth bastard?"

"Thanks. Here's your starter for ten. Do you still have legacy data readers?"

"Yes, we have to keep them. If it's magnetic or optical we can read it, though we can't promise to unpick any encryption immediately," Peter said. "What have you got?"

"An old memory stick," Grant said, lowering his voice. "Maybe storing some political dynamite. Could you handle it yourself and get back to me today? It might be nothing but I don't know."

"Send it now; I've a gap in my major discovery time this afternoon."

"Thanks, Peter."

"So what's my other test?"

"I've got an urgent Quota report to prepare and it has to be inclusive. That means all secure ministerial personal data like mine. Can I get access to that?"

"You need a different password. I'll trust you with mine but you'll have a limited time as I have to change it every hour. Is that ok?"

"That's great, thanks."

"Ok, send me the stick and I'll forward the password."

Grant selected a security box from his desk, inserted the memory stick and coded Peter's address before putting the box in the transporter. Within a minute, the box was returned with a password, coded with their agreed encryption.

He had to work fast. To speed things up, he entered a reduced query accessing only the new records now available. With that started, he left his desk and strolled round his room to collect his thoughts. On his third rotation, he started wondering what other facilities were available with this password. He tapped away, exploring the available menus. Most were the same as the ones he normally used but he also had access to the administrator's menu. There, to his amazement, were commands to change personal records. There was no time to consider repercussions and he hoped Peter wouldn't be blamed. He added a hundred years to Kate's family Quota allocation and gave another five years medical credits to Toby. Hey presto, problems solved. How easy was that? It would have taken hours to work out how to do this with his normal level of security access. He wondered how many others were changing their Quotas.

His euphoria faded as the minutes ticked by without the new report. Sir Charles wasn't going to be moved by the magnitude of the cull. He would have to spell out some of the major consequences: public protests, loss of key skills and the unbelievable horror of mass euthanasia. He started thinking how to rank these in order of impact, though he knew, in his heart, logic wasn't going to work.

At last, a buzz from his workstation. Eureka! Just what he wanted. He saw, as he expected, that Toby had been identified but more importantly so had Sir Charles's wife, whom he hadn't seen for years. Additional medical credits had been requested for her, every year. There were also several other ministers whose family members qualified for the Cull. Grant noted them, the more the merrier, for blackmail purposes.

He was about to close the program when he noticed an additional report. In his haste to initiate his query, he had left on the genetic search that had previously identified Jack Appleby as a possible kidney donor for Toby. Now there was a new name. Grant gasped. A one in a million chance but almost too difficult to contemplate the implication.

Grant pushed open the door to Sir Charles's office, barely able to contain his rage. The minister was sitting in his leather armchair scanning some papers on the coffee table in front of him, an optical enhancer in his hand. He didn't look up.

"I hope you've done your job, Spencer."

"Oh, I've done my job all right, rather more thoroughly than you wanted. Here are the names of 100,000 people in Hertfordshire to murder, and top of the list is your wife."

Grant threw the report on the table and moved to leave the room.

Sir Charles rose instantly to confront him. "What the fuck do you thinking you are doing?"

147

"I might ask you the same question. How long have you been screwing my wife?"

Grant didn't wait for a reply but he heard the shout as he strode off down the corridor.

"You're fired, Spencer."

Grant looked for the memory stick when he reached his office. It hadn't been returned. He couldn't wait. Security would arrive to expel him from the building in minutes. He snatched his mobile and left. When he reached the other side of the river, he sent Peter a coded text to meet him later that night.

He was still too angry to think about the end of his career.

CHAPTER 29

Grant sat in the car outside his flat, taking deep breaths. It did nothing to calm his rage. He couldn't remember the journey home, his emptiness was overpowering. The controlled logic that had sustained him throughout his life was no match for the storm of emotions that threaten to overpower him. He could find no way of structuring his thoughts, preparing himself for the coming confrontation. Fight or flight? He had no choice. He wasn't running away from Toby. He'd keep that thought paramount, accept the adrenaline rush and react. The moment must be faced, words said that couldn't be retracted and then perhaps he could move on and do something worthwhile.

Carolyn was in the kitchen making coffee when he let himself into the flat. She turned to him in surprise. "What are you doing home so early?"

He didn't reply, just watched as she took another cup from the cupboard. When she turned towards him her face dropped. "I know that look. Who've you upset now?"

He didn't reply.

"After all I've done to help with your career, you screw it up. You'd better apologise to Sir Charles for your cock up, whatever it is. I'm not giving up on my ambitions."

149

Grant exploded, hitting the kitchen table so hard with his fist that the coffee cups jumped, spilling liquid on the worktop. "Apologise to the bastard who's been sleeping with my wife? What sort of arsehole do you take me for? How long, just tell me that, Carolyn, how fucking long?"

Carolyn turned away, reaching for a cloth to wipe up the spilt coffee. "What the hell are you talking about? Don't you dare take your frustration out on me! Have you been drinking?"

Grant advanced round the table towards her but she moved, keeping the barrier between them.

"Why don't you just admit it?" he shouted. "I can't imagine how many lovers you've had but I know you must have slept with the man whose genes match Toby's."

Carolyn stared back, shaking her head in disbelief. "What?"

Grant felt his face burn with a fresh rush of anger. "Explain why he's a perfect transplant match for Toby. He's Toby's father, isn't he?"

Carolyn's face turned white and she edged round the table to give herself an escape route through the kitchen door, watching Grant intently. He saw the flicker of acceptance in her eyes before they flashed with venom. "Well, if he is, it's your fault. You ignored me at those Ministry events, preferring to talk to your boring researchers. Sir Charles looked at me in a way you haven't for years."

"He obviously did more than look."

"Maybe I did respond to him after all that wine. But it got you promoted and I didn't hear you complain. I've pushed you for years, got you where you are and now you've fucked up over some spurious medical result."

"I can't believe you can stand there and lie to me when Sir Charles's admitted he shagged you."

"Well, you know what?" Carolyn said, lowering her voice, "I regret not taking my chance when I had it. I could have done better for myself."

"This is your chance to try again, because I sure don't want you." Grant leaned against the worktop feeling drained.

Carolyn was quick to respond to his threat. "Well, at least you won't have to worry about Toby anymore. I'll ask his real father what we should do."

Grant leapt forward, pinning her against the door before she could move. He spat the words into her face. "Toby is my son. You won't change that. You've never cared for him. And your lover obviously doesn't care either. He's known the truth for hours and hasn't bothered to call."

"Don't you dare touch me." Carolyn wriggled free and escaped into the lounge. "We'll see what Sir Charles thinks," she added when she was beyond his reach

"You make me sick; using Toby now you think he's worth something. You can fuck Sir Charles as much as you like but don't you ever try taking my son away." Grant turned and walked out of the flat.

"Try and stop me," Carolyn screamed down the corridor after him.

Grant returned to his car, feeling a mixture of relief and despair. He had loved Carolyn once but the marriage became a convenience years ago. Toby had kept them together. He could lose her but not his son. He would go and see him.

As he started the engine, there was a flash on his message display announcing a call from Peter. Damn, he had forgotten about their meeting. He pushed the audio security button and patched Peter's call to the car radio speakers.

"I thought you wanted to meet?" Peter said. "I've been sitting in the pub for an hour now. Have you changed your mind?"

"Sorry, Peter, I've been distracted. I'll be along in 20 minutes. Did you manage to do something with the memory stick?"

"Oh, yes, and you were right. There's some highly sensitive information on it, enough to cause the government serious worry. I don't want to hold on to this stuff a minute longer than I have to."

Grant pushed down on the accelerator. "Stay right where you are. I'm on my way."

CHAPTER 30

Clive smiled. It was perfect. His eyes scanned the dimly-lit room hidden deep in the belly of the Ministry building. The restraints were heaped in the corner. He would screw them to the back wall later. The air was stale and there was a faint smell of burning. It came from the old ventilation pipes that ran across the ceiling. The Ministry had upgraded its heating systems years ago but this room did not appear on the maintenance software intelligence. It was part of a disused boiler room that had been closed for years. Clive used it as a store for his illegal downloads.

He leant against the cold concrete wall and reviewed the six-foot cell. The thin blanket, left on the tiled floor, offered little comfort. An ancient ceiling strip, yellowed and dull, was the only source of light. He imagined her hands exploring the dingy cell. He felt her fear as the seconds stretched to hours and she tried to work out where and, more importantly, why she was here.

Visualising her despair, his excitement grew. The anticipation was delicious. The preparation had to be meticulous. No mistakes. It had to be perfect.

He rose and took a last look before locking the heavy

door and pushing the empty shelving in place, obscuring the doorway. As he passed shelves of discarded electronic equipment, he made a mental note to add a few boxes of digital hard core to the empty shelves. He could not overlook something so obvious.

After climbing the cellar steps, he opened the door a crack to listen before stepping out into the corridor. Few people even knew it existed but he was taking no chances.

As he reached the outer perimeter of the building his phone flashed.

"Clive, its Carolyn."

A pleasant surprise. Had she some new intelligence on Spencer? He pictured her full lips and flirtatious eyes. She had a vicious streak but her self-centred motivation was exciting. "You've got something for me, I hope."

"No. My idiot husband's been fired."

He recognised her contempt but his spirits rose. He could hardly believe the news. Spencer would be of no help to Kate. She'd have to come crawling back.

"He's lost everything. After the government reshuffle in January he was due a top ministerial position. Now the prick will be lucky to get a job emptying the bins."

Clive lips spread into a slow smile. "How disappointing, but I'm sure you'll think of something, a resourceful woman like you."

"Don't worry, He'll regret screwing up my life."

Clive understood revenge.

"He's found out about my affair. I'll make sure you're sorry for threatening me now."

Clive gripped his mobile and forced himself to stay calm as he listened to the cocky tone of this embittered woman.

"My mistake was marrying a spineless man. Sir Charles is more my style, he has power and he's not afraid to use it. I won't waste my energy on a brief affair this time."

"He's out of your league."

"And so are you. When I tell him you threatened me. It'll be your turn to sweat." She hung up.

Clive's eyes narrowed. Stupid cow, who did she think she was? First Kate, now Carolyn. Women were pathetic liars. However, the news of Spencer losing both his job and family meant Kate would be grovelling for his help.

A fresh young face came to mind. Time he made that call. His mood lightened as he waited for her to pick up.

"Lisa, it's all sorted. Dinner first and I've a special room in mind for the two of us. It's time we got to know each other properly, don't you think?"

CHAPTER 31

When Grant arrived in the pub, Peter was nursing a pint of wheat beer. The early evening drinkers had departed and the tables nearby were empty.

"I'm sorry, I'm late," Grant said, "would you like another pint?"

"Just a half, please. I've had two already and I don't want to fall asleep on the train again."

Grant went to the bar and returned a few minutes later, with two glasses, spilling a little as he put them on the table, unable to stop his hand trembling.

"Sorry," he said, "let me wipe that up." He sensed Peter watching him as he fetched napkins from a nearby table.

"Are you alright?" Peter asked. "You don't look your usual self."

"I've just had the week from hell." Grant confessed, forcing a tired smile.

"Tell me about it. I spend most of my time chasing my stupid boss." Peter laughed but stopped when Grant just nodded wearily. "So what's happened?"

Grant shrugged, took a sip of his beer, and nervously licked the froth from his lips. He didn't really want to talk about his worries and expose his desperation but he felt he owed Peter an explanation.

"The extra access you gave me revealed some secrets. I made the mistake of challenging Sir Charles and he fired me."

"He sacked you for presenting the facts? He can't do that, can he?" Peter said. "I thought you were tipped for promotion."

"Yes, but I rubbed him up the wrong way. I don't think we'll be working together again."

"He must have issues," Peter said, waiting expectantly for more details. Grant couldn't face discussing what he had discovered about Toby.

"Does Carolyn know you've lost your job?"

"Yes, she's not thrilled. But I'm relying on you to distract me. So what's the sensitive information on the memory stick?"

Peter's expression became serious. "This won't improve your mood."

"What do you mean? What did you find?"

Peter glanced around, the pub was almost empty but he was clearly uncomfortable. "I don't think we should discuss this here. Can we go somewhere more private?"

"Ok, my car's outside. We'll be secure in that."

Peter drained his glass before following Grant to the pub car park.

"Blimey," he said, "when did you get this?"

"I got it last year with the new job. I'm not sure how long I'll be able to hang on to it now."

Peter eased into the black leather passenger seat and scanned the dials that festooned the dashboard. "You've got the entertainment package. Why can't I get a job like yours?"

"There's a vacancy. You can apply," Grant said darkly. "Anyway, the most important extra on the car is full network invisibility. No one will hear us when I switch it on."

Grant unlocked the car and they both climbed in. "Ok, you can spill the beans. What was on the memory stick?"

Peter looked relieved to get back to technical matters.

Grant remembered he had always been uncomfortable dealing with emotional situations at university.

"Well, the data wasn't encrypted so the author obviously wanted the info to be read. Do you know James Appleby?" Peter said.

"No, but I know his wife. She asked me if I could help her open it. Her husband worked on animal research but died a few months ago in a freak accident. She found the stick this week."

"That's good, so you know the context," Peter said. "I'll encrypt the document and send it to your private mailbox."

"Thanks, and you're right to keep everything secure." Grant lowered his voice when he continued, "You suggested it might be embarrassing for the government."

"I think they would have been very keen to suppress its publication. It makes frightening claims about cloned GM cattle. If its conclusions are correct, meat eaters have been poisoned for years."

"How come?" Grant said.

"Well, this guy, Appleby, claims to have found a link between eating beef and the rise in dementia. He tested cloned GM cattle on his farm, analysing their meat and organs. He discovered some disturbing trends."

"We've been eating genetically modified beef for years. It was declared safe decades ago. The Ministry of Health has stringent controls to ensure the food chain is safe. So what's changed?

"I'm no expert but it's the cloning aspect that might be a problem. Any defect in a primary animal can be passed on to thousands of clones."

Peter continued, "Appleby found some of his research animals had a mild variant of Mad Cow Disease. It didn't show up in the living animal but was detectable in post mortems. He checked where the relevant cattle was consumed and then cross-referenced reported diseases in that area over the last 20 years. He found a strong correlation with a rise in dementia cases in the over-50s."

"I didn't know dementia was rising."

"Nor did I. So I had a quick scan for reports on dementia in the Ministry of Life archives. And would you believe it, there were none?"

"Maybe no one's written any."

"I knew a guy who used to catalogue our medical research reports. He retired recently but I checked with him. He had several dementia studies. Someone has removed all reference to them. It has the whiff of a government cover-up and poor Appleby may have discovered too much for his own good."

"How worrying," Grant said, "I can think of two reasons they might want to hide the truth."

"Surely, it's just bad news."

"It's certainly that, but there are more sensitive issues. Firstly, the government gets enormous tax revenues from the cloning and meat production companies. And secondly, dementia is classified under Quota as a "life termination disease" with an acceptable excuse for euthanasia." He swallowed hard.

"Do we know if meat is affected across the country?"

"Not from this report," Peter said, "it only covers Bucks and Herts."

"I can see why you felt nervous about this, but I don't see how we can keep it secret." Grant saw Peter tense.

"I know we ought to do something," Peter said, "and you'll think me weak, but I have a family to protect and I'd rather not be involved."

"I'm sorry. I shouldn't have put you at risk."

"I'll help you on all the Quota analyses, if you get your job back, but you have to count me out on any disclosures on this stuff. I can't gamble with my family or my job."

Grant felt bad. He had already compromised Peter by using his password to amend Kate's Quota allocation. He hoped there would be no repercussions. They weren't best friends but they looked out for each other.

Peter handed over a small package. "Here's the memory stick and a summary print out. I'll send you the full report and delete all evidence of it so you'll have the only copy."

Grant slipped the items into his inside pocket and smiled at his friend. "This is the last you'll hear of it. I promise I won't involve you again."

"Thanks," Peter said, still looking apprehensive. "Is it ok if I get off home now?"

"No problem," Grant said, "I'll drive you to the station." He shook Peter's hand, "I really appreciate your help."

After dropping Peter off at the station, Grant drove on to his usual hotel. He had much to reflect on. This had been a day and a half yet it was still only 7pm. He lay on the bed and tried to prioritise the issues facing him. His job, his marriage, his son, the Quota system and James Appleby's report.

He didn't need long to decide Toby was his overriding concern. Nothing would mean much without him. He must focus on getting his son well. And he would fight tooth and nail for his parental rights if Carolyn or Sir Charles made any attempt to side-line him. He breathed a little easier having decided.

He wouldn't go back to his apartment just yet, to let Carolyn do some thinking, but he needed to get clean clothes and personal things. The shops were open so he could buy the necessary. Though he'd lost his current job, he was sure Sir Charles wouldn't convince an employment tribunal he should be sacked from the Ministry. Next week he would contact the Personnel Department.

What about Quota and the memory stick report? They were part of the same problem: a corrupt government robbing people of their life entitlement. He wasn't the first to realise that but the government had marginalised all communication channels and protest groups. And they had orchestrated the clash between the young and old to gain passive acceptance of Quota. Why was he bothering to think about it? Now he was out of the Ministry, he had lost any power to oppose them from the inside.

Without thinking, he fingered the memory stick. And the realisation was unexpected but dramatic. He remembered that old political adage: you can manage everything but events.

The disclosure of James Appleby's report could cause a national uprising. If the protests were big and sustained, the government might fall and changes become possible. How could that be done? Who could he discuss it with? He knew immediately. Adam Penn had the experience and contacts to make the most of this. He would try to see him tomorrow when he visited Toby.

Of course he must tell Kate about the report and ask to speak to her father. She might be more amenable if she knew he had sorted Mary's Quota. He sent a brief text to give her the good news.

For the first time on this dreadful day, he breathed more easily. He had many problems but he could see the possibility of taking positive action. He got up from the hotel bed and took a whisky from the hospitality bar. He drained the glass in one gulp. He felt back in control.

CHAPTER 32

Kate read the short text.

Huge problems at work but Mary sorted. Need to talk. Meet me at the hospital tomorrow after I've seen Toby.

The message from Grant was welcome though curt but said nothing about the memory stick. Obviously security was tight and he would not have risked explaining anything over the open network. She would be able to ask him tomorrow. She was relieved his work problems had not prevented him amending their Quota. Then immediately she felt guilty. Aborting Mary's exit demand was uppermost in her mind but Grant must have other worries.

Her thoughts were interrupted by Mary struggling through the door with heavy logs for the wood burner. "I told you I'd do that," she said rushing towards her.

"Don't fuss, I might be old but I can still do my bit."

Kate knew Mary was finding some of the physical jobs around the farm difficult. As Lisa was almost three months pregnant she wouldn't be able to do any of the heavy jobs either. Kate thanked God Grant had increased their Quota. Mary would be safe and they might have enough credits for a new farm hand. Things seemed to be improving at last.

After lifting the logs from Mary's arms, she swung open the cast iron cover on the burner and added them to the crackling fire. The smell of the forest filled her senses. She had never tired of the country colours and aromas, such a joy after living in the city. She closed the door on the rising flames and turned to Mary with a smile. "Sit down. I'll make you a cup of tea."

Mary sank into the worn cushions of her favourite rocking chair. "I'll put my feet up then. Bit of lemon cake in the tin, if you fancy it?"

Kate bought the tea and cake over and pulled up the stool next to Mary. "Well, I need to butter you up a bit if you're going to be here for a good few years yet." She watched Mary's puzzled expression change from surprise to delight as she realised what she was saying.

"Does that mean the Quota thing is sorted? Oh, thank goodness." Mary had bravely accepted the government's cold dictate in the hope her precious grandchildren would benefit. Kate could see the tears of relief in her eyes now she knew her future was secure.

"Yes, it's good news at last." They both laughed as Mary almost dropped the cup because her hands were trembling so badly.

"What good news is that?" said Lisa as she waltzed through the kitchen and picked up a slice of cake from the tin. "We could do with some of that around here."

"It's your Gran's call-up." Kate butted in before Mary could say any more. "Seems there was some mistake and the Ministry sent it far too early. They have so much data to process, I expect they make mistakes all the time."

She looked at Lisa to see if she had picked up the nerves in her voice but she was already rushing to kiss her Gran's beaming face.

"That's fantastic, Gran. You had better start brushing up your babysitting skills. Your first grandchild needs you." Lisa ran a hand over her stomach. "Not that it's showing much, thank goodness, means I can still have a social life."

"Be careful, Lisa. Some people would report their own family for extra credits. Don't forget that baby's not licensed."

Kate could hear real concern in Mary's words. "Don't worry, Gran, I'm not about to advertise it, am I?"

"I was going to suggest you come to the hospital tomorrow, Lisa. You need the injections in the next couple of weeks." Kate said.

"Not now, Mum, I'm off out. Not sure what time I'll be back." She retrieved a lipstick from her bag and reapplied a layer of deep red to her full lips. The colour matched the new silk scarf she had wound around her neck. She readjusted the flash of scarlet around her shoulders before adding, "Don't wait up."

"Hang on a minute. Where are you going?" Kate caught her arm as she passed.

"Meeting Jack in town for a drink. Thought he might like to spend time with real people for a change, instead of those geeks on line. Is that ok?"

Her stare forced Kate to let go and Lisa smoothed the sleeve of her new jacket carefully before smiling up at her, with just a hint of triumph.

"Just be careful."

"Oh, I think it's a little late for that, Mother, don't you?"

Lisa was gone before Kate could respond. She looked back at Mary in frustration.

"She's testing you, love. Try not to worry. She's not a stupid girl."

"I wish I had your confidence. She's already made one mistake. I don't want her making things worse."

Mary put down her tea and gave Kate a reassuring smile. "Jack will make sure she's ok. He's too cool to admit it but he loves the bones of her. Always has."

Kate glanced over at the photo of them as children and

remembered the way Lisa had looked out for her little brother at school. Maybe it was his turn to return the favour.

"Well, all this sitting around won't get us far." She rose and checked her planner. "I'll go over the test animals' stats if you could prepare the feed for the lambs. Do you think you can manage on your own, Mary?"

"Yes, yes, of course. Nice cup of tea with my favourite girl and I can take on anything, me."

Kate grinned. "Thanks. The Ministry seem keen for us to roll out the new cloning regime as quickly as we can, although Jack's taking his time. He's stubbornly sticking to his dad's procedure, no matter what the government wants."

"Chip off the old block, eh?" Mary said as she picked up the cups and cleared away.

It was nearly nine o'clock by the time both women had finished their day's work and eaten supper. They were chatting when Jack strolled into the kitchen.

"I'm starving." He lifted the lid of the stockpot and sniffed expectantly.

"I'd have thought you'd eaten. Lisa's not one to go long without food," giggled Mary taking the pot from him and putting it on to heat. "So does she want any, or has she gone straight up for more of that beauty sleep?"

"What?" asked Jack.

"Lisa. She's with you, isn't she?"

"What made you think that? I do have other female company nowadays. No need to look so shocked. I did inherit a little of Dad's charm."

The women looked at each other. Kate felt a chill envelop her whole body as she stared at Jack. "She said she was with you."

Jack shrugged his shoulders and pulled a bit of cheese from the fridge.

"Jack?"

"Don't panic, Mum, she's probably got a hot date. I'm not surprised she lies to you if this is how you react. She's pregnant not dead. About time she started having a bit of fun. After all, she's already paid the price." He cut off slices of cheese and popped them in his mouth.

Kate tried to take comfort from his relaxed response but all she could see was Clive's dark eyes, taunting her.

"It's Clive. Why would she lie otherwise? Why?" Kate went through to the lounge and picked up her phone. She tried Lisa's mobile several times but it went straight to voice message. After leaving two worried voice alerts, she slammed the unit back onto the recharging pad.

She ignored the drink that Mary had bought through and started pacing the room. "I know she's with him. I just know. How the hell do I find out where they are? She was dressed to the nines so it's probably somewhere in London, but where?"

"You're not still stressing?" said Jack as he entered the room. He dived onto the sofa and stretched his legs out. "News," he barked at the television and started scrolling through the choices.

"Turn that off, Jack, this is serious."

Jack waved his hand to turn off the news report refuting the latest Alzheimer's figures and gave Kate his full attention.

She spoke slowly for full impact. "That man is dangerous. I need to find out where she is."

"Mum."

She stopped him and continued, "Didn't you say you could track people's mobile signals?"

"But you don't even know who she's with. I can't just spy on her for no good reason; she'd never speak to me again."

"He's not all he seems. I asked him to help with our Quota and he saw me as payment due."

"Payment due?"

Kate had to sit down before she could carry on. "He came

166

onto me. I could tell he wasn't taking no for an answer but I managed to get rid of him before it got serious." It was painful but she looked Jack straight in the eye, "He's dangerous, Jack, and I don't want him anywhere near Lisa."

Jack shook his head in disbelief. "I don't believe it. He seemed a bit nerdy but nothing like that. Maybe you misunderstood, Mum?"

"Hardly, he virtually assaulted me. I'm not over reacting here, Jack." She watched her son's face harden.

"But why didn't you tell me? I would have made sure he got the message. No trouble." He looked angry.

"I dealt with it and when did you become such an expert on Clive? You only met him once."

She could see Jack looked uncomfortable and he avoided her eyes.

He got up from the sofa. "Look, she's probably not even with him. But if you're really that worried, I'll see what I can do. I've downloaded software in the lab that might do the trick. I'll get on it straight away. If it works it shouldn't take long." He gave her a kiss and smiled before leaving. "She'll be fine."

He seemed to be humouring her and Kate wondered if she was really worrying everyone unnecessarily but her gut told her otherwise. She wondered what Jack meant. His comments on Clive had been odd. Had he been in contact with him too? Surely not. Now she was getting paranoid.

The next few minutes seemed an age as Kate waited. She walked towards the lab twice but turned back. Jack was just like his dad, obsessive about that space. Twenty minutes later he was back. He had tracked her to a location in central London and checked the co-ordinates. It was a well-known champagne bar in the City.

"Well, she's fallen on her feet this time. Whoever she's with must be loaded, that place costs a fortune." His attempt at lightening her mood hadn't worked.

"I'm going to find her." Kate said and snatched up the

address he had written down.

"She's probably having a great time with some new bloke she's met, but if you insist on going, then I'm coming. Never know, might be some rich birds hanging about."

They travelled down on the Tube and at every stop Kate checked her mobile. It didn't help her mood. She became more agitated. To help calm herself she decided to ask Jack about the girl he had seen earlier. She had no idea he was dating anyone. "So, who's the girlfriend?"

"Just someone from one of the social groups I belong to. She was at the last meeting in Rickmansworth."

"Oh, a local girl, then. Does she work on one of the farms?"

His face clouded for a minute and he hesitated. "No, she works for the local Shaman Advice Service. She was at school with me." His mood lightened, "Although she wasn't so bloody pretty then." He laughed. Kate was surprised at how good it felt. It had been ages since they had shared a joke.

"What's her name? I might remember her."

"Badushi"

"Oh, yes. She was nice. You must have something in common to join the same group. Don't tell me she's into gene technology too!"

"No, such luck."

"So what is this group you go to?"

Jack started looking around and getting agitated. She realised she was being far too nosy.

"It's just a stupid current affairs group, political stuff, you wouldn't be interested. This is it, we get off here." He swung towards the door and seemed to be in a hurry to get off the train and through the crowds.

As they glided up the speed stairs towards the surface, she whispered in his ear. "Sounds like you're taking after your grandad. He could tell a story or two."

Jack turned and looked at her thoughtfully. "Yeah, I bet."

She was feeling more positive holding on to Jack's arm as they soared upwards. These tunnels had been built deep under the original Victorian tube system. It took some while to reach ground level.

She watched the downwards passengers passing them a few feet away, in silent chains of commuter gloom. A bright red scarf stood out against the rows of black suits and hijabs. She squeezed Jack's arm.

"It's Lisa. Look, Jack, I'm sure it's her."

She waved her arms and the other passengers turned in unison to look. All the security cameras were zooming forwards for a close up and she knew it would be seconds before the alarm was triggered if she didn't stop.

"Disturbance. Passenger on Level 1. Alert." The drone of the automatic security system rang around the tunnel.

Jack told her to calm down and called to Lisa calmly. She scowled as she passed and ignored them both.

"Wait for us on Level 4," Jack texted and told Kate to quieten down. He looked furious as the cameras whirred and focused closer. He shoved his mobile in his pocket and kept his head down as they travelled in mutual silence.

Five minutes later they were back on Level 4 and Kate searched the crowds for her daughter. Jack saw her first and gave Kate a warning glance before manoeuvring through the tightly packed commuters to reach her. Lisa had found a small alcove in which to huddle so she hadn't been forced to board the trains as they stopped.

"What the hell are you doing here, making all that fuss?" she snapped as they reached her.

"We'll talk when we get you home," Kate said, just relieved Lisa looked fine.

"Mum was stressing. I told her you were ugly enough to look after yourself, Sis."

As usual Jack had broken the tension and Lisa rewarded

him with a grudging smile. Within seconds they were caught up in the surge forward as the next train arrived. The journey back was quiet. No one wanted to spill their thoughts into the middle of the commuter carriage.

Kate watched Lisa all the way home and did not like the flushed expression on her cheeks. Lisa refused to look at her mother and just stared straight ahead. Even Jack gave up on his humour offensive and was listening to his tunes.

If Clive had been out with her tonight he must have charmed her completely. Lisa looked well and seemed more troubled by her than the man she'd been with. Maybe the manipulating bastard had listened to her warning or Jack's theory of a new man was right. She hoped so.

She looked across at her daughter's secret smile and a cold hand gripped her stomach. She stared bleakly as her family were propelled deeper into the dark tunnel ahead.

CHAPTER 33

Grant felt exhausted after a difficult night, sleeping fitfully and desperate to see Toby. He was on the road before 7am, early to visit the hospital, yet it was the only place he wanted to be. His route east, along Commercial Road, went through the run-down East End, still reserved for immigrants though there had been few since Brexit and the xenophobia of the 2020s. Looking back, Grant realised the country's obsession with population control had started with entry barriers for the thousands of refugees, before Quota limited the lives of existing citizens.

He parked and ran for the hospital entrance. The words of the ward nurse made him cry. "You must be so proud of your son, he's always smiling," she said, as she led him into the treatment room. "He'll be on the machine for a while. Stay as long as you want."

The pulsing green lights of the dialysis unit were hypnotic. He let tiredness claim him, just short of sleep, content to be close to his son.

"Good morning, Mr Spencer, I'm glad you're here. I was going to call you."

Grant's senses reactivated. He recognised Toby's

consultant. He staggered to his feet and shook Mr Morgan's hand.

"Sorry, I didn't mean to startle you," the consultant said. "As you can see, we've had to give Toby dialysis sooner than we expected."

"How is he?" Grant felt nervous asking the simple question.

"Stable but we need to press on with a transplant as soon as possible"

"Is it an emergency?"

"Not yet but we should go ahead within a week. If you call by the office my secretary will give you the consent form. We prefer to get approval from both parents, if that's ok?" Mr Morgan smiled before turning to leave. "Try not to worry. The synthetic kidneys are very successful: they're a better match than donor transplants, actually."

Grant sat down again. He hadn't read up on artificial organs yet. Perhaps he should just take the consultant's word. Now dialysis was being withdrawn it was the only option. Or was it?

He took a deep breath, unsuccessfully trying to kill the unwelcome thought. Hadn't he just discovered another compatible donor? It had been too much to expect Jack Appleby to donate a kidney to a child he'd just met, but wouldn't a father want to save his son? Had Grant the right to deny Sir Charles the chance to offer one of his kidneys? Yes, his inner voice shouted, I am Toby's father, I should decide. But he knew it was important Carolyn supported the decision. He would fetch her to see Toby and make her understand how they could save him. Deep down she must love her own son, even if she rarely showed it.

There was no point in thinking about it anymore. He went into the corridor and called her on his mobile.

She answered immediately. "If you are ringing to apologise, I wouldn't bother."

Grant ignored her. "Toby's very ill and he's asking for you. The consultant is recommending an artificial transplant next week. Whatever our differences I want you to see him and we can decide together what's best."

He heard an intake of breath; she was obviously considering her options. "Okay, but this changes nothing."

"Good, I'll pick you up about ten."

She hung up without further comment.

Some movement at least, Grant thought but he wondered what might be going on between her and Sir Charles.

When he returned to the ward Toby was awake.

"Hello, Daddy," his son called and stretched his arms, inviting a cuddle and dropping the bear he was holding.

Grant hugged him and pressed his face to his. "Hello, my little soldier."

Toby chuckled. "I'm not a soldier."

"What are you, then?"

"I am your best boy."

Grant lowered Toby gently down on the pillow and tried to compose himself. "Let's save Mr Snuggle before he's run over by the nurse's trolley," he said, retrieving the scruffy bear from the floor.

"Where's Mummy?"

"She's coming soon," Grant said, stroking his son's head. "Have some rest now and I'll bring Mummy to see you."

He kissed his son on the forehead before leaving the ward. He needed some fresh air. On the patio area outside reception, he found an empty bench where he could relax and let his mind wander. He watched a trickle of people approach the hospital. Lucky ones, he thought. Just like him. Only those with special contacts had access to this brilliant healthcare. He was so grateful to Kate's parents for bringing Toby here. The NHS still provided care for emergencies but anyone with a chronic illness was destined for an early Quota exit. Lost in his thoughts, he didn't notice two visitors diverting from the main path and walking towards him.

"Hello, Grant. What are you doing out here so early?"

He felt a pulse of excitement as he breathed in Kate's perfume, Chanel No.5. He'd recognised it when they had first met. He returned her smile. Jack stood alongside with a wary expression.

"You're an early bird too," Grant said, coughing to clear his dry throat.

"I wanted to be sure I didn't miss you. I thought you might pop in before work. How's Toby?"

"Ok, I think. He's having dialysis, but the consultant is advising a transplant next week."

"Oh, have they found a donor or are they talking about an artificial kidney?"

"Artificial."

"That will be fine. Dad says they do wonderful things here."

"Yes, I'm impressed. Have you heard how your mother is?"

"She's doing well. I'm off to see her now so can we have a coffee later."

"Could you spare five minutes?" Grant said and turning to Jack. "Sorry, do you mind if I have a private word with your mum?"

Kate smiled at her son. "I'll catch you up in reception, Jack. See if you can find us a drinks machine."

"Please yourself," he mumbled before marching off towards the glass doors.

Kate looked worried. "You've not had a problem with Mary's Quota change, have you?"

Grant swallowed. "No, that's sorted. It's about James's memory stick. Let's discuss it in my car. It's secure." He pointed to the front row of the car park.

"Sounds serious," Kate said, with a half-smile.

Grant did not answer but unlocked his car and activated the security shield. He sensed Kate was apprehensive and he wasn't sure he should voice his suspicions.

"Thanks again for sorting out Mary's Quota," Kate said, as she eased herself into the passenger seat.

"That's ok but I think I've lost my job." Grant confessed.

"Oh, no, it wasn't my fault was it?"

"Of course not. I had a disagreement with my boss."

"I'm sorry. Maybe things will calm down." Kate said.

"Perhaps," he said, pulling the memory stick from his pocket. "Anyway, my friend was able to read this. It was a report by James about beef production."

"Is that all? You had me worried for a moment. James was always writing reports about that," Kate said, her shoulders dropping.

"I think this was a special report," Grant said.

Kate frowned. "I don't understand."

"The report suggested GM beef was causing a significant increase in cases of dementia."

"But the government have always promoted GM food as healthy and cost-effective."

"Yes, they have. Our food supplies depend on GM production so James's report is very embarrassing for them. They wouldn't want it made public."

"But surely they would know about it," Kate said. "James used to meet government reps monthly."

"I don't know," Grant said, "but for some reason James felt the need to leave you a secret copy."

Kate was silent, twisting the straps on her handbag. Grant realised he'd worried her. It couldn't be helped. She had to know what was going on.

"I'm sorry, but I'm sure the government would have wanted to suppress this report if they knew about it."

"James never mentioned it. Could he have been threatened?"

"He may have been," Grant said slowly, knowing that Kate would realise the implication. Maybe she already suspected.

"Surely you're not implying James's death wasn't an

accident?" Kate became still.

"It has to be a possibility. How did it happen?"

Her eyes filled with tears. "I don't want to talk about it. I wish I'd never found the bloody stick."

"Oh, Kate, I didn't mean to upset you. But I think James wanted you to have the report in case something happened to him."

"What am I supposed to do with it? It won't bring him back," she said.

"I think releasing the report would stop more people getting dementia. It might bring the government down and that could end Quota."

"I wish I'd never given it to you." She paused for a moment. "What about Jack? He's still doing James's work. Are you telling me he could be in danger too?"

Grant didn't answer.

"You're talking nonsense. Give me back the stick and forget it," She thrust her hand towards him.

"Hang on, Kate." Grant said. "This needs more thought. Millions of people are at risk. We can't just ignore this."

Kate's face flushed. "Who's the 'we' here? This is my stick. Thanks for helping Mary, but I'm not going to put my family at risk. Promise me you'll destroy any copies of the report you've made."

"I promise," Grant said, giving her the stick. "I know this is a shock but please let me talk to your father about the report. He'll know if it's significant."

Kate climbed out of the car, tears streaming down her cheeks. "Just forget it." She slammed the door as she left.

Grant sighed. Their friendship seemed to have died in an instant, but James's report was too important to ignore. Would she calm down and talk to her father? Probably not, she was worried about Jack. And, he had to agree, she was justified.

CHAPTER 34

The memory stick dug a painful ridge into Kate's clenched palm as she walked back through the hospital reception. Tears filled her eyes when she paused in front of the lift. Grant's words, and the violent images they evoked, made her reach for the support of the cool steel door. It had been a struggle coming to terms with her husband's death when she believed it to be an accident, but now? Grant had more or less confirmed her own suspicions.

She forced herself to stand tall and stare at the tiny piece of hardware in her hand. Could James have put his life in danger for this? Had he knowingly risked himself and his family for the information it contained? Everything she knew about her husband felt like a fabrication. The implication was immense. Could Grant possibly be right? No. She didn't want to believe it.

But Grant knew the top guys in the Ministry, worked with them day in, day out. If he even thought this was a possibility, she should listen. Jack would have no idea how dangerous his current research was.

As the lift doors opened, she ignored the concerned looks of those emerging and buried the lethal memory stick and its secrets in her shoulder bag. As she reached her mother's cubicle in the oncology ward, she could almost hear the bomb ticking inside the zipped pocket.

Kate looked through the observation panel. Her mother was sitting up in bed watching the news streaming onto the end wall. She had missed her over the years, especially when her own children were born. Kate could never have imagined leaving Lisa and Jack, and knew now she would do anything to protect them. Maybe her mother had left her for the same reason?

Her mother beckoned her in. Kate passed through the sterile beam at the entrance and hurried towards her to hug her tight. She stroked a strand of her mother's long grey hair back into place. Her mum had fought the trend to move to shorter hair now she was in her 60s. As a girl, Kate remembered standing on a stool arranging her mum's waves into elaborate styles with gaudy slides and ribbons.

Should she tell her mother about the memory stick? Kate knew she had some ugly stories to tell about the government's attempts to keep nasty secrets and would have no trouble believing Grant's theory.

"You look great, Mum. You're off the oxygen and drip?"

"Yes, much better now, love. I've just sent the men off for refreshments. We would have waited but Jack said you were talking to Grant."

Kate glanced at her bag on the floor. "Grant had to speak to me. But I wanted to see you. What did the doctor say?"

"Bit more treatment to go but it's all positive. They're a great team here. Your dad's been sending everyone nuts, quizzing them about the new drug treatments and transplant technology. It's amazing the breakthroughs they've made since we've been away. Did Grant say how Toby's doing?"

Kate realised she hadn't taken in anything Grant has said about Toby; she had been so shocked at his suggestion that James's death had not been accidental.

"I do hope it's not bad news, you've gone quite pale?" Her mother's concern was evident as she leant forward to comfort Kate.

"No, no, Mum, it's nothing like that, I'm sure Toby is fine. I just asked Grant to look into something for me."

"Jack was saying he'd helped Mary out and upgraded your Quota. That must have put him in a very dangerous position at the Ministry?"

"I think he's lost his job."

"Poor man, that's awful if he was just trying to help."

Kate realised she had been a bit hysterical with Grant. But if it was true James had been killed for his research, she wanted the report destroyed. She found it hard to believe anyone could have come on to the farm and arranged his accident. But Grant knew the government and they could still threaten the rest of her family.

"Kate, talk to me. Something is obviously worrying you."

Jack and her father came through the door armed with snacks and drinks.

"Hi Mum, we weren't sure how long you'd be so we got you a bottle of fruit juice." Jack put the drink in Kate's hand and opened his own can of cola. "So, what did the big man want?" He winked at his mum and grinned.

Kate stood silent.

"It seems the poor man's lost his job." Her mother announced.

"He'll be in trouble if they've discovered he changed your Quota," her father said.

Kate looked at her dad's worried face. She was grateful for Grant's help. He had never misled her or let her down. She thought about the conversation in the car and knew she needed to tell her family. It was too important to keep quiet.

"Mum's paranoid about most blokes. She even had me following Lisa like a bloody private eye," Jack chuckled, taking another swig of his fizzy drink.

"Come on, Jack, that's not true. I had every reason to be worried."

"Seems like you owe Grant a lot if he's improved your Quota." Her father chipped in, looking at Kate with a worried frown. "You look awful, Kate." He pulled the chair out for her. "Sit down, love, something's wrong."

They were all waiting for her response and she could hear the memory stick ticking louder in her bag.

"I found some information hidden in my Souvenir Box. It was an old memory stick of James's and I asked Grant to try and read it."

"But, why..." Jack started to protest.

"Let your mum finish, son."

"That's why he had to talk to me. James had written a report proving the government had covered up a major health risk. Grant suspects his death was not an accident." Kate looked up to see if her words had sunk in. Jack looked stunned and her parents exchanged a look that dispelled any doubts she may have had.

Her dad put his strong arms around her. "Believe me, they're capable of anything, darling," he started, "but we need to read the report and find out exactly what they were so afraid of. Jack may be at risk otherwise."

Kate pulled away from his embrace and looked at her son. "No, I want everything destroyed. I've lost James. I don't want anyone else in danger."

Jack butted in, "The bastards. I've been working with Dad on his research and I've not found anything threatening. If there's work I don't know about, then I need to see it. I'd understand it better than any of you."

She could hear determination in Jack's voice. "No. I want you to stay out of it." She pleaded with her dad again. "I don't want you taking any chances. Promise me."

Jack looked puzzled. "Why did Dad leave you the report, if he didn't want us to use it?

"He's right, love, James trusted you. He knew you'd do the right thing." Her father pulled her closer. Kate leant against him and felt drained. She just wanted her family safe.

Jack looked furious. "If Dad died for this, then I'm not letting you destroy it."

She turned to her son and could see he was on the edge of tears.

"We owe him that," Jack said.

Kate knew he hadn't cried since the funeral and had thrown himself into his dad's research to bury his emotions. This was the first time she had seen him open up. Jack's face was rigid with emotion. Maybe he was right? She just wasn't sure. "I need to think about it."

Jack looked determined. "If Grant's here, I'm going to find him." He pushed past her and headed for the exit.

Everyone looked at her in silence.

She picked up her bag and reached inside for the memory stick. She knew James had given them ammunition to challenge the government, but at what cost? Did she have the courage to use it?

CHAPTER 35

Grant checked his watch. He had underestimated the impact of his conversation with Kate. If he could catch her in the canteen he would apologise. She must have struggled to come to terms with her husband's accident. Now he was suggesting he may have been murdered. Always too concerned with facts, he had been far too blunt. She might yet consider discussing the report with her father if he could explain.

Waiting for his coffee, he scanned the tables. Kate was probably still with her mother. He found an empty table by a window; the sight of the gently flowing Thames always calmed him. A string of boats was passing below, ferrying passengers to and from the Estuary Airport. Many travellers now preferred the river link to the high-speed train. Very few had the opportunity for overseas travel and he wondered how many trips were actually for business or national issues. Sir Charles seemed to travel more than necessary. His train of thought frequently seemed to bring him back to his ex-boss and right on cue a text appeared.

"We need to talk." Short but filled with implications. Before he could decide how to react, someone sat in the chair opposite.

"What have you been saying to my mum?" Jack said.

Grant forced a smile but Jack didn't respond. "Is your mum still here?"

"She's very upset."

"I'm sorry, I didn't handle it well," Grant said. "I need to see her. Explain."

Jack ignored the suggestion. "What makes you think my dad was murdered?"

Grant pressed his lips together and shook his head in silent apology.

"I worked with him. Tell me what you've found. If his work put him in danger, I need to know." Jack's voice grew louder and he banged his fist on the table. People were looking.

Grant leaned forward and spoke quietly. "You're right. But your mum asked me not to tell anyone."

Jack paused but he didn't look satisfied; a determined young man, Grant thought.

"I've some arrangements to make but I'll be back around 1pm. I'll talk to you both then."

Jack sat back and relaxed a little. "Ok. We'll meet you here." He stood. "I need answers." He glared at Grant and left the table.

Grant was impressed with the boy's single-mindedness.

Half an hour later, Grant parked his car in the road outside his apartment. He hoped Caroline would not make this difficult. Toby needed this operation.

She was standing by the window when he entered, already wearing her coat. She turned, picked up her bag and stared at him, her face expressionless.

"I want this visit discreet," she said, "I'm only coming if we can don't use the car. It's too easily recognised."

"Ok. We can use the tube. The hospital's a five-minute walk from Canary Wharf."

Carolyn took sunglasses from her bag and put them on before stepping past Grant and out of the flat. Throughout the walk to the station, she ensured she was never alongside him so there was no opportunity for conversation. On the tube there were enough empty seats for them to sit apart. Grant made no attempt to engage her. Past experience told him she was a master at the blanking game, but he knew that she could explode at any moment. He tapped her on the shoulder when they reached Canary Wharf and led her through the maze of tunnels to the exit for the hospital.

"It's just a short walk towards the river," he said, as they came out into the midday sun. He didn't expect an answer and none came. He wondered what she was thinking now she could see the modern hospital ahead, not the rundown building she might be expecting. Did she have a plan to scupper Toby's operation by claiming he wasn't the father? He grew more apprehensive as they approached the entrance but decided not to challenge her. He knew she always acted in her own best interests and surely removing the ongoing burden of Toby's illness would support that.

"Toby's on the fifth floor. There are no visiting restrictions so we can go straight up," Grant said and showed the way to the lift. Carolyn kept her sunglasses on so he couldn't see her reaction.

Her job in advertising had trained her for the fifteen-second pitch. She seized her opportunity as soon as the lift doors closed. "I will sign the operation paper on one condition. You divorce me and take full responsibility for Toby. It was you who persuaded me to get married and have the child when you found out I was pregnant. I never said he was yours."

The lift doors opened before Grant could reply. He had no immediate answer, although he knew in his heart that this was probably the solution he wanted.

Toby was excited to see his mother. He screamed her name as soon as he saw her. Carolyn played her part, took off her sunglasses and smiled for the first time since Grant had collected her. She picked Toby up and gave him a big hug.

"Show me your bed," she said and let Toby lead her across the ward.

"Here, Mummy," he said, pointing to the bed where Mr Snuggle's tatty head protruded from a green blanket. "And my friend, David, is next to me," he added, gesturing to a small dark-haired boy asleep in the bed to the left.

"Do you think Mr Snuggle would like a friend too?" Carolyn pulled a small bear from her coat pocket. Grant was surprised she had made the effort to buy a toy before coming to the hospital. He realised it was her farewell gift to their son.

Toby giggled. "I'll call her Mrs Snuggle. My bears can be friends like Mummy and Daddy."

Grant watched Carolyn's response to Toby's poignant remark. He was sure he saw a glistening in her eye before she regained full control. After playing with her son for ten minutes, she tucked the two bears into Toby's bed and announced her departure.

"Mummy has to go now," she said, "but Daddy will stay for a while. Be a good boy."

She gave Toby a last cuddle, a kiss on the cheek and then backed out of the ward waving. It was the believable exit of a caring mother, Grant thought. He was almost convinced she'd had a change of heart. She was waiting for him when he came out.

"Where's the form you wanted me sign?"

"I'll fetch it," Grant said and went off to find the doctor's secretary. He returned a few minutes later with the document.

"You have to sign here," he said, "but don't you want to read it first?"

"I told you before I'm handing everything over to you." She took the pen he offered and signed.

"I'll make my own way back. Get your solicitor started on the divorce. I want this sorted quickly so I can get on with

185

my life."

"Are you really sure about this?" Grant felt he needed to ask.

"I've never been surer," Carolyn said coldly, turned and walked out of Toby's life without looking back.

Grant watched her, not knowing what he should feel. Yes, he had begged her to marry him when she became pregnant but he had loved her then. She had inspired him to become more ambitious, helped him get promotion and made him more comfortable in Ministry social circles. He hadn't realised she was already one of Sir Charles's mistresses when he first met her. He'd expected her to become a proper mother to their child. They were relatively old parents and most people of their age would have seen Toby as a precious gift. But she treated him as an irritant, interfering with her career. Their marriage stopped working within months of Toby's birth. Today's outcome had been inevitable for some time but he felt sad, nevertheless. Grant looked at the form. Carolyn's signature spelt an escape for all the family.

CHAPTER 36

Kate stood beside her mother's hospital bed. She was showing great improvement. This should have been the family reunion she had longed for, but the information James had left could put them all at risk.

"Mum, Grant said he'd be back at one," Jack checked his mobile, again. "I need to know what's going on."

Jack was hungry for answers and he would not settle until he had them. Kate panicked and looked towards the door.

"Vamoose, the lot of you," her mother smiled knowingly. "Go on, now. The tea trolley's on its way and I won't get a look in otherwise." Her father bent to kiss her mother goodbye and told her to behave.

"Give your old Gran a hug before you go," she said and opened her arms to Jack who offered himself forward but was clearly too preoccupied to respond with any real emotion.

Her father moved towards the door. "Let's all get some air," he said and winked at Jack. "I'm sure I've a few more stories you've not heard." He slapped his grandson on the back and led him into the corridor but Jack stopped dead.

He checked the time again. "What about Grant?"

Kate could see Jack was not going to let it rest. "You go

ahead. I'll phone him and we'll catch you up." She followed them to the hospital entrance and watched them walk towards the river. In the distance, she noticed the commuter boats slicing through the choppy water. There was a broody sky but the clouds had parted enough for the pale sunshine to lighten the Thames.

She pulled out her phone and called Grant. He picked up straight away saying he would be down in five minutes; he was just settling Toby for a nap. He must be in agony, Kate thought, worrying about his little boy. The doctors here were good but the child was in danger. Now she was being asked to put her own children at risk. Could she?

James had drawn attention to himself and worked hard to get the evidence together. He had wanted the public to know. He must have thought the risk worth it. Walking nearer the water, she saw a couple of birds fighting over a tit-bit on the embankment. The birds were ready to fight for what they'd found. So had James.

She glanced back towards the hospital entrance. Grant stood on the pathway squinting into the pale sun. He hadn't spotted her yet. He was strong but not arrogant considering his position in the government. Could she trust him? He was obviously a loving father and had fought for his son's life, but was he using James's report for his own benefit? Did he want his job back badly enough to use her family as collateral? She thought not but she needed convincing before she was prepared to do anything. He waved and came striding towards her.

"Hi, Kate, sorry to hold you up."

"It's ok. Jack and my dad have gone ahead. Jack insists on talking to you. He's upset."

"That's my fault. The thought that his dad's death hadn't been an accident must have terrified him. I'm an idiot. I was too worried about the wider implications when I blurted out my opinions."

Kate could see Grant meant it. They caught up with her father and Jack sitting on the river wall with their legs dangling over the side. They were in the middle of a very competitive game of stone skimming.

"Your son's a bandit. He told me he'd never played this game before," her father moaned.

Jack scrabbled to his feet when he saw Grant. "So, let's hear it then." Jack's chin rose in defiance.

"It's just a theory, I don't have proof. I..."

Kate felt this was getting out of hand and she didn't like Jack's tone.

"Let's all sit down and discuss this properly." She led them to an old bench and wiped the leaves off.

"We're all here for the same reason, Jack."

Her father manoeuvred the young boy towards the bench and sat next to him.

"I'm done with talking. That's all anyone wants to do. No one listens. Violence is all this bastard government understands." His hands flew out in exasperation. "If they killed my dad, they weren't interested in talking, were they?"

Kate shook her head trying to eradicate the bleak scenarios. "This is exactly what I was afraid of. If this information is so threatening to the government, what's to stop them hurting us?" She looked at her dad for an answer.

He paused. "We're not doing anything, anything at all until we have a plan. I won't put my family in danger."

Kate felt herself about to explode. "And you know all about that, do you, having left me alone to mastermind your one-man campaign?" She managed to ignore her father's hurt expression.

"I've told you we left to keep you safe. We were the problem. I had people around you the whole time, making sure you were ok."

"Don't ask me to do that to my kids. I'll not risk having to abandon them, like you did."

No one moved. A soulful call of a river bird could be heard in the distance.

Her father stood up and came round to her. "That will never be an option. I promise you. I know how hard that was. I would never ask you to do the same, never. I will find a safe place, for us all." He kissed her cheek.

Kate felt the fight leave her.

"Mum, sometimes you have to take a risk," Jack pleaded. "Dad took a risk researching this stuff in the first place. He worked hard to get it together and keep it secret. When they found out he was on to them, he left it for us. It's his revenge and I want to use it."

Jack rose and marched up and down on the gravel as he spoke. Kate was reminded of his childhood habit. He turned and waited for her to speak. "Please, Mum."

Her father led him back to the bench. He looked directly into his eyes. "Never move in anger, Jack, it's the wrong way, you don't get anywhere. They'll pay, but we'll do it properly and as safely as we can. We need to change things for everyone, not just for revenge, no matter how much we want to."

Kate wasn't convinced. "How sure are you this is damaging for the government? I don't understand all the science but tell me if it's good enough."

"It's good enough," confirmed Grant. "James's research looks indisputable. The government must have known about the food problem years ago but did nothing. I'm an intelligent bloke but the propaganda had me fooled. They produced their own data to back up whatever they wanted people to believe. Sure we had an overpopulation problem but the way they decided to deal with it wasn't right."

Grant outlined the research and the clear conclusion that consumption of cloned GM beef had caused dementia cases to multiply. He explained how James had tracked the infected cattle to specific factory farms that had been under contract to the government, as part of their Cheap Meat for

All Programme. They knew the cause of the rise in dementia but did nothing to stop it. In fact, it helped support their exit strategy by persuading the elderly, who feared many years of dementia, euthanasia was the lesser evil.

Kate could see how dangerous this would be for the government if it got out.

"Grant's right," her father said. "We have the evidence we need. This could make a big difference to our children's lives, to everyone. I want revenge for James's murder but removing a few decision makers won't change the system. I fought against this in Europe but never had the evidence or the right people in place." He shook his head in frustration before continuing. "We need contacts inside, like Grant, and strong passionate youngsters behind us, like you Jack, but more importantly, a nationwide protest movement on the streets. By using the secure dark web, we can build a protest that will galvanise the country. When the truth gets out it will expose the government. It's not who we hurt that counts, it's what we change."

Jack stood and faced the group. "I've friends ready and able to take direct action. They'll listen to me. They have the means to attack the Quota building and destroy it completely."

Kate was horrified. She had no idea. "This is madness, Jack. Who the hell have you been talking to?"

He did not reply but stomped off along the embankment.

"He's probably exaggerating but if he's got in with an organised terrorist group, it could be serious," her father said. "I know some of these groups are all talk. The youngsters are frustrated after years of little work and no prospects." He called to Jack but got no response.

"Try not to worry, Kate. Jack needs to feel involved. It's his future he's fighting for." Grant's voice was quiet and controlled. "I'm sure I can get back inside the Ministry. I'm going to meet my old boss and he'll have to listen. We need to force the government to find a solution that's fairer. Protest is fine but any meaningful solution has to be political. I've been part of a corrupt government, but now I can use my position to put things right."

"I'm not sure we should trust your boss," her father said. "Don't tell him about the report until we're sure."

Kate watched the clouds gather over the water and felt the temperature plummet. Jack came striding back towards them, his teenage slump nowhere to be seen. They were right but she still had reservations.

"So how do I know my family will be safe? How can you guarantee that, Dad?"

Her father's face was full of concern. "It's a risk, Kate, I won't lie to you, but none of us have much of a future, if we don't do something. I promise we'll plan this down to the last detail. I'll have a hideaway ready and if it comes to it, get you all to a place of safety in France."

Jack had just joined them. "I'm not going anywhere. I know about it now so you can't leave me out." He looked determined.

Kate was beginning to realise there may be few choices left but she wasn't going in blind.

"Who else knows about this Grant?"

"I have a contact in security. I'll make sure he understands the implications. Kate, we're all doing this to protect our families. It's the only reason for doing any of it. The system failed to give my son a chance and has cut your children's lifespans. Do we have a choice?

"We don't, Mum," Jack's voice rose. "As long as it's not all talk again. We need to make the bastards listen this time."

"With your father's proof, they won't be able to ignore us. Blowing a hole in Quota headquarters isn't the only way to beat the system." Her father spoke with quiet authority and Kate saw her son considering the idea.

"Grant, are you sure you can get the right people on side?"

"Yes, Sir Charles has a lot of influence and like any politician loves to play the power game. Even he will see how potentially critical this would be for the current administration. He won't want to be on the losing side."

They all stood silent waiting for her decision. She looked at them in turn and knew she would have to trust them completely.

"Ok. Grant, give my dad and Jack a copy of the report."

As the heavens opened, she hoped she would not regret it.

CHAPTER 37

Clive's pulse quickened and he gripped the edge of his desk. He stared, hardly believing the data in front of him. Kate Appleby's Quota had been increased. Who had altered it? The criminal gangs operating in the early years of Quota had all been eliminated by his tracker software and the only ones left worked for him. Was there a European cell involved? He tracked back and could see the originator was one of the Ministry's own staff. Did he have a rival? It had been a while since he had seen off any competition.

He could feel beads of sweat forming on his forehead as he leant forward and scrutinised the data streaming across the screen. Working in near darkness inside his high rise flat he hardly noticed the London skyline that shimmered outside his window. The grey employees' block inside the Ministry of Life complex was drab but his thrills came from trawling the ministry files and playing with innocent lives.

Digging underneath the security codes he recognised the access terminal had been disguised by a data analyst called Peter. He dug deeper and uncovered an illegal trace to the cocky Mr Spencer's office. Kate had gone to him for help after all. He was surprised Spencer had been able to compromise the Quota settings; the data analyst had taken a big risk.

Clive dismissed their effort as an amateurish operation. The security probes would have discovered it within the week in one of the automated sweeps. He removed the tag and deleted any trace of it. He reset Mary's Quota and with rising excitement watched the instruction activate. She would receive a call from the Enforcers within hours. Perfect.

He switched the desktop off and turned his own security tags back on within seconds. He knew exactly how long it took the bugs to detect a rogue instruction and always cleared in time.

Clive imagined how hysterical Kate would be when the knock on the door arrived. Over the years he had seen relatives cry, plead and finally resign themselves. Some of the elderly would feign a dignified exit from their homes, assuring their despairing families all was well, disguising the anguish of a final goodbye. He was looking forward to Kate's call. Hearing her plead would be satisfying.

Just enough time for a work out, Clive thought; he could be showered and back before she called. His exercise regime was obsessive. He had upgraded his access to the Ministers' leisure facilities and used their private gym daily. He had never been challenged. The ministerial suite was hardly used, the fat politicians preferring the free bar instead.

He entered the luxurious wet room and stood naked in front of the mirrored changing area, slowly running his hands over his perfectly toned body. The skinny kid had grown into a powerful man. He had made sure of it.

While he was drying his hair, his mobile flashed up Kate's home number. He continued to rub his hair vigorously and ignored the verbal alert that followed. He would wait until he was back in the flat. She would be in a state of panic by then. He dressed and sauntered back towards the concrete high rise. He hated the bland building but welcomed the anonymity it gave him. He was one of hundreds living in the warren, but he had more power than the fat cats who drove past to their sleek riverside properties.

Inside his flat, it was Lisa's tearful pleas he heard on the recorder and was disappointed. So Kate wasn't at home. What a shame. He relaxed into his armchair and called the farm number.

"Clive... Clive is that you. Thank God. It's Gran... she..."

Clive interrupted.

"It's ok, Lisa, calm down. What's wrong?"

"The enforcers, they took Gran. I thought Mum said she'd sorted it. She told me her friend had fixed Mary's Quota."

"I'm sorry, Lisa. I offered to help but your mum turned me down. Seemed to think she didn't need it. I'll come straight away. Try not to worry, love, I'm leaving now."

He returned his mobile to the desk and poured himself a drink. Let her sweat for another hour. She should be good and ready to agree to anything by then. Sipping the iced whisky, he sighed. Things were back on track.

Lisa was standing at the door to the farmhouse as his car screeched to a halt. She ran and he caught her as she stumbled into his arms.

"It's ok, I'm here now, let's get you in the warm."

Once they were inside the house, he could see the kitchen was empty.

"My poor love, did you have to deal with all this by yourself? Where is everyone?"

"At hospital in London visiting my other grandmother. I told the men they were making a mistake but they wouldn't listen to me."

Clive led her to a chair and poured her a large brandy. "Sip this, you need to calm down and tell me exactly what happened."

Lisa explained how the government enforcers arrived

without warning, taking her gran and giving her no time to contact her family.

"I tried to call Mum but she wasn't answering. Gran insisted it was just a big mistake and she'd be home again soon." She stared up at him, clearly hoping for reassurance.

Clive looked into her eyes and feigned a look of sheer disappointment. "It seems your mum's friend completely misled you. I'm afraid people think they can bypass the system but in truth I'm the only one who can do it successfully. It was only a matter of time before they came for your gran. You did right calling me. I'd like to help but your mum made it pretty clear she didn't want me involved."

He was pleased to see Lisa's eyes were full of pain and he put his hand over hers to stop them trembling.

"But we have to get Gran back." Lisa's eyes met his. "Is there nothing you can do?"

Clive struggled to hide his delight. This was exactly where he wanted the Appleby family. He managed to force a concerned frown and offered to make some calls. He sent Lisa on a search for Mary's Quota records and placed a voice-to-voice alert to his contact at the holding hostel for the area.

"You've just picked up a Mary Appleby. She's of interest. Don't administer any drugs till I get there."

"Not sure I can do that."

Clive's eyes narrowed. "If you don't, all deals are off and I will be having a little word to my friends in security."

"You owe me."

Who does this jerk think he's dealing with? Clive sighed and continued, "I'll pretend I never heard that. I'll be along to collect her within the hour. Make sure the old woman's ready."

He shut off the call just as Lisa came back into the room. She dropped some letters on the floor. Tears streamed down her face; she looked up in complete desperation.

Clive drew her closer and kissed her. He felt her smooth skin and full lips respond to his touch. She was young and grateful, just how he liked them.

"If I'm going to get her back, I need to leave now. When your mum comes home, get her to ring me on this secure number immediately. I promise you, I'll do my best." He handed Lisa his card.

As he backed his car out of the drive and roared through the dark countryside, Clive grinned. He should make the centre in about 40 minutes. He just hoped they hadn't sedated Mary before he arrived. He wasn't going to lift a dribbling, overweight old woman into his car.

Clive drove down the narrow streets, ignoring all the speed restrictions; he could eliminate the tickets when he got back to work. The Senior Holding Centre was a converted hotel near the old Olympics stadium. He knew the procedure inside out. Most of the elderly were shown their rooms and given a heavily sedated nightcap while their paperwork and identification chips were checked.

Coaches arrived daily to transport queues of senior citizens to the ships. The new business of euthanasia had revitalised the docklands, bringing jobs and a thriving work ethic to the area. He smiled at the irony. The country's wealth had been built on the back of the slave trade years earlier and the business of population control was providing a similar boom to the economy now.

He parked in a lock-up nearby and walked the remaining 200 yards to the hostel. He made his way around to the service area and was pleased to see his contact was already in place. Clive waited until he saw the official guard leave his position for a crafty cigarette and his contact waved him in.

"You don't turn up unannounced again. It's too risky."

"For you, maybe," Clive smirked and followed the Geordie through to the back area and into the storeroom. As he entered, Mary sat up on her bunk. "I might have known this had something to do with you," she snapped.

The old bitch had guts. He would need all his charm to

calm her down. "Lisa called and asked me to help. You must have been terrified." He watched Mary sink back on the bed confused. "Give us a few minutes," he snapped at the guard and waved him out of the room. He smiled at Mary and offered her a top up of fresh water.

"No, thanks."

Clive replaced the drink on the bedside table with precision. He wanted to slap her, but forced himself to calm down. "You may not like me, Mary, but as I see it you have two options. Join the happy coach of travellers tomorrow on your one-way cruise to nowhere or call Kate and ask her to accept my help. Your choice." He enjoyed watching Mary squirm.

"I don't want you anywhere near my family after the way you treated Kate. Get out." She crossed her arms and gave him a defiant stare.

She would pay for that later.

"Kate got the wrong idea when I saw her. I've only ever tried to help. Why else would I be here?" He moved back, giving her the space she needed and relaxed into the chair opposite. It was important to get her on side.

Mary looked confused and hesitant. "I'm not worried about dying. It's Kate I care about and if you so much as touch a hair on her head, I'll gut you like one of my pigs."

Clive laughed out loud. Now he had heard everything. He would enjoy beating the crap out of her but for now she was his ticket back into the Appleby family. He smiled kindly. "It's your decision, Mary, but your family needs you and we both know I'm the only one that can get you back home." He stood and walked slowly towards the door, waiting for the only response she could give him.

"So, you'd take me back, no tricks?"

"We'd have to leave immediately, before the authorities log you in. After that, I can't help you."

The door rattled open and the guard's face appeared

around the edge. "Out now, or forget it. Time's up."

Clive looked at Mary and waited.

She stood. "Ok, but only if Kate agrees."

Clive nodded. Oh, he would make sure she did.

In less than a minute, they were standing by his car. He rang Kate's mobile number and offered the phone to Mary. She paused for a second. "I'm ok, Kate. Clive got them to release me." She listened. "Yes, that's right. I'm with him now." Mary hesitated again and looked at Clive standing over her. "He's promised to get me back home, but love, you have to ask him."

Clive snatched the phone back and sat waiting for Kate's reply.

"I don't understand what's happened, Clive, but I want her home, now."

"If you're asking me for help, a bit of gratitude would be nice." She had to know where she stood.

Clive could hear the reluctance in her voice as she murmured a reply.

"Please."

"She'll be back within the hour." He cut the call before she could say any more.

He opened the car door and ushered Mary inside. He seethed with impatience at the time she took squeezing herself down into the low seat. He slammed the door and walked around to drop into the driver's seat beside her.

He glanced at Mary as he reversed the car out of the lock up. The old woman looked deflated, showing none of her earlier bravado.

"Thank you, Clive."

The drive back to the farm was the quietest but most satisfying journey Clive had made in some time. Women were no trouble; you just had to know how to handle them.

CHAPTER 38

Kate waited at the front door, desperate to see headlights on the perimeter road. She was home from the hospital not long after she received Clive's call. Mary should be back by now. She was grateful Clive had managed to talk the Enforcers into releasing her but what had gone wrong? Grant was positive he had changed their Quota status. Had his hasty dismissal from the Ministry caused a problem?

"Mum, come in, she'll be back soon. Clive won't let us down."

She looked at Lisa's confident smile and worried how little her daughter knew this man. He had obviously charmed her into believing his heroic actions. She knew better. Clive's motives were always selfish. He only ever pleased himself. She had learnt that here in her own home. She pushed the thought of that awful afternoon to the back of her mind and allowed her daughter to lead her back into the kitchen.

"They'll be hungry, so I've made a bit of tea. Not up to Gran's standard though."

Kate knew Lisa was trying to cheer her up but she wasn't in the mood. "It's my fault, I should have been here. If only I hadn't turned my mobile off by the river, I could have got here in time to stop them."

"Really, Mum, they wouldn't have listened. Clive was marvellous and he must have put himself in danger to get her back. I haven't a clue what we would've done without him."

Kate winced at the thought of being reliant on Clive's help for anything. He was far too manipulative. Lisa had contacted Clive quickly. Lisa had obviously been seeing him, as she feared. She watched her daughter moving around the kitchen, laying out the food and drink. Her clothing was loose but at four months, her pregnancy would be obvious soon. She felt sure Lisa had not told Clive. Her face lit up every time she mentioned his name but how would he react if he knew about the baby?

The roar of a powerful engine announced their arrival. Lisa rushed towards the window. "Oh Mum, it's Clive and Gran."

Before Kate could move, Lisa's was out of the kitchen and down the corridor. Kate pulled back the curtain and watched her daughter run towards the car as Mary emerged. Lisa's high-pitched screams of delight filtered back to Kate, waiting nervously in the kitchen.

A torrent of questions followed Mary through the door. She looked dazed, ignoring Lisa's excited babble. Mary stood and looked around her kitchen. "Nice to be home," she murmured.

Kate swallowed. This woman had been her rock and it was hard to see her so broken. She looked at Mary and found she could not speak but rushed to hug her.

Lisa helped her Gran into a chair and began serving the food, chatting excitedly. Mary gave a tentative smile of thanks as Kate noticed Clive framed in the doorway. His intense eyes moved down her body. The shock turned her feelings of relief to anger. He looked smug. She fought an urge to slap him.

Lisa pulled out a seat and smiled up at him. "As the hero of the hour, you get the largest piece of cake. Come on, Mum, you haven't eaten since you got home."

Clive put his arm around Lisa and drew her nearer. "Wow, a beauty and a cook, what a lucky man I am."

Clenching her fists, Kate found her voice at last. "How are you, Mary?" She resisted the desire to pull Clive's disgusting hands off her misguided daughter. Instead she snatched at a chair and sat opposite Mary.

"It must have been terrifying." She turned her attention away from Clive and concentrated on her mother-in-law. Mary looked dazed. She had taken a nibble from the sandwiches she'd been given and was now pushing a piece of scone around the plate.

Mary's voice was uncharacteristically quiet as she started to speak. "I felt so helpless." Her voice faltered and Kate guided a glass of juice into her hands. She sipped it before continuing. "Being locked in was awful. It was like being in prison. Who do they think we are?" Kate could hear a bit of spirit return. "Sort them, tag them and ship them out. That's what they do. Our cattle get treated better."

"Oh, Clive, I'm so glad you got her out." Lisa's admiration was obvious.

Kate ignored Clive's wide grin. "Go on, Mary."

She took another sip from the glass and her voice became stronger. "When old Bernie up on Hill Farm got taken, his wife was almost relieved. He'd been suffering from dementia for years and she was exhausted looking after him. The medical credits ran out so his drugs had been cut some years ago. The entire family had suffered. I thought, when my time came, I'd choose the exit programme, but now I'm not so sure."

"Oh, Gran, it sounds horrible." Lisa turned to Clive, "But how did you manage to convince them to let her go?"

Kate was interested in his reply. She was positive it wasn't his newly discovered charm that had swung it.

Clive looked relaxed, enjoying the limelight as all three women waited for him to speak. "Easy, when you know the right people. It's about contacts in the end and I have plenty of them. There's not much goes on that I haven't a hand in." His smooth smile did not fool Kate. She knew his appetite for control and wasn't surprised.

"But, these guys follow the Quota instructions to the letter. How did you manage to persuade them to listen?" Kate could see that hit home and his smile cooled somewhat.

"You know me, I normally get what I want in the end."

Lisa leant across and took his hand. "He'd do anything for me." Her sweet upturned face was looking for confirmation and she could see Clive was not about to disappoint her.

"Of course. Your mum knows how far I'm willing to go for someone I care about." His dark eyes threw the thinly disguised threat at Kate and the charming smile, that dazzled Lisa, didn't fool her. Was she the only person in the room who could see this man for what he was?

"Yes, they seemed to listen to him alright. He got me out in a jiffy." Mary leant closer to Kate, "I was a bit worried when he first came in, but he bought me straight home."

He even had Mary fooled. How could she think this man had changed so dramatically from the animal that she had described just a few weeks ago? Had Mary forgotten?

Clive raised his voice and his eyes grew darker. "Some people just like to play games. I never promise anything I can't deliver. You can rely on that."

Kate had no doubt.

"Well, he certainly did better than Grant, Mum. I'm sure he just used you to help Toby." Lisa's forceful damnation got a nod from the others.

"That's just not true." Kate exploded. The whole evening was turning into a scene from a pantomime, with Grant the villain and Clive the hero.

Clive shrugged his shoulders, humbly accepting their verdict.

She pushed her chair away so hard it toppled over. "Well,

Mary, you look done in. I really think we should get you upstairs and in bed."

Mary thanked Clive again. As Kate walked around the table towards her mother-in-law, Lisa was giggling and hanging on Clive's every word. Kate could not stand it a moment longer, so she pushed in between them to pick up the crockery. "I should think you'd want to be getting off, Clive, important man like you must have lots to do?"

"Mum, don't be so rude. I've offered him a bed for the night. It's the least we can do."

Kate froze. The thought of Clive in her house overnight was too much to deal with. Before she had a chance to respond, he was kissing Lisa on the cheek and making his excuses.

"Your mum's quite right. You'll all need some sleep. I have to go, make sure the orders I gave at the centre are backed up on your Quota status. I have no intention of letting you down like Grant Spencer. Now he has his son sorted he won't care about you. Some people just look after number one."

He stood in front of Kate waiting. She knew she should thank him. She turned to the sink. "Well, I'd better get this done, I'm sure Lisa will see you out."

"Mum, you haven't even thanked Clive, yet." Lisa's tone was indignant.

"That would be nice, Kate. You know how much it means to hear a good word or two from you, after all these years."

She looked at his dark reflection in the kitchen window, mocking her and plunged her hands in the sink, scrubbing the oven tray. She did not trust him but owed him Mary's life. She dried her hands and forced herself round to face him. "Thank you, Clive. Mary means a lot to us all, I'm glad she's back safe."

"Oh, I think you can do better than that, don't you?" He winked at Lisa and held his arms out to Kate. Lisa did not look amused.

Kate walked towards him with heavy steps. As his

muscular arms surrounded her she felt her entire body recoil but she willed herself not to resist. This was for Mary. She felt his hips push into hers and realised he was getting aroused. She wrenched herself away.

"I'll just go and check on Mary." She left the kitchen and ran to the bathroom. She felt sick and filled her cupped hands with water from the tap and rinsed her face. As she looked through the window she watched her daughter follow Clive to the car and kiss him passionately. Kate felt her stomach contract. Was this the payback he was looking for? Not Lisa, please not her.

She would kill him first.

CHAPTER 39

Sir Charles sighed as he read the text.

Toby is our son!

The message was terse but Sir Charles was well aware of the subtext. The woman expected him to come running. That wasn't going to happen. He probably wouldn't even contact her. But he couldn't get the thought out of his mind. He was a father.

Carolyn had always known he felt cheated not having children, but he wasn't desperate to claim parental rights for a dying boy. If she'd told him before she married Spencer he may have acted differently. She had been a distraction when his wife's dementia was diagnosed, though not his only comforter. If he had fathered other bastards, he hoped they would be healthier than Carolyn's boy.

He poured himself a whisky, walked across to the library window and looked out down the drive. Spencer was due anytime. He had shown enormous affection for the boy and wouldn't give him up easily. Sir Charles would leave the child with his surrogate father, for the time being. Any scandal might affect his political ambitions and it was the best option if he wanted to get Spencer back on board. He had to convince him that he didn't care about the boy, that it was history. Spencer mustn't find out that he had still been seeing Carolyn for the occasional entertainment. He suspected she might use that to blackmail him. She was a ruthless bitch, part of her appeal in a strange way. He supposed he would have to talk to her after all.

There was a knock on the library door. "Mr Spencer's here to see you, Sir Charles," the housekeeper announced.

"Let him in."

He must focus on Spencer, reassure him about the boy and then encourage him to come back to work. To build the case for a change of government, he needed a top researcher to find the political dirt that could be leaked and cause unrest.

The door opened and Spencer came in, his face set in a tight frown.

"Thanks for coming. I know this is difficult." He decided not to offer his hand but indicated the Chesterfield chair by the fireplace. "Let's sit down and talk things through."

"Yes, I want a few things sorted." Spencer sounded more tense and angry than he'd expected.

"What will you have to drink? I can recommend this single malt." He tapped the crystal decanter on top of the cocktail cabinet. Spencer didn't respond.

Sir Charles poured generous measures for them both, brought over the drinks and sat in the armchair opposite his guest.

"I am sorry about how I reacted last week. Your discovery was as much a shock to me as it was to you. So let me make it absolutely clear. I didn't know I'd got your wife pregnant. I admit we had a brief affair, but that was before she met you." He could see Spencer was ignoring the whisky, obviously not prepared to relax.

"So now you know, what do you intend to do?" He recognised the challenge in Spencer's eyes as he held his gaze.

"Nothing," Sir Charles said, leaning back in his chair.

"You're the boy's father, always have been, always will. I am sure Carolyn thinks the same." He wanted to hear what she might have said.

"Yes, in her own way," Spencer said. "She's decided to sever all ties with myself and Toby." He paused. "Apparently we've been holding back her career."

"Oh, that's a shame. A child needs his mother." He suspected Carolyn was playing a devious game, abandoning the boy to Spencer, yet promoting him secretly as their son. "How is the boy? Is he still having treatment for his kidney problem?"

"He's about to have an artificial kidney, though you might want to consider giving him one of yours," Spencer said.

Normally Sir Charles would have slapped down this jibe but he wanted the man onside, so he ignored it. "Look, Spencer, the boy is yours. I've signed papers confirming I have no claim on him." He handed the document to Spencer who took it without comment. "I wish him well with the transplant but let's move on and put last week behind us. I want you back at work."

If Spencer understood what he was planning, he should need little convincing to return.

"I'm not sure I can. I don't think I can work on the Quota system."

Sir Charles decided to reveal a little of his intentions. "Look, I know I pushed you into a corner with the 70s Cull Project, but it was for a reason."

"What do you mean?"

"It wasn't my plan. I wanted you to expose the inhumanity of it. And you did that. Now I want to leak the report so we can get things changed."

He had confused Spencer. "I don't understand."

"Over the last year, you've convinced me Quota needs a review. I didn't tell you because I wanted you to keep challenging me. I have to give an update on the policy to the

House next week. I want to press for changes. Will you help me do that?" He watched the tension drain from Spencer, to be replaced by the look of someone who had discovered a friend in need. The deal was done; he would be back in the office shortly.

"I want you to keep this secret."

"I wish I could believe you are serious." Spencer said.

"Trust me and watch what happens over the next few weeks," Sir Charles said and walked over to the bar to pour himself another drink. "You haven't drunk any of your whisky. Don't you like it?"

Before Spencer could reply, the door burst open and he watched opened mouthed as Sir Charles's wife ran into the room.

"Someone has broken in," she screamed. "Look, he's sitting in my chair."

Sir Charles grabbed her as she lunged at Spencer. She was dressed in a strange concoction: a pair of grubby pyjama bottoms topped off with an elaborate cocktail dress complete with a dozen bracelets jangling angrily on each arm.

"This is a friend, darling. Let me take you back to your room." He gripped both arms and almost dragged her towards the door, leaving the astonished Spencer looking on.

"I'll be back soon."

Sir Charles tried to stay calm on his return to the library but felt abject horror at his wife's intrusion. He was angry with her latest carers. They seemed unable to control her. He had kept her comfortable but behind locked doors for years but now Spencer had seen her, the man whose wife he had used when his own was struck with dementia.

"I am sorry about that," he said. "As you can see my wife has a drink problem. Unfortunately she's refusing help. I would appreciate your discretion."

Spencer nodded. "I guess I'd better be on my way. I hope I don't frighten Lady Winchester on my way out."

"She'll be ok now she's back in her room. Anyway, I'm glad we managed to clear the air," Sir Charles said, though he noticed Spencer still looked uneasy despite his reassurances. "I look forward to seeing you back at your desk this week. We have a job to do."

As soon as he was alone, Sir Charles went to his study and sent a short encrypted message to a key member of his team.

Get your protest groups primed.

Then he sat back and contemplated the awful thought that it was time to send his wife away forever.

Grant drove back to London, trying to make sense of the last hour. The meeting with Sir Charles had been surprising in so many ways. He didn't know what to believe. Yes, he had his job back, but had Sir Charles really renounced all claims to Toby? Would the document he'd given him be considered legal? How would Sir Charles react if he saw Toby in the future, a healthy boy, with similar features? Grant shuddered. How would he feel himself?

Despite the apparent resolution of his personal issues, Grant was still concerned. Should he believe Sir Charles's claim that he wanted to end Quota? That could change everything. He and Adam could pursue their protest activities, knowing there was powerful support inside the government. He had almost told Sir Charles about James's report, but knew he needed further evidence of commitment before he revealed anything to him.

His thoughts turned to Lady Winchester. Grant hadn't seen her for five years. She had aged significantly, her long straight blonde hair now a tangled mess of dirty yellow. He'd been shocked by the wildness in her eyes. She seemed more deranged than drunk. Grant remembered her excess medical treatment flagged in his Cull Report. She probably had dementia and the issue of contaminated beef might be of interest to Sir Charles. He increased the volume of his car radio forcing himself to stop speculating and concentrate on the present. He'd drive home now and tell Carolyn to leave, that was if she was still there.

It was just after 6pm when he arrived back at his flat. He opened the door with trepidation, hoping she would be gone. The sound of the shower and wafts of her perfume dashed his hopes. He carried his overnight bag to the bedroom and came back into the kitchen and made himself a cup of tea. He sat drinking it in the lounge and waited for her to appear.

She looked startled when she saw him. "What are you doing here?" she snapped.

"I might ask you the same," Grant said quietly. "Have you thought where you're going to live?"

"What do you mean?"

"When Toby's better, I'm bringing him home. You made it clear you wanted nothing to do with us."

"He won't be home for a while, if at all, so there's no rush. I'll find somewhere in my own time. And I am sure it will be better than this place." Carolyn gave him a contemptuous smirk.

"You better find somewhere now. I don't want you here another night." Grant's demand didn't seem to ruffle her.

"I don't think that'll be a problem."

Grant laughed to himself. It was obvious the peer hadn't contacted her. She would have been specific if he'd offered her shelter.

"By the way, I'm working for Sir Charles again." He was pleased to see the shock reflected in her face. "I hope you aren't expecting to play Happy Families with him. I know for a fact that's the last thing on his mind." He had her attention now. She looked apprehensive.

"And how would you know that?"

"I've just come from Wendover. Sir Charles's signed away all claims to Toby." He pulled the paper from his pocket and waved it in her direction. "He never mentioned you. You're on your own now, Carolyn."

"We'll see about that," she said, standing abruptly and marching into the bedroom.

"That's right, go and pack," Grant shouted after her. "I'm off out for a drink. I want you gone when I get back."

CHAPTER 40

Kate hoped the shock did not show on her face. She knew her father was trying to find them a safe place to stay. But here, in a derelict part of the London docks, on board two wrecks?

"Those two narrow boats under the weeping willow are ours. You and Mary get the first one and Jack and Lisa can have the smaller one alongside."

She stared at the blackened hulls and boarded up windows of the two boats. "You are joking, Dad?"

"Don't panic. It looks far worse than it is. It'll keep people off if they think they're derelict. Now, watch yourself, hold on to me and I'll guide you aboard your boat."

Kate wished she had worn her trainers as she stepped over the trailing ropes and broken containers. She smiled at her father's clothes as he struggled with the ancient padlocks. He still favoured the baggy Indian trousers and cotton shirts of his youth but his long grey hair added a sense of mischief. He uttered a few swear words but then she heard the metal lock groan and he forced the door open.

Once inside Kate was amazed at the transformation. The granite worktops, new thermo-cooker and latest technology offered them better facilities than they had on the farm.

214

Mary would be thrilled. The eating area was a compact well-organised space. The two bedrooms were fine but she could see it would be far too cramped to house the children as well.

"The sister boat alongside has two smaller bedrooms and toilet facilities. They only have a kettle and a toaster. Perfect for teenagers."

That might go down well with Jack, she thought, but she was not keen on Lisa sleeping separately. Her father fished out an electronic key which activated a sliding panel, to reveal a hidden communications station.

"Wow."

"It might look a bit James Bond but we have a lot of field agents from Europe that use the boat. It's a safe stop over." She studied her father's face. It continued to amaze her that her father had been a key figure in the protest movement for many years.

"Fancy a cuppa?" he said reaching for a mug.

"Oh, Dad, no martini?" Kate giggled and sat down at the narrow table.

It took several mugs of tea to hear her father's plans. He explained he had contacts in the media and social networking providers and a web of active protest groups countrywide. They were all ready to support a revolt against Quota.

They had been involved in a few propaganda schemes and uprisings over the years but nothing that had caused the government enough damage. Now, he explained, with James's evidence and Grant's inside ministerial influence, they stood a real chance.

"I had no idea you were such a big cheese."

"It's been a struggle and to be honest your mother was the one that made a real difference. Unlicensed children in Europe were being hunted down using the Euro-Reich's guidelines, outlawing non-standard births. She established a network of safe shelters and helped hundreds of disabled children to safety."

Kate felt tears in her eyes. Her parents had taken huge risks for complete strangers. She had spent years wallowing in her own feelings of abandonment but they had given up their entire lives to give others a future.

Her father took her hand in his. "We missed you every second and it was a hard price to pay. Now you have children, I'm hoping you'll understand."

They held each other. She felt the years of questions dissolve leaving an unshakable pride. Her parents had been heroes and, like James, believed in a better future.

Her father pulled back and she saw the excitement in his eyes. "James's research gives us all a chance. He must have been a determined man; he didn't stumble across this dementia cover up. He dug and dug to get the information. I wish I'd been able to work with him, I wish I'd known him."

Kate realised how alike they were. How unselfish their lives had been. James worked for years, not for status or wealth but to provide enough food for the growing population. The government had offered him help but then covered up the dementia consequences, pushing him to increase production at any cost. At the same time, her father had been battling Quota overseas.

"I do want to break the system, Dad. I was frightened at Jack's anger but I can see why."

"We need to destroy the Quota computer but with Grant's contacts we'll avoid casualties. His input is essential. Bringing down the data systems will galvanise people but political will is paramount if we're going to change anything for families. The country needs a powerful figurehead to lead a new government or there will be anarchy and chaos."

Kate put her cup down. She still had her doubts about involving politicians. "I know Grant's been a good friend but we need to make sure the people he trusts are behind us for the right reasons. I've seen enough of government officials to worry."

Clive's face flashed through her mind but she pushed the image away. "I knew this man at university, who works for the Ministry. Clive's the one that got Mary released from the Quota enforcers. I trusted him to help me but he's a nasty bit of work and Lisa has got involved with him. I don't want her anywhere near him."

"Is he the father?"

"God no, the father's a married farmer who doesn't want to know. Since Lisa's met Clive, he's put on a sophisticated front to impress her. She's vulnerable. I should have acted earlier to protect her."

"The more you try and put her off, the more she'll be drawn to him."

"You're right and now she thinks she's in love with him. But she has no idea what he's like. It's why I need a safe place like this."

"I'll protect the family, especially Lisa, in her condition."

"How did you know she was pregnant?"

"Lisa has been asking your mother questions. She's helped enough youngsters with unlicensed births and knows how frightening it is."

Kate felt a stab of jealousy that Lisa hadn't come to her. But then again, why would she when Clive had done his best to alienate her.

"I'm worried what Clive might do. He's almost the same age as her own father and she's besotted. I'm sure he's using her as payback for getting Mary out." She was afraid her father might be tempted to use Clive's valuable access into Quota.

"He sounds like a nasty piece of work. I'll keep my eye on any involvement he has in our plans. We need people on the inside but I've seen power corrupt men and put people at risk."

Kate looked at her father. His brain was always working on the next move and she hoped his fight against Quota wouldn't jeopardise her family. She needed to trust him.

"Lisa's a feisty young woman and if she's fallen for him,

we'll have a fight on our hands."

"He's bad news, Dad, really."

"Lisa will be sharing the boat with Jack. He adores her and I'll make sure he keeps an eye out too. Now all you have to do is convince them to come."

She would give them no choice.

The next day Kate braced herself for a difficult conversation. Jack was in the farm lab and she could hear Lisa singing in the bathroom. She knocked on the door. "Lisa, I need to talk."

"I'll be out in a minute, Mum. Give us a break. When do I get the opportunity for a good soak?"

"If you let me in, I'll give you some of my body soak." Within seconds she heard her daughter padding towards the door.

"Done." She was wrapped in a towel that didn't quite make it to the sides. Time was passing and Lisa was beginning to expand. As if she could read her thoughts, Lisa pulled the towel around herself.

Kate found the bubble bath James had bought for her last Christmas and poured it into the bath. It smelt of almonds and was a huge luxury. Lisa breathed in the sweet aroma and plunged into the suds, covering her blossoming stomach with bubbles.

"How are you feeling?"

"Great, I haven't been sick for ages and feel fabulous again." She ran her hands over her stomach. "Well, I know I'm looking a bit chubbier but Clive loves it." She pushed the foam around her enlarged bosoms and smiled.

Kate winced. "Well, I wonder if he'll be as enthusiastic about your baby when it arrives. I'm assuming you've told him?"

Lisa ignored the question and turned the taps on full blast.

Kate sighed, "No, I didn't think you had."

"It's none of your business and he'll make a great dad. He's so protective and with his job we'll have no problem getting the medical credits."

Kate could hardly believe what she was hearing. "You're joking? A cosy family is the last thing Clive will want."

"And what would you know? He's told me all about your pathetic attempt to get off with him at college. Well, that was centuries ago. You had your chance. It's mine now."

Kate watched the steely determination in her daughter's face. From a small child she had fought for what she had wanted and most times James had given in. Not this time though.

"You have no idea what he's like. He almost raped me the last time he was here and the only thing he's interested in is power."

Lisa's eyelids lowered and she sank back into the foam. "Yes, he said you came on to him when he visited the farm." She sounded almost bored. Then she opened her eyes and Kate was horrified to hear the pity in her voice as she said, "But he's clearly not interested. He loves me. I'm sorry, Mum, but face it, it's me he wants."

Kate stood exasperated. "Well, it's irrelevant. We're moving. Your grandad's found a safe place for the whole family so we're leaving tomorrow. No argument. Just pack the essentials, it's kind of small."

Before Lisa had time to object she marched out and slammed the door. God, she needed to get the whole family out.

Jack was standing at the end of the corridor laughing. "I told her it wasn't a good idea; I know how you feel about your precious bath."

Kate was reminded how much he looked like his dad, that casual way of standing. "Jack, you need to pack. We're leaving, tomorrow."

He looked amused rather than shocked. "Well, I assume

she'll get out eventually, there's really no need to leave!" He turned to walk away but Kate caught his arm.

"No Jack. I'm not joking. We've found a safe haven, a barge in Canary Wharf. When these protests kick off, I want you both out of the way."

Jack's smile evaporated. "Not a chance. I'm not hiding. Those bastards will pay for what they did."

She could see the veins lift in his neck and the colour flood his face. He was angry and quite rightly so. "But Jack, I've lost your dad. I don't want anyone else in the family hurt. Please, I couldn't bear it."

His arms reached out and he held her close. Stroking her hair, he said, "Don't worry, Mum. Don't forget, I know they'll be after me. Dad didn't."

She smelt her son. He was almost a man and had his own battles. She couldn't deny him his role in avenging his father but she would protect him as much as she could.

"Grandad has a narrow boat. It's got all the communications facilities you need. He's used it before for activists. It makes sense for us to go there. The farm is the first place they'll come looking for us when trouble starts. It's not hiding. It's all part of his plan."

Jack considered for a few seconds and grinned. "Sounds like the old dog has brains as well as balls. Great! It's about time this family got real. I'd better start going through my files, there's a lot in there I wouldn't want them to get their hands on. Download time, I think." He hurried down the corridor towards the lab.

She reached the kitchen just as Mary was making some tea.

"So, how did the meeting with your dad go?"

"He's found us a couple of canal boats on the Thames. I've told the kids we need to be ready to leave tomorrow. We only need the essentials. No kitchen sink, it already has one of those!"

220

"Better start packing. I'll get some pies from the freezer."

Kate laughed and was delighted to see Mary bustle about the kitchen like her old self. She'd be happier knowing the whole family was in a safe place, although it would be a wrench for the old woman to leave this house after so many years.

"You ok about leaving here?" she held Mary's hand and was glad to see her determined smile.

"I took this old place on when it was failing. We started from nothing and we can do it again."

Kate watched Mary delve into the cupboards. Her mother-in-law was made of stern stuff. She was beginning to realise it ran in the family. She heard the bathroom door bang noisily upstairs and Lisa stomp across the landing. She feared her daughter's stubborn streak would be the biggest threat of all.

CHAPTER 41

"This is crap. We need action, not slogans. Just kill the bastards," Jack's voice broke as his anger overwhelmed him. He looked away to hide his tears. His outburst had shocked the audience into a tense silence.

His grandad came to him and whispered words of caution. "We feel your pain, Jack, but fury won't help. You'll just get yourself killed. Let me deal with this."

Jack felt the anger burn the tears from his cheek as his grandad moved to the microphone.

"Everyone here has been hurt by this government: every day our loved ones are taken; our sick children die; our jobs disappear. We have the power to make them pay and we will, but only if we work together."

The audience murmured agreement but Jack grabbed the microphone from his grandfather, his voice thin and shrill. "These men have never listened. Why should they now?" His strength returned and he grew calmer. "We have to hit them, quick and hard."

He thought he heard support from the younger members but he could see his grandfather wasn't pleased.

"We'll take action at the right time, Jack. Action needs to

be decisive and co-ordinated if it's to work."

He was dismayed when the chairman added support for his grandfather. "Adam's told us that Sir Charles will speak out against Quota next week. We must give that a chance to work. It's the first time a minister has ever questioned Quota."

"That bastard ordered my father's murder."

"So we'll let him talk then we'll have him," someone called from the back of the hall. There was choked laughter from a couple of lads.

"Stop!" the chairman interjected. "We understand your anger, Jack, but we need to make the most of the chance your dad's given us. Please let us do that."

Jack felt belittled. He wanted to hit out but how? There were tears in his eyes again. He tried to push away a comforting arm but the clasp was firm and strong. "I'll help you. Leave them to their debating," the whisper came from behind.

Jack turned to see Clive, smiling with a finger to his lips. His anger lessened. He hadn't seen him at the start of the meeting but he recognised a powerful ally.

"See me after," Clive said, before retreating to the back of the hall.

Shouting had continued while Jack was distracted.

"Give the lad his due."

"It's time they listened."

The chairman banged his fist on the table. "Ok, ok, that's enough. I won't have mob rule. We'll follow Adam's plan for the next month and your support and patience is expected. We'll review if we need to change course. Meeting closed."

"That could have been disastrous, Jack," his grandad said, catching up with him as he was leaving the building. "I know you think I'm an old fart, but trust me, I know what I'm talking about."

Jack nodded but avoided his grandad's gaze. He regretted embarrassing him but not for his call for action.

"I'm sorry," he said, to keep the peace, "but I won't give up."

His grandad smiled, "Keep that passion, Jack, but don't let it get out of hand. I need to discuss details with the others. Why not join us?"

"I don't think I'd be welcome. Anyway I have some friends to meet. I'll see you later."

"Ok," his grandad said, tapping him on the shoulder before turning and walking back towards the hall.

Jack felt deflated. He wanted action and he wanted it now.

Clive waited in the shadows and watched Jack finish his conversation with Adam on the steps. He saw him pull away from his grandfather's embrace. The boy was looking for more than comfort.

He sneered at the disappointment on the old man's face as he turned and went back inside. He had checked Adam's history: a few peaceful protests with a chain of European resistance groups looked impressive, but he lacked bottle. But he might become a nuisance, if left to stir things up on a national level. He would need to be neutralised. But Jack's earlier outburst showed true anger. Something that Clive could exploit.

As he walked towards the entrance, he could hear laughter from people inside, most had come for the entertainment value, not protest. They were unemployed and bored. Just a few, like Jack, had potential.

Clive's phone flashed. It was Lisa. He cancelled the call. The little tart could wait. He watched Jack walk towards his scooter, shoved the phone back in his pocket and hurried over to him. "I liked your speech, Jack. It had passion. Are you brave enough to follow through?"

"Of course, whatever it takes."

"If you want action, you'll be taking big risks but you

want to destroy Quota, don't you?"

"My dad paid with his life. I've seen enough of his work to know what a threat he was to them. I want to blow Quota to shreds."

Clive knew Jack's knowledge would be useful. This was what he wanted to hear. "Jack, I knew your dad at college. He'd be proud of what you did tonight. We should pool our resources. You tell me what you know and I'll make sure you're right at the centre of the action, while that lot waste time talking." He gestured towards the hall.

Jack looked pleased. "You're on. Just make sure I'm in the front line."

Clive grinned. "Then that's just where you'll be." He clapped the boy on the back and gave him a card. "Call me tomorrow. We've got a lot to discuss."

Jack's face lit up, "Great," he said.

"Just one thing, don't tell your grandad about our arrangement. He means well, but he's past it. He doesn't have the stomach for direct action and we both know it's too bloody late for banners and rallies."

"I don't think he's useless. The government thought him enough of a threat to chase him across Europe."

"Yeah, but what did he ever achieve? "

Jack shrugged and stuffed the card in his back pocket and started his scooter.

"Call me," Clive said, as the boy rode off. He turned his collar up against the chill wind and strode off towards the car park. As he reached his car he remembered the missed call. He settled himself inside and checked his phone. Lisa had left a voicemail. It was probably just another pathetic call, but he put it on speaker and started to drive.

"Clive, please, please pick up."

He reached across to cut the message but his hand hovered as he listened. "Mum's taking everyone to a safe place. God knows where. I want to be with you, darling. Save me from being holed up in some boring place in the middle of nowhere."

Where the hell were they going?

"I'm sure you'd agree it makes more sense for us to be together. I can pack a bag in minutes. Have to go but ring me, soon as you can. Love you."

The high-pitched tone ended the message and a frown gathered on his brow. So, Kate thought she could protect her family, keep Lisa safe. What an idiot she was. She had played right into his hands. He might have to change his plans but this was better than he had imagined.

He pictured Lisa in the hidden room he had prepared weeks ago and the images excited him. He had to control himself. He gripped the wheel and dictated her a text. "You are right, darling. Pack a bag and meet me in The Boot at Sarratt as soon as you can. I can't tell you how I've longed for this moment. You've no idea. Love Clive"

He laughed as the words streamed across the monitor.

Clive found a table away from the main bar. This pub was one of the rare survivors from the past; an indulgence owned by a millionaire web analyst who had grown up in the village, a nostalgic hobby that must have cost a fortune. Each to their own passions, he thought.

Lisa appeared at his table, grinning like a child. She looked so pleased to see him. He smiled back and offered her the large glass of wine he had ready.

"Can I just have a juice, please?"

He pressed the glass into her hands. "We have so much to celebrate. Don't spoil it. These are exciting times for both of us."

She looked flustered but took a reluctant sip.

"I was careful. No one saw me leave. Mum and Mary were packing and I think Jack's off at one of his meetings, so I'm all yours."

Yes, you really are, he thought.

"Well, drink up, I've ordered dinner and then I will whisk you off to my bachelor pad and have my wicked way." He ran his finger across her soft lips and was rewarded by a conspiratorial kiss.

"You devil."

Yes, he thought, I couldn't have put it better myself.

Two glasses of wine later, a giggly Lisa caught up with him in the car park. "I can't see why you insist on all this cloak and dagger stuff. Mum will just have to get used to us being a couple when we're living together."

"I don't want to risk upsetting her. You know how she feels about me. Just give her time, eh?" He helped her into the car and kissed her cheek.

The booze and the drugs he had slipped into her glass meant Lisa was asleep before he reached the A41 towards London. When she woke up it wouldn't be in the luxurious penthouse apartment he had described. The cold basement room would be a reality check for the dozy cow, a nightmare, not the dream she expected. The little bitch might provide entertainment but she would also bring him the prize he had longed for. Mother and daughter, he liked it.

CHAPTER 42

Kate jumped as she heard the front door slam shut. Those kids had better have a good reason for getting home this late. She had made it clear this morning how important this move was. She hurried towards the door and saw Jack drop his keys in the hall and swear under his breath.

"Where's Lisa? I thought she was with you?"

"No, why?" He looked puzzled as he walked into the kitchen and swung the fridge door open.

"Because she left without a word and she's not picking up." Kate checked the time again and her voice rose. "It's nearly one. Where the hell can she be?"

"I thought I had another beer in here?"

"For Christ's sake, Jack, would you get your face out of the fridge and bloody listen for a change." Kate slumped into the chair. She felt drained and Jack wasn't helping.

"Mum, she's not five any more. She's probably out with her mates. After all, if you're determined to bury us away in some old boat, she'd have a few goodbyes to say, I'd imagine."

Kate looked at the impatience in her son's face. He thought she was over reacting. Lisa had slipped out without a word to either her or Mary. She was up to something.

"I'll do a search. I've just downloaded some face recognition software. Illegal but I can't wait to find out if it works."

"Jack, the government banned that stuff."

"They'll have a lot more to worry about when we get going." His tone grew serious. "It's ok, Mum. She's probably missed the last train and stayed over at her mate's. Chill. She'll be fine." His young face shone with confidence she just couldn't share.

"Find her, Jack."

"If this programme is as good as the government feared, I'll find her no probs." He opened the fridge drawer and cheered. "Great, I knew there was one in here." He snapped the ring pull and slurped a mouthful, wiping the foam from his lip. "I've got a bit of work to do so I'll text you. What time we supposed to be leaving tomorrow?"

"I want to be packed and out of here by early evening. Your grandfather's going straight to the boat to get it ready but he'll be back to load the van. He's gone to a lot of trouble to find this place. I want to make sure we're all ready, including your sister."

"Ok, ok, but it's late and Lisa will be snoring her head off. Don't expect we'll hear till the morning now, Mum."

"I'll just wait for a bit. She might get a cab."

"Don't wait up too long, eh."

He kissed her and went off to the lab with a wave of his beer. He would probably be working for another couple of hours yet. More like his dad every day.

Kate poured herself another cup of coffee she did not want and stared into the darkness. The occasional hope of lights on the distant road made her squint past her own reflection but the headlights just flickered and died as they disappeared over the hill.

Was she panicking? She knew why, of course. Clive. He was the biggest threat as far as Lisa was concerned. Thinking about him made her shudder. Thank god he had no idea about the pregnancy. She wasn't sure how he would react.

Half two. Her stomach was churning with worry while her head was agreeing with Jack. She knew Lisa did not want to go. It would be normal to want a last night out first, wouldn't it? Once in hiding they'd be cut off from normal life. Whatever that was? But why hadn't she said something? If she had planned to meet Clive, she would have kept that quiet. Is that where she was? God, she'd send herself mad.

Her mobile alarm went and she switched to video. Jack's face illuminated the screen. "Hi, Mum. No luck so far but I'll try again in the morning, I might not have the settings right yet. This software is complicated and I need to target the street cameras and the passwords are proving difficult to crack but I won't let it beat me."

"Thanks for trying."

"You go to bed, Mum, I'll be up for a while. Try not to worry." He grinned and switched off.

Kate dragged her feet upstairs and into the bathroom. She decided a last soak was in order. She would give her father a call first thing. Please God that wouldn't be necessary and Lisa would turn up indignant and bad tempered over all the fuss. As she sank into the soapy water, she imagined her strong-willed daughter's stroppy face and welcomed every imagined grunt of disapproval.

Kate woke with a start. What time was it? She grabbed her phone. It was six am. She checked. No messages from Lisa or Jack. She dialled her father's number.

"You're up early."

"Lisa's missing."

"What do you mean?"

"She didn't come home. No messages nothing. Dad, where is she?"

"Try not to panic. Does Jack know?"

"He's trying some search software but I've not heard anything yet. Something's happened to her. I'm sure."

"Kate, we've made no moves yet. She's not in danger. I'll finish up here and come down. Try not to worry."

Kate put the phone into her dressing gown pocket and went to look for Mary. She found her in the barn packing a few last things.

"Nearly done here, although I think there's far too much for a narrow boat." She looked at Kate. "I hope that dick of a farmer next door realises he's getting off lightly, feeding our animals while we're gone." She put the last lid on the box. "Think he'll just be glad to see the back of Lisa and the baby so he isn't going to take a chance with our livestock."

"Lisa didn't come home last night."

"Oh God, I didn't mean..." Mary took Kate's hand and covered it with her rough ones. "Try not to worry about her, Kate. She's always been able to look after herself." She smiled. "Let's go back inside. She'll be home by the time I get breakfast on the table, never one to miss a meal, that girl."

Kate allowed herself to be led past the back of the barn into the house but she felt in a bit of a daze. Going through the movements, she was aware her life had been far from normal for some time now. She reached for the plates and her hands brushed the wine glasses they had been given as a wedding gift. James had the date engraved on them. So much had happened. Would she rather have known what life had in store?

She missed him so much. Her rock. He'd have put things right. Her life had been in a spin since he had died. Nothing felt right, nothing was right. She felt as if she was standing on floors that kept giving way, plunging her downwards into a darker place. No rules, no safety net. A place of shadowy people who whispered in a language she did not understand.

"Are you going to put those plates on the table or just

stare at them?" Mary stood poised with a hot pan of bacon spitting salty clouds into the air.

"Sorry," Kate placed the china onto the wooden table and watched while her mother-in-law tried to placate her with an enormous breakfast that she only nibbled at. It was too early to raise Jack so they cleaned up.

"Well, that packing has to be finished before Dad gets here." She looked at Mary. "Do you want to wait here while I finish it?"

"You can't get rid of me that easy." Mary grabbed her warm cardigan and followed Kate to the barn.

The activity helped keep Kate from exploding with worry. They had four crates filled and stacked when Jack appeared. "Shame, you seemed to have finished!"

"Suppose you've got all your stuff done, then," Mary said as she wiped her hands on her apron.

"Just a few bits of hardware, could pack it into a bag to be honest. So has my wayward sister turned up yet?"

Kate had just started to relax but Jack's question made her stomach flip. "No."

The silence that followed frightened her even more.

Her phone flashed and she dropped it in her haste to see the message. It hit the ground and disappeared into a dusty bundle of loose straw. She cried and fell to her knees pulling the dry stalks apart, clawing at the floor.

Jack bent and pulled her to her feet. "Mum, she's Ok, I'm sure she is." He knelt down and pulled the dry feed apart to reveal the mobile buzzing like an insect caught in a web.

He held the phone up and his broad grin sent a shiver of hope through Kate. She grabbed the phone off him and read the message herself. "Sorry, Mum, phone died. Speak later."

"See, told you she was fine. Dozy cow never charges properly."

Kate felt tears run down her face. How stupid. Was she losing her mind? She looked from Mary to Jack and could see the sympathy on their faces.

"So, did you leave any breakfast for me or not?" Jack laughed and poked her in the stomach. She pushed him away. Everything was going to be all right. They walked back towards the house just as a special delivery bike pulled up.

"Mrs Mary Appleby?" The rider asked, holding a letter out to them.

Mary nodded and stepped forward to confirm delivery. Kate knew it was a government directive. The distinctive 'Late-Life' logo was unmistakable. Was this yet another call up for Mary? Surely not? Clive had sorted it all.

Mary stood perfectly still and then shoved the envelope in her pocket. "Sure it's nothing to worry about. I'll read it later. Now, let's get some breakfast down you, young man." She marched Jack into the house but Kate was not fooled by her dismissive tone. This could be serious and she would need to see Grant quickly. She had never believed Clive's slick heroics. She knew him better.

Kate rang Lisa's number but it was unobtainable. She knew her mother-in-law was trying to protect her from extra worry. They would not be able to get out of another call up. God knows what Clive would want this time.

The knot in her stomach tightened as she tried Lisa's number once again. Get a grip, Lisa's fine. Now go get that letter. This was one worry she hadn't imagined. She followed them into the kitchen. The letter was poking out the pocket of Mary's cardigan. She waited until Mary's back was turned and slipped the grey woollen garment off the back of the chair and carried it upstairs.

She tore the envelope open, breaking the electronic tag. The government trace would activate and she knew she would have little time to counter it. Yes, it was as she thought. Clive had lied. The directive was immediate. Mary was asked to report to the holding station within 24 hours or they would come for her. No mention of her last experience. It was as if it had never happened.

They needed to get to the boat immediately and call Grant. He was their only hope.

CHAPTER 43

Grant opened the door to his office. If they had searched the room, they had been professional. Everything looked in place: the unsorted pile of papers, the family photo on his desk and the cushion on his chair. But something was missing, probably gone forever, the feeling of easy familiarity. This wasn't the place he had worked for years, where he had built a successful career, a place of pride. Just last week he had been motivated by his job and ambitions. Now he didn't care and whatever his achievements, they were devalued by his role in sustaining an oppressive regime.

As he approached his desk, the proximity sensor triggered a message alert on his tablet. Sir Charles! He should have guessed. The man was desperate for his help, despite their differences. Grant scanned the demand with growing fury. How could he have come back to work for this man? Well, he knew the answer, revenge, though the justification didn't lessen his anger. At Wendover, he had seen his return as an opportunity to help destroy Quota. And Sir Charles's plan had seemed a positive move in that direction until he had spoken to Adam.

Grant had outlined his meeting with the peer and Lady Winchester's condition and suggested it might be helpful to show Sir Charles the GM Food report. Adam's words kept echoing in his head.

"No need. I've read the full report. Sir Charles started the GM Food Programme and received regular updates from James."

The implication was sickening. The bastard may have ordered James's murder and anyone else who knew about the report would be in danger. Grant's thoughts turned to Kate. He must keep her safe. The strength of his feelings surprised him.

For the next two hours he concentrated on preparing Sir Charles's speech, the story of Quota in three acts: its justification, the ruthless culling of the sick and old, and proof the population had been sustainable for ten years. His thoughts were interrupted by a loud banging on his door. Before he could respond, Carolyn strode into the office, her face flushed.

"What have you said to Charles? He won't see me." She spoke loud enough to be heard down the corridor. Grant raised his hand to quieten her.

"Don't you dare do that to me!"

"He told me he wasn't interested in Toby and I'm not surprised he got rid of you. You'd be an unwelcome distraction."

Grant had never seen Carolyn look so angry but now a smile spread across her face. "I didn't get that impression last week. I had to throw him out of our bed."

Grant couldn't speak. Surely she was just lashing out?

"You don't believe me, do you?" Carolyn said, her voice fell to a whisper, "Well, you ask your cheating boss. He's been screwing me for the last five years and he loved it." She spat her final words at him. "I'll make sure I get what I'm owed."

"Confront the bastard, then. He's got one demented woman so one more won't make much difference."

Carolyn paused. "What do you mean?"

"You'll find out."

She turned and marched out of the office, her heels tapping a frenzied tattoo on the parquet flooring. Grant picked up the family picture from his desk and threw it after her. The noise of glass shattering against the closing door drowned out his words: "You bitch."

He was shaking but it was with relief, he realised. Carolyn's betrayal was cathartic. This marriage was over. He went across the office, picked up the broken frame and extracted the picture from it. After placing the photo on his desk he lined up a ruler alongside Carolyn's image and carefully tore her away from Toby. He ripped her into tiny pieces and threw them into the bin. Feeling cleansed, he returned to deal with the other vermin.

The preparation of Sir Charles's speech was almost complete. He had the arguments needed to condemn Quota but he wanted one more thing and after an hour's research he found it in an old news item, Sir Charles opening a GM food factory. The information had to be included carefully. Grant smiled. Sir Charles would unknowingly commit political suicide just when he thought he was winning power.

Grant relaxed at the office window and gazed down the river, his thoughts turning to Toby. A message from the hospital interrupted his quiet moment and was infinitely more unwelcome than Carolyn's intrusion. He felt guilty that just thinking about his son had somehow stimulated worrying news. There was a problem with Toby's transplant. The doctor suggested he should come to the hospital. He emailed the speech to his boss and left for Canary Wharf.

Sir Charles rarely met someone unknown to him in his office, least of all anyone who might be linked to an anti-government group. The late night call from someone calling himself Clive

Boland, though curt and unspecific, had been concerning.

"The protest groups can bring you down. You need to talk to me."

One of his trusted colleagues had told him that this individual was the government's double agent who had infiltrated the protest movement, a Quota operative but believable as a saboteur to the dissidents. The man might be useful but what was his angle in approaching Sir Charles directly? Was this a threat or a message of support? He couldn't take a chance. He needed the protest groups to support his plans, so he had agreed to a meeting.

At the back of his office was a secure room. Visitors entered it from another door; their meeting would be unseen. Sir Charles was sitting at the desk when Boland entered. He thought he recognised him from the admin section. There he'd been staring at his screen, not looking the type to be venturing beyond office technology. Now he sensed arrogance. Boland showed no deference. He strode towards the desk and moved the other chair to face Sir Charles closer than he found comfortable.

"I'm busy so make this brief," Sir Charles said.

"The protest group know you set up the GM Food Programme," Boland said, his stare unblinking.

Sir Charles fought to keep his expression bland as his pulse quickened. He hadn't expected this revelation. He thought all evidence of his input on that project had been destroyed. "What gives you that impression?"

"They have a report on the disastrous effect of contaminated GM food that names you." The reply was as quick and cold as the first.

Sir Charles shifted on his chair. There was no way this man could have known about the report unless another copy had been found. "Who's circulating this spurious information?"

"Spurious or not, I don't think you want it broadcast. Am I right?"

Sir Charles didn't reply immediately, looking hard at Boland. He wouldn't answer this challenge. What did this man want? Was this bluster or a threat? "Why are you telling me this?"

"You need me on your team. I am the only one who can deal with the people who have the report." Boland said and now a slight smile played across his thin lips.

"What's in this for you? And don't tell me you are acting out of any form of conviction."

"I sense there's a change coming and I want to be on the winning team."

Sir Charles leaned back in his chair. This man shared his desire for power. He didn't trust him but it would be unwise not to see what he could do. He might have to destroy him later. "So what are you suggesting?'

"The Appleby family have the only copy of the report. I can arrange for them all to be eliminated accidentally."

Sir Charles had to smile. "That sounds very thorough. How have we let you fester in Quota Admin, when you obviously have a talent for more?" He didn't wait for an answer before adding, "I won't ask for details." With a nod of his head he indicated the meeting was over. Boland didn't move. The man had attitude.

"I think I ought to mention something else before I go. I've just bumped into an angry Carolyn Spencer in the corridor. She was looking for your office."

Sir Charles shuffled his papers. "I can't think why. I hardly know the woman."

"Come off it. She's one of your tarts."

"You don't get to talk to me like that,"

"I think I do, especially as I've just persuaded her not to make a scene. That wasn't easy after she told me you were the father of her son. I think you owe me now." He paused and stared until Sir Charles averted his eyes.

"I'll be in contact again soon," Boland said. He stood

and offered a hand. Sir Charles rose too and with reluctance shook it. He wiped his hand as soon as his visitor left. It was a long time since he had been intimidated like this. His dismay was short-lived and this man's arrogance would be too. He had overplayed his hand. Sir Charles had been eliminating opponents all his life. He would deal with Carolyn too, though maybe he would toy with her a little longer.

CHAPTER 44

Kate had tried Grant repeatedly so was relieved when he returned the call.

"I can't talk. Toby's worse. I'm on my way to the hospital."

She could hear the panic in his voice but still had to ask. "I'm sorry but Mary's received another call up. They're coming in the next 24 hours." His silence was unnerving. She hated herself for piling on the pressure.

"Get her away from the farm. Hide her. There may not be a Quota system to worry about soon. I'm sorry, I have to go." He cut the call before she could answer.

If Toby was still waiting for a transplant he was in real danger. It didn't sound hopeful. As Kate put her phone back in her pocket she realised Mary had been listening. She tried to smile but it did not disguise the worry in her eyes. Kate walked over, held her close and spoke with a confidence she did not feel.

"Dad's coming this afternoon. The boat's ready for us. You can hide there for the time being. It's safe, I promise you."

Mary looked pale. Kate could see she was unconvinced. She must keep her busy until her father arrived. "We'll need food for a few days. See what you can get from the freezer and use the hydro-minimisers. We won't have much room on the boat." Mary liked a challenge.

"I hate those contraptions. They suck the life out of any food you put in. Bloody things."

Kate smiled. That's better; her fighting spirit had resurfaced. Mary straightened her cardigan and marched out with a sense of purpose almost crashing into Jack who was standing in the hall. He looked troubled.

"Mum, I can't find Lisa. I tried face-recognition but I need access to the street cameras." He paused and then blurted out. "I've asked Clive to help, so he's driving up now."

She fought hard to keep her fear under control. She didn't want that man in her house. At the same time, if it helped find her daughter before the protests began she would have to deal with it.

"Mum?"

"He's a clever man, Jack. If anyone can find Lisa, I'm sure he will." She made a show of tidying the cushions and changed focus. "I've spoken to your grandfather and he's coming to collect Mary. We need to get her to the boat, find your sister and get her on board too as quickly as we can. By the way, don't mention the boat to Clive. I want to keep our whereabouts secret."

Jack gave her a hug. "Ok, Mum, but with Clive's help we'll find Lisa. She'll be fine."

She forced herself to relax. Jack led her to the sofa and sat her down carefully. His face held a determination she had not seen before and he lowered his voice to a whisper. "Mum, this public uprising is long overdue. The groups are planning some major protests outside the Ministry tomorrow, they're arming themselves big time." He rose and his tone grew angry. "The bloody government won't know what's hit them."

Kate looked at him in horror. This was a dangerous game and her family were smack in the middle. She needed to take control before it got out of hand.

Jack was already headed for the door. "I'll get my file. Clive will want to see what I've done so far to try and find Lisa." His voice broke a little as he left the room: he was concerned for Lisa but Kate knew Clive would be the immediate threat.

She texted Grant immediately, saying she hoped it went well for Toby and that she was taking his advice and moving Mary to the boat. She feared for both their children now. The riots could get nasty and she had no idea where her pregnant daughter was. She spent the next hour calling all Lisa's friends but no one had heard or seen her for weeks. There was only one person left and as she looked towards the perimeter road she saw his car speeding towards the house. She hoped she was wrong.

A few seconds later, Jack burst into the room announcing, "He's here."

She was irritated by Clive's arrogant stride as he sauntered into the lounge, shoved the floral cushion on the floor and settled on the couch. He pulled the stool towards him and slammed his dirty trainers down on the ancient tapestry. "I could do with a drink, Kate."

"I'll get you a beer, mate." Jack was out of the door before she could stop him.

Clive patted the seat next to him, a clear indication to sit down. She moved towards the armchair opposite.

"So you think you can find my daughter?"

"You really should be more hospitable or I might change my mind." Kate heard the threat in his voice.

Jack returned with two open cans and gave one to Clive. "I tried all the software scams but the bastards have the street cameras locked up tighter than a nun's arse." He slumped next to Clive on the sofa, laughing. The two men grinned. Kate felt sick. This was not a man she wanted Jack to emulate.

"If you want to find her, bring your stuff and come back with me. That girl's pretty stubborn, if she's made up her mind to stay missing. She will." Clive looked towards Kate and his eyes had a chill to them she had seen before.

"Great. Let's go then, I've got my data." Jack came across to kiss her cheek. "Don't worry Mum, I'll be back with Lisa soon; this bloke knows all the tricks."

Yes, thought Kate, that's what frightens me.

Clive waited until Jack had left the room, drained his can and rose. He smiled. She did not like the cold confidence in his eyes and tried to get out of the armchair. He moved quickly and pinned her hands down. He leant forward, grabbed her head and forced his lips to hers. She froze. His breath quickened and his tongue flicked a parting caress as he pulled away.

"Don't worry, Kate, I'll have her before you know it. That's a promise."

The words hung in the air as she watched him swagger out. Kate was convinced he already knew where she was. She followed him outside and tried to smile at Jack who gave her a cheery thumbs up while he waited for Clive to join him. They climbed in the car. As the vehicle disappeared up the drive she fought the desire to race after it but she knew Clive was their only chance of finding Lisa, so she let them go. Once Mary was safe on the boat, she would follow them to the Ministry. She had to find her daughter. She wiped a tissue across her lips and could smell Clive on it. The thought of her daughter's future in his slimy hands nauseated her. She needed a shower before her father arrived.

"I had trouble closing the van doors. Mary's taking everything. Now she's trying to stuff more food in the back." Her father stood, hands on hips, watching Mary put the last of the vacuumed trays in the vehicle.

Kate smiled and walked up to her father. "Jack's gone back to the Ministry with Clive to help find Lisa. She's still missing. He thinks he can track her down."

Her father held her shoulders. "I'm sure she's with friends, but the Ministry's the last place Jack should be going right now. The mood is grim. If the political temperature doesn't change, it could get nasty." His face became serious. "I've been trying to talk some sense into the protest groups but a few won't listen to reason. They've armed themselves with some pretty serious rocket bombs. They're capable of blowing the building if it comes to it."

Kate shook her head. "Jack won't listen either. Half the population have been dreaming of this revolt for years. The government has gone too far. Everyone will be behind the protest groups this time."

"I know, but if the speech in the Commons works we can disable Quota peacefully. Whatever we think of Sir Charles, let's hope he wins them over tomorrow."

Kate nodded and took a last look around the farm before closing the door. She was leaving so many memories. This had been her home for all her married life, such happy times with James. Jack and Lisa had grown up here. Now she wasn't sure she'd ever come back. They were all in danger. There was no choice but to leave for their safety.

She climbed into the loaded van and sat beside her father. As they pulled away she gripped Mary's hand and watched her home get smaller in the rear view mirror.

An hour later, they were in Canary Wharf. The massive office buildings were silent, unoccupied, abandoned after the last great recession. By the quayside, they unloaded the van and Mary fussed about on board the narrow boat. Her original horror at the boat's neglected exterior had obviously changed to respect as she happily busied herself finding a place for all their possessions. Once everything was put away, they sat down to a hot meal and made up the beds for the evening. As Kate lay down to sleep, listening to the soothing water lapping the boat, she prayed Jack would find his sister and they could all be safely snuggled up in this tiny hideaway. She texted him to join them as soon as he found Lisa.

The next morning Kate rose early and was up and dressed, waiting on the quayside for her father. He told Mary to stay put and helped Kate into the small motor boat tied at the back. As the sun appeared between the tall buildings they headed towards Putney Bridge and the Ministry of Life building.

They could hear the chanting of the mobs well before they could see them.

"It's getting nasty, Kate. I really think you should go back and stay on the boat with Mary." Her father said as they docked and climbed onto the towpath.

"I'm not going anywhere until I find out where Lisa is. And I still haven't heard anything from Jack. I'm worried he's in there with Clive. I must know they're alright."

Her father gestured towards a corner café, up the hill from the Ministry. "Ok, but stay in there till I come back. The owner's a good friend; you'll be safe. Promise me you won't do anything on your own."

"You go, I'll be fine." She forced herself to sound confident. A couple of men pushed past her, their focus on the road ahead, oblivious of the women and children trying to reach safety inside the shops. A young man stopped, picked up a broken brick, stuffed it under his jacket and ran to catch up with the others.

"I have to try and talk some sense into these men, they're set on violence. Don't move."

She nodded.

"I mean it, Kate. I know you're worried about Lisa but we stand a better chance of finding her if we do it together." He looked into her eyes and kissed her cheek. "I'll be as quick as I can. If it gets worse, promise me you'll take the motor boat and head back to Mary."

She stood on the corner nodding, but was already scanning the crowds milling down the road.

"Promise me?"

"Ok." Kate knew this was one promise she could not keep. She watched her father disappear into the crowds and waited until she was sure he was out of sight.

She looked up at the imposing Ministry building that filled the skyline. The crowds were grouped around the entrance, kept at bay by the military police guard. A long line of shields and anti-riot beams crossed the entrance. No one was getting in that way.

Kate started walking along the perimeter and doubled back behind the service buildings. She knew there must be another way in. She remembered James moaning about the underground tunnels he had to use to deliver his research material, a network of warrens the public never saw.

As she crept around the last of the outbuildings, she saw an armoured vehicle turn into the slipway. After a few seconds the steel doors rose in a shuddering groan to let it through. This was what she had been looking for. But how was she to gain access? She slumped against the concrete pillar and burst into tears. It was hopeless.

She took out her mobile. She would rather get inside without Clive knowing but decided to risk contacting Jack; maybe he had found Lisa already. If Clive knew where she was he would have his own agenda and it would not include helping her family to safety. He had fooled her once. She was not about to let him get his hands on her children now.

She called Jack's number and waited.

CHAPTER 45

Grant stood as the doctor entered the waiting room. "How is Toby?"

"He's safe for now, but he needs the transplant urgently, and we are having problems preparing a synthetic kidney."

Grant swallowed hard. He hadn't realised the situation was so critical. "How long have we got?"

"That's always difficult to say but probably only a few days. We're keeping him stable and carrying on with our process but if there are any new donor options, we must consider them."

Grant groaned inwardly. There were no feasible new options. "Ok, I'll see what I can do. Can I visit Toby before I leave?"

"He's in isolation but you can look through the viewing window. I'll take you through."

Grant welled up when he saw his son. The boy was his whole world and he was powerless to help him. If only he had been his real father and could donate a kidney. He watched the child sleep, hooked up to the machines that were keeping him alive. Tears fell as he pressed his face against the cool glass. He tried to think of any alternatives but he couldn't find an answer.

His mobile alarm buzzed. The Quota debate was starting within the hour. That would not help his own son but could stop others suffering from lack of medical credits. He knew he should be there. He wiped his eyes and blew a kiss to his son.

Ten minutes later he caught a river taxi to Westminster. Despite the heavy rain, there were tens of thousands of protesters. He saw several incidents of soldiers being pelted with bricks and the majority of the banners reflected the mood of anger.

QUOTA OUT - GOVERNMENT OUT
OUR LIFE OR YOURS?
NO MORE STATE MURDER

News of Sir Charles's Quota speech had spread and the prospect of a change raised demand for it. Adam and his friends had been more successful mobilising the protesters than Grant had expected. He hoped they could be controlled if things didn't go their way. With difficulty, he pushed through the crowd to the access gate of Parliament. A group of heavily armed soldiers guarded the entrance and Grant spotted snipers on several of the nearby roofs.

"Where do you think you're going?" A soldier demanded, raising his taser and ignoring the official pass Grant waved at him.

"I'm a junior minister. I need to get in for the session." Grant said.

"Not until I've identified you." The soldier focused his mobile scanner on Grant's face before gesturing him to advance through the security arch. "Ok, you're cleared."

The atmosphere inside Parliament was as frenzied as outside. MPs and their advisers were in loud debate everywhere.

"Spencer!"

He walked across the lobby to where Sir Charles was standing with an aide.

"You took your time. Do you have anything extra for my speech?"

"No," Grant said, "though I've seen a newsflash from China this morning, announcing they're welcoming more immigration. It might be worth mentioning this to illustrate how they messed up population planning."

"Is that all?"

"Yes. You've got everything else in the download I sent you."

Sir Charles walked away to greet one of his cronies.

"Good luck," Grant called after the retreating peer and he meant it. There was no response. He joined the line waiting to access the public gallery, acknowledging a couple of reporters he knew.

The Times man put down his recorder. "Not sure why I bother. You'll just censor everything anyway."

"Who knows," Grant smiled. "Today might be different."

When he reached the gallery, he waved his pass to get a front-row seat. This should be the performance of a lifetime, he thought. I might even get to play a part. The MPs filed into the chamber below, odd snippets of their conversations rising above the continuous drone of the mob outside. He watched Sir Charles enter; his confident stride looked close to arrogance in Grant's opinion. There was cheering from the opposition but not much from the government. They clearly recognised Sir Charles's initiative as a self-serving quest for power.

After a short introduction by the Speaker, Sir Charles rose to lead the Quota debate.

"I come to the House with humility, with regrets but with hope for the future. You entrusted me with the management of population numbers and I have done the best I can. I believe the Quota Project has met its objectives and I will prove that to you. Now, if you care about the well-being of the country and the happiness of our citizens, it is time to return life choices to the people."

Sir Charles paused and looked around the chamber, gauging his support. There were murmurs of agreement but a shrill intervention came from above.

"Call yourself a caring politician? What about your wife with dementia, contracted from your food programme? And what about the sick son you've disowned and abandoned?"

Grant turned to see the ushers advancing on Carolyn. He hadn't noticed her sitting two rows back. Sir Charles's attempted retort was lost in the uproar. He was gasping for breath, as he kept shouting to be heard. His moment of triumph was gone and he knew it. His face turned white and he groaned before collapsing.

The Speaker banged his hammer furiously. "Silence, silence. Get the medics for Sir Charles. Give him air."

Grant realised Carolyn's revenge could destroy the Quota debate before it started. He wasn't going to let that happen. This might be the only chance he would get to persuade others to talk about Quota change. He jumped on to his seat. The shock of Sir Charles's collapse had brought a moment of quiet reflection amongst the MPs.

"Ditch the politician but not the debate!" He bellowed. "We don't need him but we do need change."

He acknowledged nods from many MPs. With limited time before the security guards reached him, he turned to the public gallery.

"I worked on Quota and was hoodwinked like the rest of the nation. You've all lost family members unnecessarily." He raised his voice. "We don't need population planning now. This government have kept Quota to support its own corruption. Look outside, the people want change. Let's kill Quota now." His clenched fist came down on the ornate rail he was braced against.

The roar from the gallery urged him on. The guards were almost on him. He leaned forward and shouted at the senior ministers below.

"Quota's unjust and backed by some with their own agendas. If you don't listen, the people will make you pay, just like she has." Eyes followed his pointed finger to Carolyn who was struggling with three ushers trying to evict her.

Grant continued, "Sir Charles made terrible mistakes. Don't make even more." The guards reached him seconds later and dragged him from the gallery as the noise erupted below.

They marched him to the end of the great hall. The biggest guy winked when he opened the side door and pushed him forward.

"We're on your side," he said, releasing Grant's arm. "The bastards took away my mother last week. Destroy Quota for us, sir."

As Grant made his way down the corridor, he spotted Carolyn being questioned in an anteroom. The door was open so he walked in.

"You've done some stupid things in your life, Carolyn, but that beats everything."

"The bastard had it coming. Nobody ignores me," she screamed.

"I don't think that's likely. You'll be famous as the woman who started the Quota riots. Your selfish revenge has ruined any chance of a peaceful solution."

Grant closed the door on Carolyn's horrified face and walked away. He assumed the mob had heard what had happened. The din from outside was frightening. He doubted if Adam and the protest leaders could keep control. Crossing the entrance lobby, he passed the paramedics attending to Sir Charles and overheard them querying where to take him.

"He's asking to be taken to the Canary Wharf Research hospital, mumbling something about having a son there?"

Grant interrupted, flashing his pass. "I'm Sir Charles's assistant. He does have a son there. It's probably the best place to take him." Already he was thinking this might solve Toby's problem. If Sir Charles died, a donor kidney would be on hand.

"Thanks, sir. He's critical, we need to get him out of here quickly." The paramedics strapped Sir Charles onto the stretcher.

Grant followed them as they carried the peer to the waiting ambulance. Sir Charles looked grey-faced and beaten. Grant was about to join them in the ambulance when his mobile flashed with an urgent video call.

"I'm at the Ministry of Life." Adam was struggling to speak, his voice almost drowned by the background noise. "We've heard the debate failed and the protest here is out of control. There could be an attack on the Ministry building. Grant, get here as soon as you can. Kate needs your help."

"Why?"

"I'll explain when you get here. I'm in a cafe outside the main gate." Grant saw the desperation on Adam's face as the video faded.

He nodded to the paramedics and closed the doors of the ambulance. A boat was the only way he could get to the Ministry of Life; there was chaos everywhere. He pushed his way through the crowds towards the Thames. Some owners were hiring out their boats at extortionate prices. He paid one willing to take him up river.

CHAPTER 46

Clive looked out of the window at the crowds below milling around the Ministry of Life. From the thirty-second floor, they looked like a swarm of demented ants as they waved their banners. They had no idea the building was about to erupt.

"What's the sequence for the cameras? I know Lisa's got friends in the university area." Jack's question irritated him. Clive turned from the window and studied the boy's gangly body hunched over the glass table. He was busy resetting the street cameras in an effort to track down his precious sister. The boy was bright. Shame, he could have used a scientific brain like his. Clive's gaze returned to the street below. By the end of today Jack's brain would be drifting through the air, a cloud of tiny spores like the clueless insects below.

"Clive?" Jack was poised, fingers stretched across a stream of numbers and street codes waiting for his response.

"Same sequence as the dock area. Lazy bastards just repeated the pattern across the lower districts. I told them it was a mistake."

Jack grinned, tapped in the long code and continued working. His attention was fixed on the screen. Clive walked quietly across the room. The boy was concentrating on the complicated codes in the notebook. Clive took the syringe from his inside pocket and crept behind Jack. In one smooth movement, he plunged it deep into the boy's freckled neck.

Jack's eyes rolled and his face hit the desk. Out cold. Clive dragged him into position under the main terminal. The lad was moments away from tracing his sister on the Ministry's face recognition system. He would have seen her entering the building right behind Clive less than 48 hours ago. If he had left him at the farm, he would have worked the sequence out in hours. As he thought, the boy was bright.

He looked at his watch. Time to check on Lisa; he would need to keep her alive if he was to enjoy her after all the fuss died down. As he tied the boy up, he heard a buzzing. He cursed. That was an oversight. Clive lifted Jack's body and pulled the vibrating phone out of his jeans. It was Kate calling. He checked the signal. Local. She must be in the city. Now, mother and daughter, that was the game he'd always wanted. He smiled and answered the call.

"Hi Kate, it's Clive," he kicked Jack's body back into position, "Jack's flat-out working on the codes but we think we've found her, in the University district. Do you want me to interrupt him?"

"You sure? I rang her friends earlier today and they hadn't seen her?"

Clive frowned. "Pretty sure, but he's checking it out now. Where are you?"

There was a slight hesitation before she answered, "I'm outside. We need to find her. The streets are heaving, it's getting dangerous."

She was here. Imagining the two women was exciting him already.

"You can come in here. Go around to the service area at the back. I'll call you when I can get you in. Right now isn't a good time, the security is tight, but give me half-an-hour."

"OK, but hurry, it's crazy out here. Can I speak to Jack?"

Clive looked down at Jack's body on the floor. "Not a good idea, he's tied up at the moment."

He cut the call just before his raucous laugh bounced around the silent room.

Kate stared at her phone. He had cut her off and he sounded far too confident, happy almost. Maybe they had found Lisa. Maybe she had him all wrong. She shook her head. No, he might fool everyone else but she knew him too well. She needed back up.

She worked her way back through the crowd to the café area. She had half an hour. If her father was back he would know what the mob was planning and help her face Clive. Kate was almost knocked off her feet as more people joined the crowd by the entrance. When she approached the café on the corner she could see her father arguing with a group of men. They looked like they might just strike him but stormed off when he stood his ground.

"Dad, are you all right? What's going on?"

"Oh, where the hell have you been? You're going straight back to the boat. It's not safe here. The debate fell apart and they want the government out at any cost. Grant should be here any minute. Some boats are moving on the river so I'm hoping he managed to get one."

"I've spoken to Clive. He thinks he may have found Lisa. He's in the Ministry. I'm going in to talk to him. I'll need your help."

"No, you're not. That building could go up any minute. They reckon they've got someone on the inside who is going to blow the Quota computer sky high." He grabbed her hand. "I'll walk you to the motor launch. You need to go straight back to the boat with Mary."

She pulled her hand away. "No, Dad, not till I know Lisa's safe. Jack's in there too. He could get hurt. If that building's a target, I have to get him out." She glared at her dad and his face softened.

"Adam." They turned as they heard Grant yell.

Kate saw Grant pushing his way through the crowds towards them. He was pale, his usual calm manner gone and his jacket ripped at the seams.

"Thank God, I found you. It's chaos."

Kate felt the mob surge forwards and was almost dragged away but her father hooked his arm around her and pushed his way through a side door into the café. It was a mess. All the chairs had been overturned and crockery smashed on the floor.

Kate faced Grant immediately they were all inside. "Jack's in the Ministry with Clive. He has promised to get me in. I must see Jack is safe."

She could see Grant was about to protest, but Kate continued," I don't trust Clive any more than you do but I need my boy out of there."

Her father's voice was full of concern. "The groups are intent on revenge. They've threatened to blow the building. They won't listen to me or anyone now. It's too late."

Grant shook his head and walked through the debris on the floor, kicking it across the room. "This could have been avoided. Why wouldn't they listen?"

He swivelled around and gripped Kate hands. "You must stay safe. Leave it to us. We'll get him out. I'm sure I'll be able to get through security. I'll take Adam. Between us we'll check the building; there are only a few places Clive could be working from. We'll find him."

Kate wanted to believe him but could she? Grant gave her no chance to decide. He dropped her hands and was out of the café with her father running to keep up.

She rushed to the window and watched them approach the armed guard at the entrance to the Ministry building. The guard was shaking his head and pointing to the response vehicle making its way down the street. They were dispersing the crowds with tasers. The security guy pushed Grant and her father away and after a few angry words she watched them turn back toward the café.

Her mind was made up. It looked unlikely they would get in; she would have to take Clive up on his offer.

"Gone back to the boat," she wrote with lipstick on a menu and propped the message on the counter. She slipped out of the café through the kitchen and edged her way round the back of the government building avoiding the angry mob. She headed towards the service entrance Clive had mentioned. He was the last person she trusted, but if he was the only way into the building, she would do exactly as he asked.

Kate had to find Lisa and get Jack out.

CHAPTER 47

Grant followed Adam into the café. They picked their way through puddles of broken glass. No one was there.

"I hope to God Kate headed back," Adam said, grabbing a chair and pulling it upright. He slumped as the energy appeared to leak from his body.

Grant reached for his mobile to call her but paused as he spotted a note propped up on the shelf. He leant over and grabbed it. "She says she's left for the boat," he waved the note at Adam. "She'll be safe."

Adam looked up. "That's unlike her to give in so easily." He took the note and studied it. "Let's hope she's telling the truth. Now it's up to us to find the children. Do you know of any other way into the Ministry?"

"Possibly. We certainly won't get in the main gate now." Before Grant could say any more, an avalanche of water forced its way through the flimsy louvered windows. There was a second explosion as it hit the entrance doors, smashing through the glass panels towards them. They backed away and took cover behind the counter as the water gushed through the room.

Grant raised his voice above the noise. "The security

forces mean business. If the terrorist groups arm the rocket launchers it will be all out war. I need to get into the Ministry and try to disarm Quota before they blow the building. It's the only thing they'll listen to now." He signalled towards the kitchen door.

They crawled out the back and crouched behind the commercial bins, ducking as a couple of bricks flew over their heads. A stream of angry youngsters roared down the road towards the water cannons. Grant shouted to Adam. "You talk to the protestors. Tell them what I'm going to do. Get them to hold fire and wait."

"But I need to find the children."

"I know that building inside out. If they're in there I promise you I'll find them." Adam signalled agreement but Grant could see the pain in his eyes. "You stand a better chance talking to the mob leaders. I doubt they'll listen, but you have to try. The fiasco in Parliament today was the last straw."

Grant motioned upwards and they both peered over the bins. He could see a determined line of protesters huddled behind sheets of plastic advancing towards the Ministry gates. The water cannon changed direction and scattered them like insects. Adam looked grim as he turned to Grant. "Find Lisa and Jack first. We'll deal with Quota once they're safe."

Grant nodded. "No one's safe but if Clive has Jack or Lisa, I'll find them." He left, heading for the Ministry building as Adam picked up his phone and tried to contact the protest leaders.

Grant zigzagged through the crowds. He could see the water cannon had pushed the mob back across Putney Bridge but the building was still within range of a rocket launcher. The sky was red with the glow of many fires. The population was sending a clear message tonight. The back streets were less crowded as he made his way towards the run-down garage under the railway arch in Lower Richmond Road. The ministerial drivers were based here years ago. Inside, there was a tunnel that connected to the Ministry building; he hoped the entrance had not been sealed.

The mechanics in reception were busy watching the media coverage of the riots, discussing the protesters' tactics. Grant managed to make his way behind the cars parked at the entrance and into the building without being noticed. He found the underground tunnel on the right, but the heavy metal doors were rusted and would not budge. He found a mallet on one of the workbenches and, when he heard a series of explosions outside, hammered the heavy padlock until it fell to the floor. He sneaked a look through the office window and could see two men in oily overalls, gathered around the news monitor, swigging beer and cheering. They had not heard a thing. He slipped through the steel doors unnoticed.

It was a long walk through the maze of tunnels to the Ministry. A dirty light filtered down through open drain covers above. He passed old tyres and abandoned car parts flung into gullies. The dull melody of water dripping down the walls echoed around him as rats scurried by his feet. Every few yards inquisitive claws would cling to his flapping trouser legs. Shaking the rats off slowed him down, so he ignored them and ran faster through the rancid puddles. He just hoped the exit was still in use the other end.

As the tunnel narrowed he reached an iron grid that crossed the exit. A shabby notice swung crookedly off the right-hand gate. It had not been used for years. He tugged at the central handle and swore loudly and rattled the rusty chain. There was no time to go back. He had to get through. He repeatedly smashed the chain against the linked fence and hung his entire weight on it. Water had rusted the chains enough for him to pull them apart.

Grant sat for a few moments to recover his breath before making his way up the internal staircase to the lower floor. He knew this would lead him into the service area of the building and he would be picked up on the security cameras. It was a chance he would have to take. Just as he was about to open the entrance door, his phone flashed with a message from the hospital: Toby's consultant. Not more bad news, surely?

He opened the video link to Mr Morgan's grave face.

"Sorry, Mr Spencer, but Toby has taken a turn for the worse. We're trying to stabilise him but we may have to risk an artificial kidney if we can't find a donor organ by tomorrow. I know the situation in the city is horrendous but we need to discuss options. Toby's been asking for you." He sighed before his image faded to black on the screen.

Grant slumped to a sitting position on the stairs and he stared at his phone in disbelief. He knew the route to the hospital would be impossible while the riots continued and Kate's children were dependent on him as well. He had no choice.

Kate ran down the steps of a basement flat along from the Ministry building and waited for Clive's response. She felt bad lying to Grant and her father about her plans but they would never have agreed. She watched angry feet thud above her and wondered about how to get her kids to safety. The city felt like it was about to explode.

When it came, Clive's message was short and precise. He told her to walk towards the service entry door A12 and wait. He was disengaging the security system so the timing was crucial.

She felt uncomfortable. He had her entirely under his control but it was the only way she could get inside. Her head felt faint with worry and she realised she had not eaten since early this morning. Her body must be running entirely on adrenaline but she needed every bit of energy she could summon.

In the distance she could hear the rumble and screech of police and armoured vehicles, their sirens piercing the noise of the crowds in the streets above her. The light was fading and the city was in uproar. Part of her felt excited that they were fighting back after years of acceptance but the price terrified her.

She ran up the stairs and across the street. It took her a few minutes to find the entrance she wanted. Her breathing was rapid as she leant against the service door waiting for the signal to enter.

Clive's alert 'Go' flashed across the screen. She pulled at the door handle and heard the soft click as it opened. Inside, the corridor was in darkness; she stared and reached out her hands unable to make out a thing. Her wrist was grabbed, wrenched forward. She screamed.

"Shut it," Clive hissed inches from her ear and dragged her along at breakneck speed. He pushed her through a doorway and into a lift. The doors closed and in the gloom she saw the floor numbers flicker past on the electronic strip above. She felt his fingers close around hers and she bit her lips into silence. It seemed an age until the lift stopped and the doors flew open.

"Follow me," was his terse command, as he hurried down the dark corridor. She had to run to keep up. They swerved in and out of several empty offices and down a back stairway before he reached a maintenance entrance at the back of a lift shaft. He unlocked it and pulled her through just before the lights flicked into life. She was breathing heavily.

"You're out of condition, Kate," he smirked.

She looked around the room. Plate glass ran the entire length and judging by the rooftops she imagined they were near to the top of the building. There were several desks, monitors and a huge interactive screen on the back wall.

Clive walked up to the screen and keyed in some numbers. Immediately the entire wall sprang to life. Green numbers slid across the walls and ceilings. Names, numbers and faces babbling as they faded in and out of the room.

He raised his arms, "This, is where the magic happens. This is Quota Control."

Kate walked closer and realised there were hundreds of faces, merging and disappearing, disembodied heads and entire identities scrolling down the walls.

"You do this? You control this?" Kate could hardly believe it. A man like him orchestrating people's lives, futures.

He was beaming. Clive zoomed in on a face, a middle-aged man, slightly overweight and balding. His data showed he worked in a transport depot for underground trains. He had a wife and three children. Clive tapped in some commands and she was horrified to see a red alert flash across his record 'Immediate call up, credits dissolved.' His face deleted from the screen. Gone.

Clive laughed and raised his hand to the control panel again. "I saved Mary, but someone had to pay the price."

"No," Kate cried. This was unbearable. Surely this wasn't possible? "You can't."

"Oh, but I can and have." He switched off the panel and all the faces swirled into the corner of the room and disappeared. It was like a bad dream. This couldn't be happening. If he was capable of this, what had he done to Lisa and Jack?

Her mind focused: she must stay calm. She must not show fear. He thrived on that. She needed to know where her children were, and fast.

Grant heard the drone of engines slowing and saw the lights go out along the tunnel. The power was off. He stuffed his phone in his pocket and realised this was his chance to get in without being noticed. The security cameras and alarms were out but he didn't know for how long.

He wrenched the heavy door open and peered inside. Sure enough, the whole entrance was in darkness. Some people were shouting at the other end of the corridor but he could not hang around. He ran to the steps and started climbing. He decided not to chance the lift, even though it worked on emergency power, and took the stairs three at a time.

By the time he reached the tenth floor he was breathless. The security centre was on this floor and the lights were on here. If he could access the scanner he would be able to check who was in the building. If Clive had brought Jack and Lisa here the body scanners would pick them up. He guessed the building would have been evacuated after the threats, leaving only essential personnel.

As he got nearer to the security unit, he could hear the guards in some panic.

"I still think we're stupid staying. I'm not waiting until this bloody building's incinerated."

"Our orders are to stay put and secure all entrances and exits."

"Orders... who are you trying to fool? This place is finished. The mob won't stop until they turn the building to rubble. Look at the monitor. A block has already lost power. You can do what you like but I'm leaving."

Grant listened as the guards got more and more agitated. He heard a thump and peered around the corner just as one guard was running down the corridor. He crept over to the counter and could see the other bleeding, out cold on the floor.

He paused to check the guard was still breathing and walked across to the heat scanner. The grid showed which floors were showing live status. He could see he had five to check. He would start with the closest. As he walked towards C block, the lights started to flicker back on. The power must have been reinstated. He would need to move quickly.

The phone in his pocket vibrated. Adam's face appeared. "Grant, I've managed to reach two of the more violent groups, one has agreed to wait but I can't convince the other leader. I am going to keep trying but they are planning to arm the rockets in an hour's time. I can't get them to wait much longer.

I've spoken to Mary and Kate never made it back to the boat. I have an awful feeling she might be in the building."

Grant sighed. One hour was tight, especially if he had three people to find now. He hoped Kate knew what she was doing.

Clive looked at Kate's face. She was hiding it but her entire body was rigid with fear. He could almost taste it. She had changed little from their university days. Her hair was shorter but her eyes still excited him. They were wide-eyed with alarm now. He could see her breasts rise and fall beneath her woollen coat. She was so sexy. Her fear made her more so. Taking his time, he moved around her, inspecting every curve, every line of her body.

"You look warm, Kate. Take off your coat."

She stepped away pulling her belt tighter. "I'm fine. I want to see Jack. Now." Her eyes narrowed and she looked towards the door.

"No rush. I told you he's busy chasing up the location alerts on Lisa." He pulled his phone from his pocket. "He'll call as soon as he's confirmed it." He stuffed the phone back and moved closer to her. Reaching for the buttons, he started to undo her coat. The fine wool was soft and his fingers followed the contours of her arm from shoulder to wrist. Silky tuffs collected under his nails, he could feel her tremble as he enclosed her fingers with his.

She pulled away and walked towards the door. "Where is Jack? I need to talk to him."

Her eyes blazed with a determination he remembered too well. During their research years she would not give in. It was her insistence that he was on to something that made him work harder. His cure for dementia would never have been found if he had not wanted to impress her so desperately. Then she let him down. His recollections faded and he remembered why he was here.

Maybe he should let her see her son. It might make her realise what she was up against. Those green eyes looked far too confident. He needed to change that.

"Ok, but remember you asked."

Clive had lost patience. He dragged her to the exit. He had turned off all the cameras in this block but it was no time to take chances. As he pulled her into the computer suite, he turned the floor level lighting on. He did not want the room illuminated from the street below.

He looked at Kate whose eyes were searching the entire room but finding nothing. He smiled.

"Jack's a bright boy. Brave too. He wanted to bring down the Quota system so I thought I'd give him his moment of glory." He pushed her forward through the desks and monitors towards the clearing where Jack was lying under the main terminal desk.

He gripped her arms as she screamed and struggled to get to him.

"There are enough explosives inside the terminal to destroy everything in this room and a couple of floors above but I made sure I've backed everything up. I will continue the Quota programme with the new political leaders. We'll need some kind of population control and I'll be the one to deliver it."

She tore her eyes away from him and called her son, "Jack, Jack..."

Clive was surprised at her strength but she was no match for him. He slapped her across the face to quieten her hysterics and pushed her into a chair.

"One move towards him and you'll both go a little earlier than planned. You can't help Jack but you can save Lisa."

She looked up and spat in his face.

He laughed. She had spirit, he would give her that.

Kate looked at Jack's immobile body. She was relieved to see his shallow breathing. She glanced up at Clive who was grinning. He was a maniac. She had always thought him strange but had no idea how delusional he was. She wanted to rip the smirk from his face but that would not help her son. She needed to be clever, as manipulative as he was. He must have Lisa too. So what did he want from her?

She waited for her breathing to normalise and spoke quietly.

"So, what do you want, Clive?"

He did not reply but dragged her towards the exit. She hated leaving her son on the floor but she had to find out where Lisa was before dealing with Clive. She would kill him if she had to. The thought calmed her and she allowed herself to be led from the room, silently telling Jack she would be back for him; willing him to hang on.

Clive led her to another lift and they plunged downwards in silence. His face was hard to read. His flat features rarely showed emotion but if she could detect anything it was arrogance. Standing straight, he wrapped his knuckles on the lift wall, appearing almost bored with the wait.

She realised this was just a game to him. He was used to playing with people's lives, after all he did it for a living. The control was paramount. She knew it was important for him to think he had complete control over her. Maybe that was the answer.

The lift juddered to a halt and they exited in what she presumed was the basement as she could see no floor numbers or windows. He led her along several bare corridors without a word. Eventually he unlocked a door and pulled her down some concrete steps into a storage area. Shelves lined the room and filled the centre. He headed straight to the back of the store and pulled a shelving unit away from the wall. After making enough of a gap to slip behind, he pulled her forward.

With an old-fashioned key he unlocked the hidden door,

opened it and pushed her inside. She found herself in another narrow corridor; her body almost touched both sides. She groped her way along the rough walls, the dull yellow light above gave everything a grubby glow.

Clive started to manoeuvre his way in front, pressing his body against her. She gritted her teeth and closed her eyes. His hands were stroking her thighs and he seemed to stop for a moment, lost in thought. She coughed violently, an involuntary reaction but it seemed to break his train of thought and he squeezed past her.

She followed him into a bare cell. Lisa was sitting on the dirty floor, pressed into the corner of the room with a thin blanket over her lap. Her hair was matted and the smell coming from the container in the corner was fetid. It was a few seconds before Lisa looked up.

Kate ran towards her and fell to the floor wrapping her arms around her sobbing daughter. Lost in their embrace they did not hear Clive leave but they both fell silent as the key clicked in the lock and the single bulb above plunged them into darkness.

"It's ok, I'm here." As her comforting words drifted into the darkness, she started to plan.

CHAPTER 48

Sir Charles's eyelids felt glued but with effort he forced them open. He couldn't focus, just saw a blur of bright lights.

"Can you hear me?" the voice was strong, comforting.

"Where am I?" he tried to spit the words out but his dry mouth refused to co-operate. The last thing he could remember was preparing for the Quota debate. Would he miss that now?

Someone was removing the mask from his face. He didn't have the strength to stop them. He tried to speak again. This time, he managed a rasping sound, every word separated by a gasp for air.

"Don't try and talk. You've had a heart attack. You need to rest," the man's voice again.

"How long?" he turned his head and blinked his eyes until he could make out a man in a white coat standing by the bed.

"A few days while we assess what treatment you need."

"Treatment?" he tried to raise his right arm but found it tethered to a tube. He could hear the rhythmic beat of a machine behind the bed.

"We must check for blockages in your arteries."

"I can't stay," Sir Charles said, as a brief pulse of energy surged through him. "I have an important speech to give." He attempted to sit up but could only raise his head a few inches.

"I think that can wait," the doctor insisted and cradled his head back onto the pillow. "You rest. We can talk again when you're stronger." The mask was refitted and the doctor left.

He tried to be positive. Maybe he'd collapsed at home. No one need know. He would delay his Quota initiative for a few weeks and could still win power. He pressed the button in his hand and a warm feeling spread through his body. Drowsiness overwhelmed him.

"You've had a good sleep, sir." He was woken by a gentle touch. A nurse adjusted his pillows, helped him sit up and removed the mask. "Do you feel able to have a visitor?"

"A visitor? Who?"

"Your wife. She's been waiting for more than an hour. The doctor says you can have a few minutes together."

"It can't be my wife," he protested.

The nurse smiled. "I'll send her in." She smoothed his blanket before leaving the room. A few minutes later the door opened and a woman in a red dress entered.

"What the hell are you doing here?" he groaned.

"I knew you'd be a terrible patient. That's probably why no one else is waiting outside."

He sighed. Bloody Carolyn. She'd haunt him to his grave. He groped for the help button but it had slipped off the bed.

"I wouldn't bother calling the nurse. I told them I was your wife so they've given us some quality time," she laughed. "That's a joke considering the state of your real one."

The room was flooded by a sudden bright flash of light followed by a distant rumble.

"What's going on?" he said.

Carolyn strolled over to the window and raised the blind. "It looks like the mobs have made it to the Ministry of Life. Your Quota Review is going up in flames, literally."

"We haven't had the Quota Review."

"Sorry, Charles. You tried but collapsed before the debate got going."

"I don't believe you. I couldn't have."

"Think what you like. The Quota protesters were never going to trust your self-serving reform, anyway. They know real changes only come through force."

Sir Charles moaned. The explosions and flashes continued. "So you've come to gloat?"

"No. I wanted to give you the chance to do something good for once."

What was she talking about? The pain in his chest seemed to be getting worse. He was too tired to argue and pressed the drug button for another dose. Carolyn came closer and pulled some papers out of her bag.

"This might be your last chance to give our son a future. You just have to sign these." She pushed the documents in front of him.

All his life he had been in control. Now he felt helpless, his very survival in the hands of others. He had no family apart from his demented wife and he suspected his political friends had already changed their alliances. Only this demanding woman had any interest in him now.

"Sign what?"

"Paternity Affidavits. Sign and I'll leave you in peace." She manipulated a pen into his hand and rested the documents on a tray in front of him. Why shouldn't he acknowledge their offspring? Euphoria spread as the morphine worked its magic.

He'd sign and maybe deny it later. He let her guide the pen across the papers. She kissed him but he was confused when he saw her smirk as she withdrew.

"Thank you," Carolyn said, "I'll leave you to the doctors. See if your influence extends to the almighty." She snatched the signed forms and stuffed them back in her bag. "You can relax now you've sorted out your inheritance." She turned and marched out without a backward glance.

He tried to think what she meant. Something sounded wrong but thinking was such an effort. He pressed the button and felt his muscles relax. The drug was his only true friend. He couldn't think past the next wave of morphine as it flooded through his body.

CHAPTER 49

"Look at me, Lisa." Kate crouched next to her daughter and stroked the fringe away from her tearful eyes. The dark concrete cell was cold and she had been cradling Lisa's shaking body since Clive had locked them in. "We're going to get out," she cupped Lisa's chin in her hand to get her full attention, "but you need to listen and do exactly as I say."

It took a while to calm Lisa down and get her word perfect.

"We don't have much time," Kate took her daughter's hands, "When you're out, get help for Jack. I don't know how long he has." The words dried in her mouth as the image of her son came flooding back. "He's..."

"He'll be ok, Mum, he has to be!" She felt Lisa grip her arm, the colour returning to her face.

Kate stroked Lisa's hair, trying to comb some order through the matted waves. In the distance she could hear footsteps and then the lock rattled. Clive was back. Lisa started trembling again and Kate gave her a tender kiss. "We have to be strong now, Lisa." She waited for a nod and saw her daughter's grim determination grow. She released her, pulled herself up and turned to face the door just as it creaked open.

The bulb flickered and Clive's body filled the doorway.

"How sweet, mother and daughter, such a special bond, seems a shame to destroy it. Let me think, youth or experience, which to enjoy first?"

He stepped into the room and Kate moved towards him, shielding Lisa. "It's me you want. Let her go."

A slow smile spread across his face. She felt sick at the excitement in his eyes.

"You think it's that easy do you? Maybe once, when we were young I would have listened but you betrayed me. You're the same as the rest, selfish, fickle, whores." His smile vanished and he grabbed her. She heard Lisa gasp.

Kate knew she had to control her disgust. Her children's lives depended on it so she forced herself to caress his face. She pictured her son, helpless upstairs, and summoned all the love she felt for her family and poured it into the kiss she delivered. She felt the bile rise in her throat but fought the panic.

"Clive, I was young and stupid. You intimidated me." She moved away and forced herself to sound flirtatious. "Are you telling me you had no idea I fancied you?"

He looked confused for a second.

Kate smiled. "I knew you were way too bright for me and destined for greatness, everyone said so."

It was working, he was lapping it up. "I knew you would crack the cure. The professor was a snake taking the credit for all your work. Dementia was a global problem. He knew it would be worth millions."

"Yeah, and he paid the price."

Kate realised then that the middle-aged research scientist had not left for a better deal abroad. She watched Clive smirk. He had got rid of their professor. Is that why the research was never followed up?

Clive sounded boastful now. "Shame about the work but I wasn't about to let him get the credit. It went down on the same plane as he did. The entire world had to pay the price with him."

Kate disguised her shock with a smile and boosted his ego again. "You could replicate it surely? A cure for dementia could save millions. Use your intellect for something extraordinary, Clive. Forget Quota. Your work would save lives and make you famous."

He started laughing, hysterically, doubled up against the wall for support. She glanced at Lisa, who was pressing herself into the corner of the room, her knuckles white, clutching the blanket to her chest.

"You've no idea, do you? For a bright woman you sure are dumb." His sarcasm seeped into his words and he leant against the cell wall slapping his knees in delight.

"Do you really think the government would have implemented that cure? A population out of control, medical resources overwhelmed and food at a premium and you think they wanted to save lives?" His laughter rolled around the concrete cell. "Dementia was the main tool in their armoury, the only thing the population feared more than dying. It made Quota a plausible answer. Without it the politicians could never have got agreement to their Planned Exit policy."

Kate listened horrified.

"It was their trump card, years of senility or a painless exit? What would you choose?"

"But surely, if they'd had the cure, if it hadn't been destroyed in the crash, they could have prevented so much suffering?"

This time the smile was grim. He looked up and stared straight into her eyes. "I explained it to them in very simple terms. Politicians like straight choices. Nothing complicated. Once they saw the logic, the plane crash was easy to arrange. There were enough terrorist groups to blame."

He fell silent and got to his feet, appearing bored. "But, that's old news. I'm interested in what I'm looking at now." His eyes left Kate and settled on Lisa huddled in the corner.

Kate moved towards him and started unbuttoning her

dress. "You're a powerful man, I like that." She took his hand and slipped it under her cool cotton bodice, touching her bare breast. She shivered. "See how excited I am. I want you Clive, I never realised how much until now." As he drew closer and kissed her neck she looked towards her daughter. The door was open but she hoped Lisa had the courage to stick to their plan.

"No, he loves me." Lisa stood and glared at her mother. She was doing well.

Kate strode towards Lisa. "Shut up." She hissed, and held her breath willing her daughter to play her part.

"You had your chance, Mum. It's me he really wants." She could feel her daughter's breath and watched as a rivulet of sweat slivered down Lisa's forehead. It was now or never.

Kate mouthed 'I'm sorry' and slapped her daughter's face. A tremor crossed Lisa's lips but her eyes looked steely. Kate dreaded what she had to say next. "Do you think he'd be interested in a pregnant slut like you? He's worth a lot more." Watching her daughter's lips quiver was unbearable and she had to plant her feet firmly on the ground to stop her legs shaking.

"Pregnant?" Clive's voice rose. He pushed Kate away and moved nearer Lisa, spreading his hands across Lisa's stomach. Kate realised he might think the child was his.

"She's five months gone. It was the married farmer up the road."

Kate watched the disgust seep into Clive's eyes and she pushed her daughter towards the door. She faced Clive. "She's a waste of space. An unlicensed birth, they won't even let her keep it when they find out." Kate moved closer and kissed him again. "She's dirty goods," she whispered. "Let her go, we don't need her."

He looked confused and pushed her hands away. For a moment Kate thought she had gone too far.

"Do they know?"

"What?"

Clive turned and shouted at Lisa, "Do they know about the child?"

"No." Her daughter shrank back against the wall.

He walked away, stood in thought at the other end of the cell then turned.

Kate realised she had no idea what he was going to do. This wasn't the reaction she had expected.

"They'll take it. They'll use it, like they did me."

She looked at the sorrow in his eyes, the first time she had seen evidence of any real feelings. She could use this and moved quickly towards him. She wiped the tear from his cheek. "I had no idea. How old were you when you were taken?"

"Six. Six years old." His shoulders trembled.

"Your mother must have been heartbroken."

His face flooded with colour and the veins throbbed in his neck. "The bitch gave me away. Sluts all of you," he lunged at Lisa and screamed in her face. "Your child will pay for your stupidity, that's not right."

His hand whipped back up to strike her but Kate was quicker. She grabbed his wrist. "Think of the child, Clive. It could have been you."

She watched a flood of emotion cripple his face but he dropped his arm.

"You've got me, Clive, you've got everything you wanted. Kill me, destroy Quota but don't murder the child. It's innocent."

She watched him struggle and then nod. One look and Lisa was through the door and she watched her stumble up the narrow corridor. Lisa was free. Kate had to act quickly in case he changed his mind. She closed the door firmly. She must keep to the plan and concentrate on Clive. She needed his complete attention. She leant against the back of the door and removed her coat, undid the remaining buttons on the front of her dress, keeping her eyes on Clive the entire time.

She moved towards him, slipping the garment over her shoulders, letting it drop to the floor. Clenching her teeth behind the smile, she started removing her black underwear. She watched his eyes follow her every move as the goose bumps prickled her skin. Controlling her shivers, she gathered up the blanket on the floor and patted the rough material into a bundle before placing her knees on the edge and sitting back on her heels. She bowed her head. This had to work.

He came forward and lifted her chin with one finger. "So it begins," he said and undid his zip.

CHAPTER 50

Grant headed towards B block to continue the search. He checked the time. It was taking too long. After uploading the new section of architectural plans into his mobile, he realised the building was a maze. This area had been closed for years. A moving dot registered on his screen, a feed from the security unit scanner. It looked too big to be a rat. He moved the scanner upwards towards the ground floor instead but hesitated. It might be worth taking a look.

He refreshed the screen. In the basement the red dot was moving up the internal stairs at the far right of the building. If he ran he might just get there in time. He closed down the scanner and raced towards the stairwell.

As he swung the service door open, Lisa fell into his arms, crying hysterically. Thank God he had checked.

"Jack, we have to find Jack."

Grant guided her towards the nearest office and sat her down to try to make sense of what she was saying. Eventually he understood: Jack was unconscious on the Quota Control floor. He knew that was Clive's section and the bastard had Kate imprisoned in the basement.

"Lisa, I'm going to get you out. Stay well away from the

building and I'll call your grandad to tell him where you are. Do not come back whatever happens. Do you understand?"

She was shaking from head to foot. "It's Mum. Clive is assaulting her but she made me promise to get help for Jack first. You will get them both out, won't you?"

He nodded but if Adam's prediction was right, there was little time to save both of them before the rockets hit. Where Kate was in the basement he knew from the plans the walls were thick concrete. Unless it was a direct hit, she would be safe for a while. Jack was in immediate danger and could be killed any minute. He hated to think what that bastard was doing to Kate but knew he had to try to reach Jack first.

Lisa hung on to him, refusing to leave the building but when Grant convinced her time was running out she relented. He watched her reach the main road and the security guards before he plunged back into the Ministry.

The lighting had completely failed and he had to find his way up the stairs by light from his mobile. Five floors later, he was sweating and breathing erratically. A message flashed through from Adam saying he had Lisa with him but the terrorist groups were going to blow the building in ten minutes. Get out now was his final plea before the screen faded to black. He knew that was not an option.

Ten floors to go, he wished he had kept the gym membership going. His legs were trembling now but he grabbed the railings and forced himself up, step by step.

Another urgent message scrolled across his phone. Carolyn, but he had no time to listen to it. He was about to swipe it when he saw his son's face flash across the screen. "Daddy." He stopped and sat down on the cold stair, trying to retrieve the message.

Toby's face was replaced with Carolyn's. "Your son has a chance. No thanks to you. His real father has agreed to donate his organ and signed his fortune over. I will have the last laugh even if the little cripple doesn't survive." Her laugh faded out with the image and Grant felt the nausea rise in his throat.

He leant across the banister rail and retched. The cold bitch was using her own son to score points. He dropped to his knees and froze. Everything went into slow motion. He raised his hand to try to use his phone but his fingers felt twice the size. It rolled out of his hand and dropped through the gap in the railings. Dull hopeless thuds echoed up the stair well as the device dived, bouncing off the floors he had climbed.

He felt the tears on his face as he dragged himself upwards in darkness.

CHAPTER 51

Clive looked at Kate and knew he had won. Her daughter had surprised him though. He frowned, lying little cow, bringing another unwanted child into the world. When would they learn?

He glanced down at Kate, crouched naked at his feet. He tugged impatiently at the zip in his trousers and felt the saliva brimming his lips. She would pay, big time.

Kate lifted her face towards him. She didn't look so damn cocky now. "Clive, I'll do anything but let Jack go."

He could see the desperation in her eyes. His answer was a swift kick to the head. She flew backward, sprawled across the floor, blood dripping from her mouth. She reached out for the blanket heaped in the corner, scooped it up and head cowed, dabbed at her lip.

This was how he wanted her. No family to rescue her now. "That little prick was no better than his dad. They thought they could fight the system. Fucking heroes or what?" He knelt down, his face inches from her. "They killed your bastard husband and there won't be an atom of your son's body left to bury. I am the system and no-one beats me." He glared into her eyes. It was time.

Kate felt strangely calm, her body cold. It was simple. She would kill him. She slipped her right hand into the folds of the blanket and groped for the knife she had hidden. It had to be done right. She would only get one chance.

His excited breathing grew quicker as he leant towards her, smiling, so sure of himself. She drew the knife back and plunged the blade into his side, right up to the handle.

He collapsed towards her. She flinched as his blood splashed on her naked stomach. In horror she pushed him away and ran for the door, pulling the thin cover around her bare body. Ignoring his screams she pulled at the door handle. It was stuck. She realised she needed the key to open it. Turning, she looked at Clive clasping his side, the blood running through his fingers and pooling on the floor. She was used to saving lives not taking them. Feeling faint she leant against the door.

He winced pulling the key from his pocket and held it up. "You brave enough?"

A bloody stain crept across his shirt, but he lay on the floor taunting her. Her legs were shaking and she was close to vomiting but she needed that key.

Clearly in pain, he dangled the key from his finger as a grim smile stretched across his face.

She edged forward gradually and reached for the key. He snatched her hand and wrenched it down to the floor; she felt a bone crack in her wrist and he pressed the rusted key hard into her cheek.

"You're going nowhere."

He held her in a vice. Kate felt the anger build. She slid her hand down and reached for the cold metal, twisting the knife. His scream filled the room and she grabbed the key as it fell from his fingers.

She blocked out his cries and with shaking hands tried to line the key up with the lock. Just as she did, the wall at the opposite end of the room blew in. Debris hit her legs and she collapsed. She heard a roar behind her and turned her head. Clive was almost hidden under bits of broken concrete. She pushed shards of rubble away from her lacerated legs and pulled herself up.

"Help me, Kate," he pleaded but she jammed the key in and turned it. The door swung open and she did not look back.

CHAPTER 52

Grant almost toppled down the stairs with the force of the blast. A crack splintered the outside wall and smoke poured up the stairwell around him. The rocket attack had begun. It sounded like one of the lower floors had been hit.

He wiped the dust from his eyes and squinted down the stairwell. Time was running out. He dragged himself up and climbed towards the eighth floor. A series of new explosions continued to hit the building and debris scattered over him as a great hole appeared in the stairway just above his head. A ball of flame flicked towards him and the air sizzled. He screamed and touched his face. His skin was peeling.

"Jack, I'm coming." He heard Kate's voice and looked down to see her hands on the rails a few floors below. He must stop her getting any nearer. The stairwell above was a furnace. He ran down the stairs, his face burning with pain.

Kate was pulling herself up a few steps at a time. "Shit, Kate, what happened?" She had a bloodied blanket around her and was cradling an injured arm.

"Jack," she murmured. "I need to get to Jack."

He lifted her up. He had no choice. "I have to get you out."

She fought him all the way down. Biting, scratching and pleading with him but he kept going. The door was missing on the ground floor and he stumbled through the shattered glass towards the medics who were already on the scene. When they took her from him, she was unconscious.

Kate came to and stared at the smoke filled skyline; parts of the ministry building had disappeared. The crowds around her were covered in a thick grey dust. She squinted through the waves of debris that rushed towards her and tried to count the remaining floors. Jack was in there.

The cry when it came was primeval. A scream hidden so deep, it tore through her body. The pain forced its way up her throat and with its hot fingers ripped her lips apart. Her baby, her son.

"Mum, it's me. Lisa."

Kate heard the voice from what seemed miles away. She opened her gritty eyes to see her daughter leaning over her. "We're in the ambulance. The doc says you'll be ok."

She felt empty. Why?

"Lisa, let her rest now." Another blackened face appeared. "Kate, you've lost a lot of blood. Hold on. We'll be at the hospital in five minutes."

She knew that voice. It was Grant. He had stopped her saving Jack. She wrenched the drips out and tried to reach him. Her arms flopped to her sides and she could only raise her head inches from the bed. "My boy," she whispered.

The medics reached for her arms and she felt the injection prick her skin. As the energy seeped from her she turned her head. Grant had tears in his eyes.

CHAPTER 53

Kate stared out of the window across the farmyard. The new lambs followed their mothers over the field. It was six months since the attack on the Ministry of Life.

Quota was gone but at what price to her family?

Her thoughts were broken by the baby's cry for attention. He kicked his legs and cried louder inside the nest of blankets on the sofa. Kate smiled and walked over to pick him up. Jimmy had Lisa's wide smile but Jack's dark hair and dimples. She laid him against her shoulder and breathed in his special scent. She stroked the downy hair on his head and let him snuggle into her shoulder.

At just two months, this beautiful child had wedged himself into the centre of the family. James would have been so proud. After a difficult birth, Lisa had pushed Jimmy into the world, his fists clenched and his face red with indignation. Yet another Appleby fighter. She turned to see Lisa watching her.

"Mum, the car's charged. We need to go now."

Today the Pro Life Party, which she had helped form, was holding a rally in Hyde Park. She was much better at dealing with crowds of people since she had been taking such an active part. Who would have thought she could talk to hundreds, address Parliament and appear on television? Together with Grant and her father, she had helped turn a nation's distress into determination for a better regime.

She rubbed her nose against Jimmy's. A huge grin pushed his cheeks into tiny pouches and his eyes lit up. His delight and complete trust in her hit home. She had nurtured Lisa back to health after the bombing and the birth. Lisa still had nightmares about Clive. She had been tormented by that bastard. His face flashed in front of her. Clive had taken almost everything she loved. Thank God, he couldn't take any more.

Jimmy started to cry. She held him tight. "That's ok little one, it's alright. You're safe now." She cradled him and whispered, "You're an Appleby. A fighter."

Over the months, she had watched Lisa strive to secure the baby's future. Her determination to change the law on un-licensed births had been relentless. Kate's own belief they could change things had inspired Lisa to do the same. She had appeared before government committees to broker new guidelines. It ended the cruel practice of removing un-licensed babies from their mothers.

Jimmy closed his eyes and relaxed in Kate's arms. She followed the contours of his chubby cheeks with her fingers and kissed his pink lips. Things were improving. James and Jack had started the revolution. It was far from over but battles were being won every day.

"Come on, Mum, we'll be late if we don't leave now. Grant's speech is scheduled for 2pm and he wants us on the platform with him." Lisa was rushing around, stuffing bits and pieces into a backpack.

This was the party's first national rally. Her father had the programme pinned over the kitchen walls. He had been talking to the media for weeks, like a kid planning his own birthday party. It was the political party he had been fighting for all his life.

Kate wrapped the baby and put him into the pod Lisa was carrying. Working to form the new political party had given her renewed strength over the last months. "Let's go."

It was good to have her parents living on the farm. Her mother's cancer treatment had been successful and Kate felt closer to her parents than she ever had.

"It's lovely weather for a picnic," her mother said.

"And I packed the lunch," Mary added.

Kate realised her clothes had fooled no one. She had lost a lot of weight since the riots, travelling up and down the country giving talks.

"It will get better, Kate, but you need to build your strength now."

Kate remembered the way her mother-in-law had thrown herself into work around the farm after James had died and would be in the kitchen cooking meals into the early hours.

"We need a fairer future and they need our help," Mary laughed. "After all, they're men, what do they know?"

She was right. It was her family. She had fought to protect them, now she had to fight to keep it together. They walked towards the car where her father was struggling to get everything in the boot and complaining loudly about the lack of space.

Kate watched the baby sleeping peacefully in his car seat as they drove into London, her mind tormented by memories.

Lisa seemed to sense her thoughts and squeezed her hand. "We can do this, Mum."

"Yes, we can." Kate said.

Her father talked as he drove. "Our VIP seats are ready on the platform and Grant's reserved some more in the front row for Mary and the others."

He was a strong man, Kate thought. He had shown courage and conviction throughout his life. She was pleased her parents could stay now the political situation had changed.

"By the way," her father said, "Grant called to say he's bringing Toby. The boy has made a speedy recovery after the kidney transplant. It will be great to see him, won't it?"

Kate swallowed. She hadn't talked to him properly since the fire.

"I didn't realise they'd found a donor," Mary said.

Kate had refused to gamble her son's life, yet Grant had risked his to save her and her children. He had put her first when his own son was dangerously ill.

Kate steadied Jimmy's seat as the car bumped across the cordoned-off enclosures in Hyde Park. They passed lines of commuter coaches parked-up and she smiled at the bored expression of the scruffy teenager wearing a luminous orange tabard that waved them forward. His tattooed arm pointed them towards the last spot in the row.

She fumbled in her bag for her sunglasses. She took a few moments to compose herself before stepping out of the car into a hubbub of noise. The sound of musicians tuning their instruments trickled through the trees from the grandstand. Streams of people were navigating their way through the cars, clutching seats and blankets.

Her parents found the reserved seating. They sat and Kate relaxed, letting the sun warm her. She closed her eyes and remembered the good times.

She was startled by a child's scream. An excited Toby was waving a bat at her and shouting, "Cricket, cricket."

Kate's heart melted at the sight of the happy boy. She looked up. Grant stood in front of her, smiling and offering his hand. She clasped it and gave him a hug. "Toby looks so well."

"Yes. Sir Charles signed over one of his kidneys and it's working a treat," Grant said, looking into her eyes. "And how are you, Kate?"

She saw his concern. "I am good, thanks to you. I'm so sorry I haven't called you."

Grant shrugged. "I'm sorry about Jack."

Kate felt her face tense at the mention of her son but fought to keep her composure. "Why don't we have a tour of the fair before the rally? It looks like Toby has found some playmates," she said.

Mary and Lisa were playing ball with Toby. What a joy to see the boy healthy and Lisa too. They could have lost them all.

She took Grant's arm and they strolled past the stalls, toured the exhibits and watched the energetic dance displays. "Is Toby living back home now?" Kate asked.

"Yes, I have a full-time carer. Toby loves her."

"What's happened to Carolyn?"

"She stayed with Sir Charles after his operation, hoping for payback. Ambitious as ever."

Kate nodded before forcing herself to ask the question she had been dreading. "And is Quota really over?"

"Yes," Grant said. "The work you and Adam have done gathering support has been crucial. I am leading a working party to see what we do now. We still have population issues to solve, but Quota won't be the way we do it."

Kate gave a sigh of relief. Her family's sacrifice had not been in vain.

They returned to the main stage. The area was a mass of faces and the buzz of excited voices filled her ears. Lisa waved at them from the platform. She knew they were late. Kate's legs shook as she climbed the steps. She avoided looking at the crowd but glanced at Grant and his damaged face. His good looks hadn't been marred by the fire; if anything it had added depth to his smooth features. His only concession, she noticed, was to grow his hair longer in an effort to cover the white patches and thick scars on his neck. He caught her gaze and gave her a thumbs up. He was a brave man.

She readjusted her sunglasses and kept her eyes focused on the few feet of stage in front. There was a hush as she rose with her father and took the mic to address the crowd. "Thank you for coming. I am proud to introduce the Pro Life party."

She looked out at a sea of yellow t-shirts and laughed as their images burst into life on screens surrounding the audience. Kate's gaze was drawn skywards as the huge egg shaped balloons hovering above burst and hundreds of miniature golden daffodils floated down towards the crowd. A cheer rippled around the field and the band blasted out the party anthem.

She and her father outlined the proposals for the new global dementia treatment that would allow elderly citizens to continue working into later life. She spoke of the plan for older part-time workers to train young paid apprentices and end the misery of generations of youth unemployment.

Grant took over to explain the party's polices on exploiting medical advances. He also spoke about the new programmes of food production, based on James's research into Super Foods. These plant substitutes could remove the need for expensive livestock and imports.

She had to reach for her tissues when Lisa took the microphone. With Jimmy in her arms she got a standing ovation for her speech calling for the closure of the un-licensed birth programme and the end of forced adoptions.

Grant returned for his final speech. He took time to wave to his son in the front row. She realised he was the future, in more ways than one, and it was right Toby was here.

"We've all lost somebody under this regime and I would like us to take a moment to remember them. And I would ask you to give a special thought to our personal hero, Jack Appleby, who can't be here in person but wants to say a few words from his hospital bed."

Kate grinned as Jack's face appeared on the gigantic screen. When she had seen him yesterday, he hadn't mentioned a word about speaking. He was hooked up to machines but managed a wave. He spoke slowly but determinedly.

"I'm proud of the part my family played. Quota was corrupt. We are not numbers. We all count. This new party must speak for us all."

She could see the strain on his face as he finished but the crowd responded with a roar. Jack had been in intensive care since the Ministry of Life attack but Grant's heroic return to the building had saved his life. His intimate knowledge of the Ministry's layout had enabled him to find a quick alternate route to where Jack lay.

"He insisted. And although the doctors were against it, what could I say?" Grant smiled as he took both her hands. "Please stand and take the applause for him," he whispered into her ear before supporting her to her feet. "I'm asking for a minute's silence for the ones who didn't make it."

She looked across the hundreds of bowed heads before her as the silence filled the air. The flutter of the leaves in the trees was the only noise. She thought of James and smiled. Thunderous cheers and clapping signalled the end of the silence.

The band burst into life as Lisa walked towards her with Jimmy and they hugged each other. Through blurry eyes she saw images of James and the others that had fought the system appear around the arena. With her family gathered on the stage and new hope growing for a better world, she knew it was time to move on.

ACKNOWLEDGEMENTS

To Linda Spurr, Mary Crowner and Angela Hunter
who have been with us from the beginning
and our beta readers who kindly read the entire novel
several times. We could not have got here without you.